GW00393218

A

Magical Creature

Series

Copyright ©2021 HDA Pratt

The right of HAD Pratt to be identified as the Author of the work
has been asserted by him in accordance with the Copyright,
Designs and Patents Act 1988.

Apart from any use permitted under UK copyright law, this
publication may only be reproduced, stored, or transmitted, in any
form, or by any means, with prior permission in writing of the
Author or, in the case of reprographic production, in accordance
with the terms of licensing Agency.

All characters in this publication are fictitious and any resemblance
to real person's, living or dead, is purely coincidental.

Nimfa
&
Master

A magical creature Story

By

HDA Pratt

Books by HDA Pratt

A Magical Creature Series
Flighty
Nerdiver
Nimfa & Master

A Night Creature Trilogy
The Sleepless Night Creature

The Elemental Cycle
Worthy

Acknowledgements

I dedicate this book to
Fiona Pratt
The sister that always has my back

And so it begins

Master

From every angle liquid splatters against me. My skin which is as rough as death itself absorbs it all, my laugh echoing in the space we fight in. The battle I have waited for since I gave Flighty that cup so long ago now has finally come. My joy bursting around me as I send another fist flying through the air at our enemy shivers up through my arm as the wind itself seems to join in on every hit I make. These elven demons thinking they can defeat us spur me on, my rock ancestors begging me to win back what was meant to always be ours.

Hitting hard and true, my fist connects to its intended target. The elf's simple body cracks under the weight of my stonework. Sailing down hard, the elf twice my size starts to turn to coal, the brown blood that has leaked from its nose, urges me on to hurt another one. How have these creatures convinced all other kinds that they are the rulers of this land, they are so puny.

Spinning before the elf even has a chance to fully die, its body in mid transformation of turning into the awful substance its soul has hidden as I drop into the earth, earth mother listening to my thoughts instantly. Her warming touch circling my all around as I slide through the ground, my blind sense of the worth arching out above to tell me where to pop up next.

Triggered to the right, my thoughts connect to earth mother, her mind reading mine with the place I want to be. Sailing as fast and as true as I can in this battle, I fly up out of the ground rolling as I do, catching an elf on the head sharply. Falling together, my newest victim doesn't even realise what's happening before his whole body has turned to sand. My own body not even thudding to the grassland beneath in the time it's takes for him to vanish from this world, my phase under the earth is like any of my kind, hidden and surprising to the elven army attack Nerdiver's pond.

Hitting the earth with a hard thud, I push of the ground and pounce up to a pair of elven warriors, armour shining brighter than the stars from the night sky. The crest on their sparkling silver breastplate signalling the mirror Queendom they have come from. The rulers of this ancient forest, I wonder at how these weak creatures live so long. Are their youngling's not taught how to fight, or at least well or have my kind not fought them in such a long time that they are not ready to defend and kill against my kind.

Swords raised at the ready, I give myself no time to think, I just attack. Brave screams of those who think they could win this echo down to me, as I feel a presence flash behind me, my fighting fairy comrades doing an alright job at destroying the elves too. Three in all, the fairies are quick, dashing in a blur of their dust, their colours hitting the elves in an array of different attacks. Flighty spinning around one elf, he fires his two different coloured dusts at one enemy turning the substance into dagger just before they hit the creature. How he has got gold dust I do not know but I revel in the fact my black curse still plagues him. Our pack is still intact, burning on both our chests, I can see the orange flame burning on his bulky chest as all he is wearing are trousers which look to be scale like.

Smashing two punches to the left, I crack one elves knee cap in two, while another elves shoulder blade shatters under my heavy fist. Spinning slightly I swing mg elbow out behind my back, the elf with the destroyed knee cap receiving my pointed body part to his chest, caving the intricate design that represents everything their horrible Queendom stands for. Beauty, light and dominance, the mirror Queendom is filled with elves all begging and fighting over the ideals of being the most beautiful, the most-bravest elf there queen has ever seen. I tell you what though; these cheap armour and weaponry will not stand to defend them against the likes of my kind. The hard rough rock trolls can take a thousand hits before we even get the slightest chip in our stonework. Cyth's crowned mother should have concentrated a little more on the quality of the armour these elves wear than just the design.

Giving me the need to bring up my other arm in the instance defence the second warrior slashes down its simple clean blade towards my forearm. Flimsier than a flower petal, the blade may as well not be in his hand. Nothing like Cyth the crowned Prince's blade, my mind flicks to the question of how the queen will react to the fact her child is no longer an elf but something entirely higher and more powerful. Take now for instance, I hold up my rock hard forearm deflecting a puny elves blade made by no one of power, while he spins and slashes in one spot cutting the elves that would have been his friends so fast that I catch in the corner of my eye what looks to be fire emanating off of his slim line pale green skin. What marvel souliune's can do to the creatures of this Tylimantrica. If only every soul mate connection changed you like it has for Nerdiver and Cyth.

Breaking into pieces on impact, the blade that doesn't even scratch my stone, flies behind the two of us, its broke pieces spinning away as it aims at the elf's battling around us. Reaching forward I quickly grab hold of the surprised elves sleeve, pulling him so he smashing his body against my tiny one. His caved in chest begging for a breath, I spin us in one smooth movement, catching a glimpse of Flighty, my oath bound friend blasting two different elves directing in the face with full blown power and rage. How he cured the darkness I gifted him with I do not know but the power he now wields looks like it may benefit me for the better. Feeling inside that I will rule this world soon enough, I know I will bring every race who has put the rock trolls down to bent knee, to pledge allegiance to the one true goddess earth mother, all before I send them back to her dead. A guiding hand that has always been a companion of mine in the back of my head, begs me to kill more. Unlike the goddess the guiding hand has no moral keeping anything alive. If I full let myself succumb to the guides wishing, nothing would be alive.

My newly locked in place friend staring up at me as I move to shift out position, panic reads all over his chiselled face. Carry our spin on, I let go of him slightly go so I can continue spinning him, dazing him enough to push him face first to drop hard onto his already broken comrade. Lifting myself up onto my tip toes, I spread my arms wide, tipping slightly so I lean over the crumbled earth beneath my large feet. Letting everything in my stone slab of a body fall down to the ground, the two feeble elves stuck in so much pain they don't see the death that's is about to come to them, my angle of a stance and boulder of a body taking no chances of letting them escape.

Killing two elves with one stone, I land on the heap of bodies, both turning into a quick grave, their bodies forming so I'm now lay face first in a pile of mud. Regretting my finishing move, the sloshy and inconvenient mush I'm now in suffocates my laughter I had for this fight only moments ago. Taking any delight I had in wining this fight, the muddy carcasses annoy me for the fact they both have hearts as gooey as this. My connection to earth mother below blocked, I try lifting my arms up to no avail. My breathing blocked too, and yes breathing is something I need, earth mother giving us oxygen through her life force when we are below land level, I begin to actually panic. Pushing myself down into the slimy goo, I try shuffling though this yet my whole being is truly engulfed by these dirty souled creatures.

Roaring, I cry out for Earth mother beneath me in my mind, my best go at pulling the mud around me gets me no closer to the soil just beneath this muck. No easy fix will help me out of my predicament but panicking will only worsen my chance of getting out of this. How pathetic would it be to die in this goo when there is no other way the elves would have killed me but by my own arrogance.

Nerve break pain stabs into my stonework back, an axe suddenly hitting me deep while I'm down. Feeling the hard metal work into my back, it truly digs deep into my stone shell, breaking my impenetrable skin easily. Crying out but this time with no sound, all I can think is the worse part of this feeling is that it isn't made form a fight of hand to hand combat but from some weak solider that is kicking me while I'm down. The mud substance pouring into my opened mouth from my scream, I push my lips together trying to get the mud out and ignore the harsh repeating pain. Doing my best not to scream out again as another swing of the axe sails higher into my body the next stab digs deeper than the first. Trying to push down into the mud harder, I aim to push my fingers forward so I can just scrap the top of earth mother. Clearly made by a far superior blacksmith to the weapons of the elves I now lie in, I wonder if the metal in my back is just like Cyth's. The sword I saw him fighting with earlier cutting down elves just as easily as I was, his ex-race ready to be wiped out if they do not see sense and join us. The axe wielder wanting to keep hitting me try's to pry his weapon out of me, my agonising scream letting the mud all around me go dipper down into my throat again.

Yanked back hard, my body flinches, my face moving at an angle I didn't know it could, as I feel hands wrap around my shoulders. What is this elf doing to me, I can't help but panic trying as I try my best to make my body as heavy as I can. I will connect with earth mother a pinkie is all that is needed for her to pull me in. Ripped hard, I come up into the air, the mud in my mouth firing out like a jet of fire, I roar a breath in and out readying myself as best I can to kill whoever thinks they can touch me.

My mud spatter enveloping a creature before me, I don't see who it is as I pull myself out of the locked grip on my back.

"Hey watch it!" A pissed off voice screams at me, the voice sending a shot of navy fairy dust to my eyes.

Burning instantly into the core of my eyes, realisation cinders me that the two creatures helping me are Spitfire, Flighty's sister and Ellamight, a warrior elf who is on our side, though for me all elves are on the opposing side. Spitfire, rightly named has dust that has not been tangled with by a Souliune or the realisation that fairies have more raw magic than all of us. Instead her fairy dusts burn quickly vanishes allowing me to look at my two saviours, and growl a sharp acknowledgement for the help.

Gruffing an inaudible noise as my thank you, I turn ready to resume fighting, the new cuts in my back begging for revenge.

"You are welcome, Troll" The elf's voice kisses at my ears, sarcasm mixing well to my gruff of a thank you. Repeating my only version of a thank you, I call for earth mother to phase me straight down into the perfect brown earth of freedom. Master thanks no thing for help, not even earth mother.

Feeling the echoes of the upper world again, my back ebbs at the new gashes someone has be able to mark on my skin. Setting my thoughts on a single opponent who has a different weight distribution to the rest around it, I find my assailant easily, it's need of holding an axe in two hands rather than one with a shield or sword like the rest of its kind, help me find them easily. Ready myself for payback, I command my goddess to fire me at the creature.

Holding me underground, the soft touch of mother warms on my new cuts, her kind act if warming the ebbing away from my new scars keeps me from the fight. My need for payback screeching in my mind, I make sure she understands that I know the earth has always looked after me far better than the mother who decided to let herself turn to rock and let our kind die out, but right now is not the time for healing. ***Now is not the time*** I scream in my head.

Pushing up, I catch an echo of the elf I'm searching for, Nerdiver's pond not giving me much earth to use when fighting around here. Bursting up out of the dirt, I aim my body high so I can link my legs up and around the elves neck in one harsh lock. Using my body as the counter weight, I lean backwards pulling the elf so its falls backwards with me, its slim arms flailing with my surprise attack, it's axe long lost in the battleground.

Male, female, this creature means nothing to me, all it means is the war I've always wanted is finally here, and my new scars are only here to help burn my anger at this race fiercer. Stretching my arms out as wide as I can again, I enjoy every single moment of this free fall, the air flowing around me with just as much excitement as I have at how destroying these creatures feels. The grassland coming to meet my face quickly it cushions around the sides of my face, just before dirt catches the back of my head like the touch of a dear old friend.

The earth separating on my instincts I'm pulled down into mother, the elf's head coming with me as I let my locked legs free. Leaving the perfectly tall creatures head deep in the earth alone, I sip away with the thoughts of getting back to the battle as soon as I can. My revenge feeding the rage of how I will bring these elves to the brink of extinction, just as they have to us but only they will not have a comeback like we will. My kind may have decided to let themselves turn into rocks that dot the land but our future will never be that again. Nimfa will have to choose one of us to mate with and the next generation of rock trolls shall be mine.

Lord and Master of the underground, it listens to me instinctively pushing me up when I want go up, pulling me down when I want go down. Listening to me now, I burst up out of the ground as I send a punch straight into the nuts of a perfectly white majestic elf. My fist hitting harder than anything he could comprehend to make a swing at someone, he sinks to his knees giving me the perfect time to send a second punch his face. His weak body turning to dust before even touches the ground, I truly do not understand how these creatures have become the main masters of this world.

Brushing off the dust at my feet, I do a rolly polly, my grey skin making me look like a stone ball as I barrel through three enemies at once, my mind not caring for the help I am receiving from my comrades. Springing up I use the momentum of my roll to fly up to a fully armoured elf and kick him in the teeth. They may be far taller than us rock trolls but we are sprite little buggers.

Circling me in one the now weakening army finally work together, seven elves jumping upon me, their swords flashing faster than my mind can comprehend. The elves quick speed and power overloading me in a second, I now find myself locked into all of their arms, my body held above the ground so I cannot escape. Kicking out, I feel my rage burst out that this creature dare pick me up.

"Hold tight warriors!" An elf in a commander helmet shouts. "Fall in and protect the unit! Let's get this troll out of here"

Using my kinds name as an insult, I try flapping all my limbs held tight by these giants. Sighing with a huff, it angers me that they are much stronger than they look when they are not being punched at.

Circling the group who have me held in place, another ten soldiers fall into place like a synchronised band, the hordes of soldiers that keep on coming out of the woods that I can see up at this height, means this battle could go on for days. The fret deep down in me panicking that I may now be out of the fight for good, I do they only thing I can do.

"Demon!" I scream, my vocal cords of two rocks scratching against one another burst around me as my own command for my monsters help shudders through every creature beneath me.

Stopping dead, every solider around me barley breathes, they themselves haven't had enough time to process the whole battlefield like me, so whoever Demon is, it cannot bode well for them. I on the other hand relax slightly, the sound of the battle still raging in the background; I burn from the inside like a volcano ready to erupt. I will not give up, even if it's fifty to one.

A deep sigh from behind my head comes from a solider in the outer ring, his noise signalling my monster has heard my call, my freedom will be with me in a matter moments. The solider who made the sigh, begins a chorus from his comrades all making the same noise as my demon has me standing on my feet again in seconds, it's darkness of a presence disappearing back into the fight before I even have a chance to tell it to carry on killing.

Not all considered bad by how Nimfa would view them, some of the now deceased elves around me have left pure white marble statues of themselves, with one glass and a second made of crystal. Somehow one has even turned into sapphire, the point where my demon has burst through his chest in killing him looks so magnificent, I wonder why elves don't kill each other more to gain these beautiful artworks.

Poking the huge gem, it doesn't shift at all the pure of hearted statutes always seeming to be rooted to earth mother in a protective way. Even though she is on my side, the elves that live by the rules they use too follow, ones connected to nature and full of love, our goddess still holds them dear to her heart when they die. Much to my annoyance, Earth mothers need for an equal fair world can never come about if they are still around.

Sulking out of the ring of five statues, I kick the rotten carcass of one elf that's turned into moulding wood, the joy of being able to do this filling me with such flight I roll at my closest enemy with a fist full of power. Once I feel connected with all of the last remaining of my kind, a kind that shall be ruling this frail world, not nearly hanging on to it. I know we will be unstoppable, although it all depends if I can ride us of a certain troll first, one Nimfa has her orange eye on while me her pink.

Seeing my side all working as one unit, every single one of my gifted comrades fighting on my side may finally see what I've meant by my hatred for the elves. They are here for selfish reasons, one to take over any freedom we could have for ourselves. Unfortunately for the Mirror Queendom, being the ruling power of Tylimantrica and fooling all of our kinds into thinking we are nothing, sadly means our true power is stronger than any of them working together. When you're at the top, there's only one way to roll, and that's down.

Having not fought us since before my great grandfather was alive, the power flowing through all of us tingles in the land. Take Flighty for instance; having finally found his dust he has soared to heights that even I couldn't have imagined. Nimfa and her mastery over the elven magic has given Nerdiver the ability to be with her Souliune and creates a new power in this world and of course I have to have noticed a newer fairy I've never seen before fighting next to Flighty with such raw power. Her dust burns through the elven army with a single thought. Whoever she is I know for certain the elves known nothing of her and the power all fairies have inside.

Spitfire really must talk to her and Flighty if we are going to win this war. But all of this makes me question how there are only ten of us left rock trolls left and millions of elves. Why now did Earth Mother decide to send us on this path, a path where I will bring our rule back, and Nimfa will be on her throne... a seat of rock power thriving for a Millennia. Why not before the elves let the world of magical creatures diminish to nothing.

Appearing next to me as if she knew I was dreaming of her rule, Nimfa My goddess, the one true Queen of all rock trolls flies up out of the earth, her grip grabbing hold of the closet elf to us, which just so happens to be one I just punched in the gut. Wrenching the skinny boned creature down to the ground, her fist snaps shut like an animal trap around its neck. Before the midnight coloured elf has time to transition into the goo like substance it soul truly is, my queen Nimfa returns to the earth mother, vanishing just as quickly as I like doing. The last piece of her to go is the gorgeous threads of her moss hair flowing into the earth like they are un-growing out of the grass, the teasing tendrils begging me to follow.

A knuckle stronger than my own stone connects with my jaw, my face spinning like I'm on a spike as Leach runs by me, his blue sandstone body crying to be pummelled into the minerals I'm sure he's not even made of like the rest of us rock trolls.

"We got a fight to win Master!" Walking backwards away from me Leach motions around us, before dodging two separate sword swings from enemies that are moving so fast he doesn't even see them coming. "Pay attention" He scuffs at me, his feet sinking only slightly into the ground as he closes his eyes and makes five perfectly balanced attacks at the elves around him. His senses are so true that each of his attacks on the elves, makes my senses feel minimal, my connection with the earth not being as strong as to how he uses the vibrations while actually fighting.

Hearing Leach's cry for me to get back in the game, four of these annoyingly perfect creatures around me jump into action. Death to them and their perfect angles, I feed my hate for them with my hate for Leach, the repulsive sight of their angelic features, these perfect beings doing nothing to the beauty of this world if you ask me. They only show the fakeness creatures can harness. For a rock troll Leach's features are far to angelic for my liking as well, his height being abnormal for a male troll, as he is the tallest of our kind, even taller than Nimfa, which is unheard of.

Concentrating on the elves around me as they work together, all four bring their axes down on my shoulders, the previous axe master of the group clearly informing them all that this metal works best on my kind before I buried him. Agony searing through my stone skin as each axe imbeds into me, I feel each individual axe lock into place, my skin cracking tightly in a way that it holds onto the items that would dare pierce my shell. One elf moving forward to dig her dislodged axe in further, she brings her hand forward to my skin, the feeling of her light fingertips stinging to the touch, my hate for this kind growing with every attack I face.

Calling out to Earth Mother, I feel my gut tug as my need to be moved with four weapons attached to me. Grabbing hold of two of my enemies, one a pale green colour like Cyth and the other a bright white, I bring them down as I fall into the goddess's safe embrace. Crying out as I let them go, the earth forming in around them forever, I leave them below popping back up to the world, before I prise two of the deep pain coursing axes out from my body. Leaving behind deep gashes crying for me to help myself heal, these wounds are far deeper than any scratches I received in my lifetime, the small scratches on my back are nothing compared to these.

Throwing the axes to the side, I pull free the last two axes locked into my stone, black blood dripping onto the grass from the carefully crafted metal edges. Feeling my blood pool in the four deep gashes on my broad shoulders, I spin my new weapons in my grip, turning on the awaiting elves for my powerful revenge.

Slashing in an up movement, the axe in my right hand finds an empty space, the elf flashing around behind me; her joint talent that matches Cyth's only now making itself apparent. Swinging my left axe low, I spin on the spot gouging two thick cuts into the elves legs in front of me, hi collapse to the ground is slow, giving me time to aim another attack at his pale blue skinned comrade, flashing away from my attacks.

Knowing blue is not a common colour in the elven race; I wonder what else this elf may have up her sleeve. Swinging my axe as fast as I can, she dodges every attack, moving me well away from her newly damaged friend. Not caring, I chase her knowing I have done too much damage for the elf on the ground to ever feel okay again. My focus fully on my new enemy, I realise she has no armour on, only simple leather trousers and waistcoat, her cockiness at not being attacked shining clear. Her hair hangs long and waving around her, it is only slightly lighter than her skin colour. Trailing around her body which every movement she makes, her hair begs me to yank onto it. Letting myself chase this creature, my needs to destroy the strongest of their kind burning through me like a fire of terror.

Phasing down into goddess, I wait and sense this fast elf movements, her steps making me move under the ground at a speed I have only used when speeding my way here to this oncoming attack. Darting up to test her here and there, I swing each time, my swings inches away from her fleeing body as her speed starts to irate me. one swing hitting home, I only manage to cut a strand of hair off, the falling thread reflecting in the air like a jab at some weakness I may have.

If this battle never stops however I can honestly say I will not mind. I will relish in this fight as long as I can, even if that means the hordes of this race just keep coming. Smashing my hands or axes which are now I'm my grip, I hit at any elf even if they may now be on our side or not. The pleasure I feel radiating down through me into earth mother, the power she has feeds into my kind readying us for this moment returns to her tenfold with every creature we take out. For as long as I have waited for this moment, the moment to take down these creatures that destroyed my legacy, my future, my birth given right to rule this world. I will only let it last another minute for this elf to get away from me, will ruin everything.

Flying deep down into the ground, I aim myself to take this oddly coloured elf out in one final attempt. Sensing her speeding around the tight circle that is Nerdiver's pond I wait to see when she will begin to slow. Earth mother working her magic, the deep gashes on my shoulders begin to warm, the searing pain I haven't noticed yet which has been plaguing me all this time, makes itself known, Mothers healing touch doing all it can in the moments I wait.

Her foot work taking a slow step I shoot, the edge of Nerdiver's water watching behind the stone next to me, movement matching into the space between me and someone who is speeding just as fast as me up to the surface. A final slow of foot fall onto the grass just above me, I break out of the earth in the same instance Nerdiver and her horrible lungs let loose. Breaking the water line as I emerge from the soil, my axes rising to make a killer blow, Nerdiver's glowing white hair radiates around her in all her glory, my Nimfa's gift to this new race of creature will always make me question why, why give her such a gift.

Dropping my axes, my attack on the elf before me is forgotten as Nerdiver's scream of pain shudders deep into the elf's and my cores. Fleeing before Nerdiver's siren call can cut so deep it kills, the mermaid hybrid and I give calculate looks at one another, myself trying my best to hide the pain she had just inflicted on my eardrums. Why did Nimfa gift you with the hair you wanted with the feet on land you wanted. My eyes flicking to her stomach as she stares into me, I see the price she has paid the view of all of her insides being on display.

Siren calling at me again, Nerdiver swims away from me her own focus on the protection of her pond her deeply rooted hate she has for me and what I did to flighty coming second to protecting the Seerer down below. A sword coming down hard on my left-arm, it snaps straight away, these feeble weapons truly are no match for my kind.

With my people no longer around to carve their weapons for them, these elves are fools to even think they can defeat us. My brother rock trolls all popping up around me, five of us attack anything we can see, our fists digging into our opponents as each of our swings get more and more forceful. Returning to my new axes, I attack the oncoming onslaught again and again, this battle will definitely be ours, even if the elves don't seem to have figured it out yet.

Leaving my men to fight alone on this side of the pond, the ground beneath me opens with a single thought to earth mother, her kind touch always welcoming me with a warm embrace as I drop in. Hugging and healing me in such a way only a mother can give, I think to the elves now stuck in this embrace forever, there immortal lives now being a curse. Screaming is futile, or at least the elves brought down into this peaceful place by me and my kind will now have figured that out. A place of friendship and connection for my kind, the earth is the perfect prison that even an immortal cannot escape. Earth mother doing what she wants now with the race that has left there lives of believing in her behind, I would not want to be on the wrong side of her. I just hope she knows everything I have planned is for the greater good of her land.

Earth mother how you protect me, the power that you let me lead will help us rule this world. If it wasn't for you I would not know my path, the destiny I've been chosen to receive. I promise you Earth mother as long as you allow my connection with you to be as strong as it is today, I will not fail you. The world on top will rue the day that they thought they could manipulate you into lying idly by while they destroy your life essence again.

Your chosen goddess Nimfa has the power in her blood, a connection so deep with our ancestor queens that she knows old magic's that even the mirror queen will not know. Nimfa and I have the drive thanks to you, to bring back our race, a far stronger race that we will mould into a kind so devoted to you and the way our lives should be lived, that no one could forget your power again.

The soil around me squeezing for just a moment I feel the goddess warm slightly, her touch sealing up the gashes on my shoulders, my want for her to leave the grooves, a reminder to myself of this battle we will win. Her joy coming off the space around me in waves of warmth, I sense the ground above as my thoughts please mother whole heartedly.

Hoping she can forgive me for the darkness I have and the guiding hand whispering in my ear. I will her to understand the things I will have to do to make sure these wishes come true. I take this moment of silence to prepare myself for the continued fight above. I know the darkness I put in Flighty is partly to blame for the forest turning dark, but we would not be where we are now if I hadn't of tainted that cup.

The battle still raging up above earth mother's soil, heavy beating suddenly echoes around my head at each step my kin makes to win. My pulse beating in time with the march I feel them making, the tips of my fingers beg for me to fight again. Gripping harder onto my new chosen weapons, my axes remind me of the tiny one Flighty used the first time we met. Reacting to the want in my heart, the cocoon of soil soothingly wrapped around me throws me up back up into the world, the faces of demons I must destroy coming eye level to stomach level.

Swinging out, I see a flash of the blue elf fleeing back into the woods, the single most beautiful voice I love in this world mixing with words I now hate the most in the world.

Nimfa

"Master the battle is done" I sing out, using my goddess given right to command all that is around me. "We have won" His swing half way towards an elf on our side, I dread inside to think how many of the innocent pure of heart elves he has killed during this battle.

Turning to me, his grey stonework moulds into obedience, his axe wielding fists falling down to his sides as his pure black eyes train to the floor. The internal fight he must be having at stopping himself from killing every elf surrounding us, playing out. Losing his new battle easily, Master's eyes clock to mine, the need to wipe out the race that has ruined the rest of the creatures in our world burning so fiercely inside even his will to follow me isn't strong enough.

"Every elf must be punished my queen! I do this for you!" Swinging his arm back up, he turns back to the sand skin coloured elf who has relaxed thinking the time of helping us has come to an end for now.

"Thimen! Frezzon!" I shout, the fantastical power in my soul connecting to the elven magic I wish to wield, my need to use elven magic without preparation is risky, especially when I do not connect it to my rock troll magic. Not having a choice or time, I only hope the ancestor queens of each the races can see that I only do so to save an innocents life. The power inside clocking into action the moment the words leaves my lips, Master freezes mid-air, his jump from the earth means his arms are arching with the trajectory of where his axe is aiming to hit. A death kill would have been imminent.

Dropping to a fall in fear with no armour or energy left, the elf Master is about to attack, shuffles back, my gut telling me this is the first battle he has ever seen. A youngling in his races kind, the fear is written over his face, only further sparking my worry. If we scare these creatures who chose to pick the right side, they may turn on us; my vision of all creatures living equally will be shattered for ever. Unlike my wanting subject Master, I do not wish to rule this whole world, I only wish to rule my part of it.

My kind deserves to be brought back from the brink we are on. Earth mother has given me the power, shown me the past and the path we must take, she has chosen to mould my body and soul into the queen my race has needed for a long time. I will not have a suiter obsessed with power ruin our chances at a peaceful life in the Queendom we deserve.

"I said the battle is down!" My voice comes out like two boulders been thrown against each other, the noise echoing up to the tree line circling this pond. My feet on the soft grass, I let mother take me down only to resurface me meters behind where I was, my new position being the same exact stone I stood when I gave Nerdiver her legs. "We have won!" I shout, gaining a round of cheers thrown back at me.

Letting my magic stop, I feel the wain it will cause me if I hold it for too long, my plan for this area will not happen if I am far to drained. Master unfreezing, the elf he was trying to attack is no longer near him; instead four of my subjects Thadus, Nack, Demich and Xen surround him firmly. "You may go Master" I say nodding my head with a single dip; I know letting him leave on my authority is less embarrassing than him having to ask to leave. The hate he has for this kind is like a virus, and I will not have him give it to the others of our kind. I have worked too hard to get all the creatures here at this point, letting him near them could destroy it all. "Do not forget to take your demon"

"My queen" Master guff's, his voice scratching out of his throat as he commands his demon to come to his side. The Black orchid on his cheek just by his eye drops a little, the one thing on him that shows me how he's feeling truly deep inside is the sure sign I am losing him to something. A darkness is creeping in and I do not know if he will even make it to the end of this war.

Not seeing where his demon has vanished to, we all wait with a kind of heavy weight crushing all of us. Where this demon has come from I don't know but all I know is it's not the first Master has ever had. This one however is new and darker than any I have ever witnessed.

Like a cloud of hate and pain all blowing through in one, Master's demon spins out of the darkest part of the forest, the tainted trail Flighty made on his journey to Nerdiver moths ago. Like it never stops moving, the demons features are completely blurred with swirls of black smoke tendrils spinning around it, black dots that could look partly like fairy dust sparking off of it. Not letting his demon time calm down so I can get a real look at it, Master vanishes into the ground quickly, a collective wash of peace running through everyone as Master and his dark demon finally go.

"Thank you all for heeding my call. Fairies, elves, mermaid and of course my rock trolls! Today was a battle a long time coming but I wish it hadn't. Truly. To every elf that saw sense in this battle, we thank you form the depths of our hearts." A hundred I would say in all, my soul warms that so many of these warriors saw sense and didn't follow through on the commands of one crazy elf's orders. Knowing deep down this is not the queens wish, I know we must do something to ride her Queendom of the filth plaguing it. Cyth's mother needs help being brought back the goddess's will and we are the creatures to do it.

"To take your own lives and destinies into your own hands, to defy orders, commands and do what is right. Elves I tell you know you have turned to the right side! This battle was just the beginning, for what awaits us ahead is hard. If we do this right, this war does not have to carry on half as long as the injustices in our world. Every creature has the right to rule there part of Tylimantrica. And for those of you that didn't know, that is the world we live upon." Silence descending on every creature before me, I know I must give a history lesson. Knowing after this hard battle, with all of these awaiting elves, friends of mine and different types of bodies lying dead around us, this is the moment everyone else needs to learn the truth. This world needs to be equal for all of us. We are the creatures who shall be tasked with this feat before us, but everyone should know what they are binding themselves to.

"Tylimantrica was once a dark place. One filled with smoke so thick you could not see through it. The ground so heavy you couldn't walk upon it without your lungs becoming diseased. The land had lost all of its plant life; nearly all its animal life and in their place... All that was left were black menacing structures that fed off the life that was barely alive deep deep down in the deaths of our land. Destroying anything they could, even each other, these structures even started sucking the life out of the oceans, taking every part of the world they could and even the creatures that lived here." Holding all their breaths in tight, I feel every single creature around me can see exactly what it is I am describing to them. Our world broken, heavy and lifeless.

"The legends of old tales tell you one story of this kind, great adventurers and feats that they achieved in there might. But how a world can fall, change when one creature becomes more powerful than all the rest, when one race decides it only care for what they achieve what they do to this world. They change, they morph into the destroyer of a world before they even realise the world is doomed. Humanoids, the heroes of old we once thought help our kinds come into this world." Transfixed at my words, I feel the weight of my words hitting these creatures, the truth of our past and hopefully above all I hope they see the elves are moving in the direction of Humanoids, in the direction of killing everything and everyone in Tylimantrica.

"Our kinds came about when they had devastated the world to a point where only a few of them were left. Only a few of them lived so no harm could keep coming to every life around them. In this break, life made a comeback. The land that was abounded, the structures that were falling apart feeding back to Tylimantrica. Trees started to sprout, rivers started to reflow in new channels, volcanoes brought fresh earth up to fertilise the land again. But where did we come from?" I ask, giving them all a stern look to see who truly knows our beginnings, not what the last few humanoids told our ancestors what happened.

"We came from the humanoids of old. We once were of their kind, at least us elves and probably mermaids were. Sacrificing the last of their race in a bid to bring back life to the earth, humanoids performed the first true magic, a magic that only a certain few to this day can tap into. Where was this feat done, the centre of the mirror Queendom's throne, the pinnacle of power in our world, in Tylimantrica as you call it. Everyone knows that. Even the fairies who are happy in there little colonies, there magic barley being able to sting anyone of our races, theirs is the last bit of the true spark. Humanoids were never evil like you are trying to make out. Your kind and that of the fairies probably came from the residue left by the magic that created us. That is why you are lower than us, why there are less of you and why your kind has decided to lie down and let your species disappear from this world" Gasping at his disgusting words of our race, two of my closest rock trolls Zeit and Thadus spit at the ground near him, the outrage that this elf thinks he can say about us is palpable. If Master was still here he would certainly be dead.

A young one, so young I am surprised the elf is even wearing armour, though I know for an elf he probably isn't as young as I think. I laugh, trying my best to defuse the building tension between my race and the elf's surrounding us. My own disgust that he truly thinks what he just said is true, I push it deep down, my job here is to show these elf's of the truth. We need these eleven as much as they need us; I just need to convince these particular elves especially ones like him. Most that what he has be fed all his life is wrong. But how. Believing in absolute certainty of his words, a few of his kind nod, the calming sense that we had won the battle is leaving, the ones who joined our fight are now at that crossroads I knew they would be at, though can I be the one to step them all in the correct direction.

Feeling the pressure of this moment build, my feet sink slowing into the rock beneath me, Earth Mothers soothing warmth flowing through me to remind me, I am the chosen rock queen for a reason. I need to use my rock troll talents to show these creatures why I am right, make them believe in me.

Waiting for my reply the older more mature elves look to me for the truth, Flighty's grandmother one of my oldest friends giving me a stern look that could match my own, her small way of trying to encourage me. The first creature to which I helped discover a power deep within, Prilance is the first fairy to be immortal in hundreds of years. Her name meaning pure brilliance, she is destined to be the one to unlock the secrets to her kind's magic, though we decided together long ago that no one of her kind could truly find out how or why this is possible unless the fairies figure out they are more than plant keepers by themselves. Feeling deep within, I know this is the moment we have been waiting for, Flighty has more gifts than she could imagine her grandchild manifesting and Spitfire, even her names calls for what power she has waiting to be unlock inside. Never in any of the creatures out here's lifetime has our kinds been working together. This is the time to make it happen, this is the time to change our world.

Looking back to the elves all dotted around the statutes of their descended pure of hearted friends. I see something inside all of them that tells them that the truth they think they have known all there long lives, the history they have devoted themselves to is a false one.

"Nerdiver" I call to my friend, using earth mother I turn on the stone edge of her pond, letting everyone around me wait on hinges.

"Nimfa" She returns, gliding through the water to meet with me, her Souliune watching me closely as he too awaits the truth about our beginnings.

"I believe there is a youngling elf you wish to bring up to the surface, one you saved from the beginning of the battle?" Giving me a surprised look at how I know this, I smile my huge mouth at my friend. "Earth mother told me, she is who told me to bring everyone here." Moving to ask who Earth Mother is, I place my big hand against her mouth. "All will be explained in moments but first let's return her to her people. This is something she also has to hear. Then before I finish my story, bring every creature of your depths below up, it is time we take Knollica to your new home. We must protect him, and here is not the right place. The castle your prince has made for you is the best fortress any of us can fortify."

"The palace of Chifferen. I agree is probably the best place for everyone to be, but it is not ready." Nerdiver informs me, my own view of the castle only being from the outside means I have no understand of the complex inner workings.

"This pond has not been safe from the moment Cyth brought you here. We must move once my story is completed. I will try to cleanse this place of the darkness creeping in, but to truly cure it, Knollica's powerful essence that calls everyone here must be gone." Knowing what I say is fact, Nerdiver leans back slightly, her mind spinning as she tries to think of an alternative of where we can take them.

Flashing round to our side of the pond, Cyth looks at us both, giving his Souliune a looks of such intense warmth I wonder if the rock troll I choose for my partner will ever give the same to me. "Chifferen is easily modified to house and cater for every creature up here and down there. The tree I chose all those years ago is so connected to elves and whatever Nerdiver and I are becoming that it will mould quickly to us. All we have to do is ask for what we need form it. Go my breath and ready everyone. I will speak with the elves and have them prepare to be ready to leave once our history is truly told." Both moving without another word to me, Nerdiver dives down while Cyth flashes around the grassland as quickly as he can, my rock trolls forming a circle away from me as this happens.

Dipping into the earth quickly, I spring up near Flighty, Spitfire and Prilance, their first chance to speak and catch up after years of not seeing their grandmother finally happening.

"You shall come and train with me before we do anything else." My oldest friend tells her granddaughter, Spitfire wanting to have the gifts her family has unlocks showing clear on her face.

"I wouldn't want for anything else, yet I must go with Ellamight, we have a quest to complete. I only came here to find Flighty and now that I have, we must be leaving." Ellamight flashing just as quickly as Cyth, she appears with us, her own conversation with Cyth being brief.

"Our quest is on hold." The majestic black elf says to her friend, her painstaking beauty even for an elf must have made it hard for the mirror queen to let her son move on to find himself and not father a new heir to the throne with her. Pale white hair, Ellamight's skins looks to sparkle whenever Spitfire is looks at her, the deep connection between them being apparent. "My Queendom is under the rule of a usurper and I cannot in good conscience complete my quest until this is sorted. The mystics will have to wait."

"You are trained in the Elven magic's?" I ask, my interest truly sparking.

"I am, though my training is not complete. Cyth is the only one to have completed his quest by the queen, for mine is one far different than diplomacy. And it shall have to wait another hundred years it seems if this war goes wrong." Soothing her friend's clear pain at not completing her quest for the Queen, Spitfire flies to her eye level, a deep meaning passing through them, yet I see they do not touch.

"Well in that case may I ask for your help? I have come over here to ask for Flighty's but the three of us would make this even better." I think aloud, my ever changing idea on how I will cure this place meaning I may need Nerdiver too.

"Of course I'll help in any way I can. What is it you need help with" Explaining my plan for how I am to show the truth and heal this space, I move on next to my subjects asking for each of them to move into a position around the circular wooded area. All eight in place in seconds, I centre myself at the ponds edge, the forests trail Flighty's darkness created dead ahead.

Flighty and Ellamight both in place too, we create a triangle around the pond, the small elfling Nerdiver saved breaking the water's edge as Nerdiver bring her up in her arms, her tiny fragile body then quickly swimming over to me on the mermaids command.

"They will all be ready to leave when we are. I am assuming I am to bring them all up out of the water with my gift." Nerdiver asks as Cyth reappears next to us, the young elfling shuddering at his flashing speed to us, her fear of being here being very clear.

"You assume correct my friend. I would suggest getting free of the water and gaining your legs back. I also need you to do something in a moment if you are willing." I say, Cyth's hands already waiting to help Nerdiver out of her pond for the last time.

"Of course I will help, especially if it helps us all understand our origins more" Nerdiver says giving me a hard stare, meaning she knows I've hidden things from her.

Soothing the young elf by my feet, I ask if she wishes to hear a story of how we truly came to be. Nodding, I warn of the dark beginnings, but the longer she is back above water the taller her spine straightens, her elven light growing fast. Explaining all I have so far to the rest, I then shoo her off to the closest elf so I can finish the tale in true rock troll glory.

"Creatures big and small, thin and tall, round and tuff. Each and everyone one of us are unique in our physique. Alone but connected, we all feed off Tylimantrica and she feeds off of us." Two elves to the my side give me questioning looks, my new way of explaining that our world is a she can only come from two of the male persuasion. "Yes a she, Tylimantrica is female. How do I know this you ask, well ask any rock troll. With our connection being so true to the earth beneath you, Earth Mother Tylimantrica has shown us all who she is and what we need to do. For unlike the tales of old, Earth Mother tells us only the truth, has shown us the truth."

Spreading my arms wide, Ellamight begins to whisper under her breath, the elven words trickling from her mouth whistle around my ears with power. Today I solely give myself up to my rock troll ancestors, the elven part of my plan can be left to the elf.

"Humanoids long buried and gone, fed all of us creatures lies filled with the deceit there plague had ruined the world in. The falsehoods cleansed by Tylimantrica came when she awoke, our creations coming from the time her magic's seeped back into this place. We are not made from humanoids of legend bestowing the last of their magic into making us. NO!" I shout my arms coming together before me, Ellamight's whisper gaining in sound, her voice starting to fill with power.

Bringing my hands to clap together once, they spark, tiny white fireflies flying from the tips of my fingers. Each of my subjects following my lead they repeat my movement sparks of their own bursting into the early afternoon glow of the world. Each of my rock trolls sparking a different colour; we make a rainbow of power around this broken area, the statuesque bodies of the elves awaiting our help.

Flighty taking his queue, his tiny little body bounds up into the sky, my own love of seeing a fairy fly singing in my heart. His hands fly out on either side, my laser vision truly has to focus on him as he begins to spin on the spot, his fairy dust beginning to sprinkle down around the whole pond area.

My voice shocking some of the viewing creatures out of the show happening everywhere, Prilance chuckles at her granddaughter for not being on her guard for the rest of my tale.

"When the humanoids of old, began to die out and the world had time to heal, Earth Mother naturally grew stronger, stronger than ever before. When she once had given mankind a tiny amount of power hidden in the depths of her being she hoped they would bring the world into a new age. Instead the land named after herself began to crumble, siphoning her of everything she could give. You see each and every human kingdom fed from her light, taking all they wanted without giving any in return." Clapping my hands, my sparks ignite again, more fireflies escaping my pale stone skin.

Flighty's choosing to only sprinkle his golden dust brightens everything, the flickering dust floats down glowing around the pond area as do my set of fireflies. Coming forth like a soft breeze in the wind, Ellamight's words echo around us all, our combining effort contributing to something far bigger.

Every creature feeling the power building around us, something this powerful has not touch Tylimantrica in an age. The might it took to gives Nerdiver what I owed is nothing to the presence of magic growing around us now. I know every elf to question me before feels something deep inside, and when this is complete not one will question again.

"Growing back in a slow timeframe, our goddess watched and understood what she had allowed to happen with her gift to humanoids. There greed and solidarity in being the strongest race on the planet made them take and take and take. Tylimantrica couldn't let this happen again. She wouldn't let this happen again. Her power growing in life, she knew she was more powerful in this rebirth than ever before, her new plan was to create creatures equal but unique. In power, in life, every creature made to balance the rest." My words flowing in time with what Ellamight now shouts, her voice so pure so filled with the essence of her kind, I hope I tap into it when evoking the magic my own queens taught me.

Flighty's dust still blazing brighter, for every word I now say, I clap, more fireflies springing to life, the creatures I am making mix with Flighty's golden dust. It all floating around this space, the movements of the tiny glowing dots seeming to softly circle everyone here but their true aim is for a hidden purpose.

"Mermaids came from the sea; Tylimantrica imbuing a coral reef so unique and strong willed that the last piece of coral refused to die from the humanoids destruction. For every creature here to balance each other out, a unique beginning had to happen." Feeling Nerdiver's burning gaze on my body, I refuse to look at her, my many years of coming here pretending I know nothing of the mer-kind when truly I know it all. I could not tell her just as Knollica did not tell her. Her destiny up until this point was for her to discover.

"Fairies came from the skies, in earth mothers blasting of a new creation she sent a rainbow of dust up into the winds, the first fairies souls wanting to exist so much that they formed their bodies just how they form their children today. With the mixing of dust. For when one creature was created, all of us were created!" I tell our history louder, my clapping hands and that of my people powering on the fireflies to circle closer and closer to the elven statutes frozen in death, the hidden purpose now showing itself.

The crystal, Diamond, marble, sapphire statues, the list goes on for what these good souls are made from, have become. Ellamight, Flighty and I's magic now focusing in on these fixtures in the world, our way of cleansing this place from the darkness Flighty and Master brought here becoming apparent.

"Rock trolls; every one of us knows our origin. Our connection to Earth Mother crafted our need to exist when the last ten of us were born, our ancestors lying down to rest. The goddess called us home, our ability to travel underground coming from Tylimantrica's want for us to understand that we all need to be equal; all need to love on an equal playing field together to keep this world strong. The way we speed through the ground is how our kind came to existence. Absorbing the broken structures of the dark soul sucking building left of the humanoids; the goddess turned the dark power in to light. Giving the structures meaning and purpose, but above all light and life we were the slowest to be made. Over the case of six months earth crushed the structures into rock trolls, her cocoon of strength nearly sacrificed as she bore us all." Stopping my clapping, I rub the tips of my fingers together, pure white sparks dance around my hands. The more I do it the further up a trail of sparks kissing up my skin, my kind carry on clapping their fireflies almost taking over every statute in sight. Flighty's dust sprinkles down to cocoon the fireflies in their place, Ellamight's words sealing the task we want to accomplish together, the blazing light of each statue cocooned in a power that burns like a signal to the world.

"Lastly, in the moment of pure power earth mother had, she formed a new tree. Not just simple a simple like the ones standing around this pond. No... elves, you have always had a strong connection with trees, like the fairies have with their dust. Or at least they do when they unlock the power hiding in themselves. Like the Rock trolls are power comes from our own stonework, and mermaids their connection with the water is so strong because they are joined with it like that first strong willed coral. The trees Tylimantrica imbued with power as she grew them, the power Ellamight, Flighty, my people, Nerdiver and I will now bring back to this world together, comes from all of us!" Shouting those words, the sparks sizzling around my body lifts my green-blue moss coloured hair, the power ebbing out of me is concentrated into the need I have for it. My kind of power comes from our will, just like fairies, though ours is physical, my body must touch what I wish to change, our magic is hard just like the earth.

"Nerdiver..." I sing Ellamight's words of power ending as the mermaids name is called. The elven part of this spell is done, the fireflies and Flighty's dust spin and spin and spin around each statue, so fast they are now a blur. My own sparks spinning around my body moves at the same speed to match them.

Finishing his part of our joined planned, Flighty floats down to join his awaiting family behind me, his and Ellamight's power still flowing into me for this spell, our joined effort will pay off and these elves will view the truth in my words.

Stepping away from the ponds edge, the elves in my way move easily my hands reaching out to the closest statute near me. Nerdiver on my tail, she brings a ball of water in her grasp, her part being key to this all working. This feat of performing the magic our Earth Mother once did, will take from all of us, even if three of the creatures helping me are destined to bring new creatures into this world, this power will change us.

Pushing my hands forward hard my sparks fire at the fireflies and the fairy dust circling a white marble statute the look of terror from the elf before its death freezes it in time. My will to give this creature peace and to mould it into what the goddess wished for them to become when they died, a symbol of hope and that the pure hearted may gain rest forever in a form of light. My plan is one better; I wish to give this world a hub of light, a place darkness can never taint again.

My hands burning as I rest on the stonework skin before me, I feel our races connect, my rock troll hardness, this elves beaming grace, the fairies dusts spark for freedom, though something is missing I feel it. Flighty and Ellamight are still connected to me, our bodies radiate with power, the connection of the last creature needed to complete this spell waits behind me.

Reading the scene before I have to try and scream at her for help, Nerdiver takes the ball of water in her hands and covers them both with a layer of it. Stepping right up to my back, she places her hands on my shoulders, a cooling wash of power simmering down my body onto my arms as I feel final the missing piece join our spell, the cooling press water brings.

Being just what we needed, the cleansing part to this cleansing ritual has come. Passing by over my hands, the water stills the burning that is coming from the power around me, calming and cleansing the pain of this pace, of this statue beneath my hands. The water somehow growing, I feel Nerdiver's flow of power connect to mine, her water enveloping all of the imbued power here, the four pieces of the puzzle coming into together to heal a place in need.

Rather than breaking or changing into what I thought, this statue absorbs everything we have given into it, my sparks soothing the fireflies and dust so they carve into the rock. The water helping push everything down to smooth out the stone once again, its own substance is last to be absorbed.

Letting go, both Nerdiver and I step back, her tall slim body close to mine as she keeps her hands rested on my shoulders, our magic happening before our eyes. Not just the on the statute we touched, every pure hearted statute that dots this area now has water wrapped around it, mixing with my peoples fireflies and Flighty's dust, my white sparks helping the fifty statues all around us to begin absorbing all our magic. The tree line seeming to have moved back without any loss of trees, this area has grown to allow what is about to happen next. Every statue now imbued with the water, one at a time absorbs the magic we have called here on Tylimantrica's behalf and showing us what creatures working together can do.

Morphing as one, the bases of the statutes dig down, each of the different textured the elven forms grow roots and expand out, clustering the elves and other creatures in this area to squish together. Growing up, they statutes begin to tower fast, growing higher and higher so they over take the trees in the outer rim easily. Still each made of the different stone the elf turned into; the statutes morph each of their arms so they move up as their faces move to look down upon us all. Growing thicker in body, each one changes so they become a trunk, stronger and more powerful than any tree on this world.

The arms breaking and spreading apart, branches trickle out and down growing so each branch in this place intertwine to the new elven tree next it to. The faces still there, each of the elf's lips mould into a smile, a sign of piece flowing from the morphing towering structures into all the loving creatures below.

Sprouting spuds, each tree beginning to bloom, the nature of it happening before our eyes bursts in my chest as I watch on in awe. With each spud bursting, a new leaf enters the world, each tree's trunk turning into a brilliant shade of white, the texture of each tree turning smooth burning with the power of our goddess. Leaves growing, each spud turns into a leaf, the leaves of each tree being made of the stone the original elf turned into.

One tree has sapphire leaves, while others have glass ones, each tree now dotting the place with are so bright and tall no dark creature will ever think to try and come back here. An array of textures and colours now filling this area, the trees around me shine the truth of every word I have said, while one last gift our magic bestowed finishes our cleanse. The sparkling leaves that twinkling in the setting sun call for us to look at each different tree individually.

The elven rock races moulded in place for eternity before opening their mouths, the sun setting in the perfect moment for my people's fireflies, mixed with fairy dust sparkle and mermaids calming water to enter the world. Beautifully buzzing around the newly grown trees bestowed with power that may help a different soul one day, the place couldn't be more magical. Light reflecting through each leaf, the area dances around with life, a calming trickle of water escaping the fireflies that now float above our heads very now and then, washing away fears and worries from anyone who comes hear.

Watching as two elves, badly hurt from the battle get droplets of water on them by fireflies, they begin to heal, every hurt creature here getting the same treatment. Seeing we have done our task, this place is now for health and love, a place where any hurting creature may find piece. Something deep in my soul knowing now is the time to say my last words to all.

"The tree Tylimantrica once created to form elves into this world has now become the new life that these good hearted elves deserve to be. This place will be a place for healing of those who deserve it. For those who misuse this gift we have bestowed on the world together, will no find access. Elves and creatures all around me, I ask you now, join us in our battle for equality. Every single one of us makes up one part of this world. But together we can make it thrive. Together we make it whole."

Feeling in my gut that what we have done today will spark the beginning of what earth mother has always wanted, I watch the new elven trees closely, the faces of the dead returning my stare with a warning that darkness always follows the light.

Wishing the magic we performed here will bring new life to the elven race, I only hope it's for the better, though something tells me, these trees will not be the last big magic that will be performed in my lifetime.

For the road ahead

Nimfa

Holding a whole ecosystem of underwater creatures in mid-air while walking on legs you haven't had that long must be hard. Holding a whole ecosystem using water to keep everyone safe, while everyone else on land stares at you... Nerdiver really is a trooper. Not only have we only rested one night but the healing properties we have given the elven trees can only do so much. All four of us creatures are in need of so much more healing and rest, I myself need some time to get my energy back, but time is of the essence.

After I performed the spell on Nerdiver to give her what she was owed, I fell straight into the goddess's embrace and slept for days. Only resurfacing when I felt the impeding army coming, I knew I needed to call every creature willing to help me into action. Right now, the only thing keeping me and I'm sure the rest of the marching creatures going is the idea of the Palace of Chifferen giving us a place to revitalise.

Moving on ahead yesterday, Cyth and half of his rightly chosen Elves left us to make the much needed work on Chifferen started. The better prepared the Palace is for our arrival, the easier transitioning Knollica and his people to their new surroundings will be. I know Cyth hadn't planned on having anyone else in his or his Souliune's Palace, but it was the safest and easiest place I could think of for us to protect Knollica. Nerdiver is his protector and for the rest of her life his safety is in her hands. He may have released her from the duty, but Nerdiver's destiny coincides with her keeping Knollica out of the hands of anyone wanting to use his knowledge for personal gain. Earth Mother has made it very clear to me that the mustard coloured henddropus bobbing around in Nerdiver's ball of water is chosen by her and other higher beings to help this world shift in the right direction. It is our job to make sure he can do that and it is my job to help every creature forefeel there destiny.

"Are you going to be able to keep this up all the way my darling?" I ask, my own need to dig deep underground and fly to her palace without this long drawn out walk playing on my mind.

"Uhuh" Nerdiver nods, her long hair tide nicely away from her face as she clenches her teeth shut, the power she is using draining her with every step. Knowing there is nothing I can truly do but feel for the girl, I know the little energy she has left is being used for this move. The last of my own energy will be used the very same way when we get to where we are headed. Doing my best to give morale support, her best friend the black haired fairy bobs on the other side of Nerdiver's orb of water, our flank as a final defence if we are attacked.

Ordered by Ellamight, the head elf has rings of guards surrounding the middle parade over anything else. Starting with ten around us and the numbers rises as they spread out, we march at Nerdiver's pace; the noise coming of the elves is somehow pure terrifying silence. My want for their armour to make a constant clang with every step being something I never thought I would wish for, I see why there armour has no effect on helping in a battle. To be soundless and protected at the same time in impossible. One was chosen over the other, it's a just a shame for them it was the wrong one.

Feeling so enclosed by the elves, I have never been so truly encircled by so many at one time. Trying my best to focus my mind on the task at hand I go through a sort of list. All queens need to plan out for the future or all hell will break loose.

First we need to get these creatures somewhere safe, somewhere I can perform a protection spell, binding it with elven and rock troll magic. Then next I need to have a meeting with most of the main creatures that have helped me today, the ones who came to aid. Our next plan of action needs to be carefully thought through, but quickly executed on. Our rest is important for the battle ahead but it is a battle we cannot let fall on the back burner. The fleeing elves would have returned to the mirror Queendom by now and we cannot leave it to long go before we strike. Darker entities are on the horizon and the elves need to be at peace with us when that happens.

Bringing all of these creatures here will be for nothing if I cannot get them to agree on my plan. Queen Glassadena of the mirror Queendom must be in trouble, for I feel in my soul that she is like me. She is missing her connection to Earth Mother. Otherwise she would talk to her, tell her of her plan, of her view of how this world should be. If only I can stop this raving lunatic elf controlling the mirror queendoms army and speak with the queen herself. It's time for a change, and I hope bringing all these creatures together, before her, will show her the change that is possible. Working together can shift this land for the better, I known the elf queen must look for answers, answers I have for her. Sister Queen's like me and Nerdiver are what we need to survive to grow, I hope Glassadena sees that.

Nerdiver's groove, named by our youngest Elfling before we all crashed out from exhaustion, is the name given to our healing pond of haven. If used properly, I saw on our exit of the groove, the direction Flighty came to Nerdiver's pond that fateful darkened day; the dark streak he made in the forest has now been shifted into the path of light. All the trees and even the grass on the ground have turned a brilliant white, a signal to those that need help from the groove to follow it for entry. We have moulded and shifted Tylimantrica after only our first time of teaming up. What we could do if every creature in our world steps up.

My people can return, given the right timing and outcome. What could the future hold for us all, for the next few steps on this easily broken ground wading out ahead, it may call for victory or it may call for disaster.

"I do thank you young Flighty for helping me with our spell. You have certainly grown far quicker than your grandmother in what you can accomplish with your dust" Flying over the floating pool of water between us, Flighty lands on my shoulder. A move I am sure would never have been something he would do before discovering how powerful he is.

"I am honoured you asked me. Grandmother informed Spitfire and I that you are the reason she is immortal. Understanding that it was both of you and hers decision that she not give any others of our kind the knowledge on what our true dust is, my personal dislike for the rest of the colonies doesn't mean we may need them in the weeks to come. If training them and letting them know what we can really do means freeing the forest, I may be able to bite my lip" A burst of loudness coming from Nerdiver, Flighty and I look at her, her struggle with the water in front of her becoming clearer with every step. "What are you laughing at?" He asks.

"You!" She spits through her teeth. "Bi...bit...tting you...your lip!"

"I could try!" Flighty huffs the buzz of his wings moving so suddenly it flutters a breeze down my shoulder.

"You are right youngling. Prilance and I did agree not to tell the rest of your kind because the world was not ready to go to battle over finding out that everyone is just as strong as each other. Only our strengths come from different places and of course when I say everyone is as strong as each other, some are gifted higher. Take the lights of you Flighty" I say quickly to bring him back to topic, Nerdiver cannot truly be part of this conversation if we are to make it to Chifferen without fail.

"Your dust. Your grandmothers power- you are on a higher level that not all of your kind will reach. Immortality is a fussy chooser just like everything in the world. The colonies like every race have stronger flies I assume, faster and more talented that others?" I ask

"Hmmm... yes" Flighty growls, his hate for his people being so clear.

"Well, when the time comes and your family trains the rest of your kind, many will not be even halfway powerful as your family. You are all special you see, chosen by destiny to be more. Though I have to ask... Why do you hate them so deeply? Nerdiver told me of their torment before your power came home to you but it seems more. Like the mention of the best flyers for instance?"

"It is more than that I admit. My hate is something I will never get past. If they couldn't expect me without my dust then they do not deserve me with both of the dusts I now process" Dust sprinkling out of both his tiny hands, it's harmlessly trickles down my body, my curves giving it waves of route before they hit the ground. "As for the flyers, my jealously comes from not being able to do it in the past. The best flyer" His voice stops, gold dust now only escaping him, my feet pressing the fairy dust into to pathway we walk along.

"If this is to hard youngling" I press not wanting to hurt our newly forming friendship.

"This dust, the gold that is the light in my life was a gift. The brightness that became the saviour of my darkening soul came from another. My naturally born dust would have been just like grandmothers actually"

"Prilance's perfect purple colour!" I clap with excitement "I remember you being born. The day she told me her colour had finally been brought back into her family line was a day she was so warmly proud of. Only you had no dust. I remember that day so clearly. For that day was the day Earth Mother told me and Prilance of a destiny to come"

"Well this gold dust is from another fairy, one who only wish to help me... maybe even want me" Flighty says, his voice filling with a sadness I do not think even the coldest of ice could weather.

"Flighty-" Nerdiver begins to say.

"The gold light that holds back the darkness is me comes from the creature who tried to help me when I had no dust. Instead I used my darkness to kill him!" Tears falling into his hands, I feel my own eyes let water free, mine, Nerdiver's and even some of the soldiers around us cry freely with Flighty. His pain so clear and open to us that we cannot help but feel it.

"Flighty..." I begin having to stop myself to take a breath of clean un-crying air.

"This fairy you say you killed. Would he be happy with what you are now doing with his dust?" I ask the plainest of questions, one I know the answer to but I want to know if he does.

"How wouldn't he be happy! He's dead!" He burst, flying out in front of me to show me how much that question hurts.

"Flighty." I say calmly raising my arms to try and defuse the fire cracker that his emotions are. "Although, I do believe as much as we may be in need of the colonies help. We will have to do with just three fairies. Your sister has much to learn in a small amount of time, and if I am correct, which is rare that I am not" Bursting out with laugh at my expense this time, the water around Nerdiver's pool wavers, her control slipping as Flighty and I take her attention away from her main aim with our overpowering emotions.

"Like I was saying" I say flipping my hair away from so I can motion for Flighty to get back into my shoulder "Spitfire has a lot to learn from you and your grandmother. She like you and like Nerdiver are Souliune's ready to shift the world into a new era. First though we need to balance the world to let it happen"

"W...w...World... Shifters" Nerdiver pants while in the same moment Flighty bursts with confusion at my statement.

"I have a Souliune? With who?!" He frazzles my redirection from trying to soothe his pain working.

"Sorry what did you call yourselves?" I ask, knowing there is only one place she learnt this kind of information.

"We are." She stops walking to take a breath, concentrating all she can on holding the pool before her. "w...we are... The World shifters" Stopping dead next to her I wait, panicking on the inside worried the water is going to fall while she gets out what she needs to before carrying on with our march. "You are included Nim, each of us are. We are going to shift the world in a big way. That is why some of us have Souliune's but for you, you will shift the world for the better by bringing back your kind. I sure one of your children will have a Souliune like us who join with another kind, but for now I know Tylimantrica's plan is to repopulate the rock trolls first. Knollica has foretold it. We are already moving in the right direction for it to begin."

"Is that what he told you when you went to get him for this move?" Flighty buzzes, his tiny body easily fooling a creature into thinking he's an easy target.

"Yes but also when I hurt my head at the begging of the battle. He healed me, told me the truth. Knollica is here to help us, just like we are here to protect him"

"Healed you! He can do that" Flighty gaps, the Henddropus's axing green eyes staring straight at the three of us as he listens to our conversation. At the centre of everyone, the powerful oracle does radiate power, the sliver suckers on his tentacles glowing gold whenever a fish or undersea creature swims close to them. How I would like to have a conversation with him. For now though, I hold myself back from trying to reach into Nerdiver's pool. Action plans are for the battle ahead and the shift we shall make to the world can wait. First we need to get these creatures somewhere safe.

"Our questions Flighty and I assure you, I myself have many will have to wait. Nerdiver I feel you do not have enough energy to get the whole way if we keep you talking. I will move up to the front and see how far we have to go." Dipping her head once, I give it to this creature for how hard she has been working for the last few days. From what Prilance told me of the battle when we started this walk, Flighty had told her Nerdiver began the battle alone at first, after already walking all this way to her grove.

"Wait a second" Flight flaps his arms before flying to spring up before me. "Who is my so called Souliune?"

"Like I said Flighty. Questions will have to wait for another time" Calling to the goddess to phase me into the earth, I drop into the ground, my knowledge of who Flighty's Souliune is, is for him to discover alone... not for me to tell him.

$$\mathcal{N}$$

"A perimeter has been set up around the edge cluster of the woods. Every elf on guard has sworn allegiance and sword to our cause. They wish to free there queen and kind from the lies and treachery the mirror Queendom has become infested with. I myself have done the same. This coming battle is for all of our people's freedoms, though it needs to be discussed." Holding my sight with such power in her voice, I see how Ellamight is an elf chosen by her queen for greatness. I just hope what is to come will not ruin the new era her and Spitfire are destined to be a part of.

"Nerdiver has placed the water pool full of creatures in a sealed off space until Cyth and others can expand a perfect location for them to settle in. The bath Cyth created for Nerdiver overflows into the waterfall you see when you enter. Once the new tunnel system has be created, it will be time for us to all gather and work out our next step" She finishes off, a true solider in how she explains everything to me.

"Agreed Ellamight, a plan is very much needed and I thank you for the update but before we can plan our next move we must protect this place first. I know it is surrounded by strong warriors ready to defend with their lives but we need every solider we have ready to fight the oncoming battle for your land. This means, trained, armoured, healthy and not sleep deprived. Ellamight I have asked you here not long after we have weaved an incredible spell of power upon this world already. I know it takes its toll doing such a powerful spells though I am asking it of you now once again help me."

"Help you? What is it you wish to do?" She asks so seriously I see the tiredness creeping into her features. Assuming I am probably looking the same, I know that for both of us, the spell we now need to invoke will mean we shall probably sleep up until Cyth has prepared the permanent home for Knollica and his people.

"We need to weave around the circumference the soldiers have made and form a barrier spell to protect this palace. Not just for the next few weeks but for the rest of time. The soldiers on guard should not be twenty but we should only be in need of two. One on either side of the bottom step to the entrance of this palace. We need every warrior as rested and prepared as we will be. We have brought Knollica here to protect him, and just like Nerdiver's grove, his ancient power calls dark forces here. We must make it so nothing can pass on this land unless the king or queen says so. Our newly forming creatures who own this castle deserve to have the protection of the ancestors. We need to be certain Knollica and his people are safe alone when we go to the mirror Queendom. I wish to make it so any attacking creatures will only be faced if the Mellifine's agree entry is allowed by them"

"Mellifine? Really?" She chuckles her head leaning back at my new word for what Nerdiver and Cyth are on their way to becoming.

"What else would you call a mermaid elf hybrid?" I quiz her, the main reason I called her here being put on the back burning if it allows me a few moments to try and convince her to start her process with Spitfire. Who knows what they will become when there Souliune finally begins.

"I guess I haven't thought about it really. Seeing how Cyth has changed so drastically since the last time I saw him if I'm honest hasn't truly sunk in. What is Tylimantrica's plan for them; I understand bringing a new era in after the darkness that is sweeping this world. I myself have grown up in the elf Queendom all my life. I know the destruction they are creating. Why do you think I have stepped away from it so much? I know my queen is not aware of any of this; her concentration has been trying to tap into where we thought the power of creation started. I know once she is told of the truth, once she hears from me what I felt when our races united, she will understand that is where our worlds magic lies. She doesn't want to use it for destruction, not like the Kia, who to this day I do not understand why she let her use the queen's power. Ruling for as long as she has, you can understand she may have let her aim slip on her rule of the queendom. But if you look at how she released Cyth to be with his Souliune, she knows what is best for our world. I just hope what Tylimantrica has planned, it will not cost too much." Pain simmering under her voice, I wonder what quest Ellamight's queen has given her. If she still hasn't achieved it in the long time that Nerdiver was trapped in her grove, what kind of quest is it for. Could it somehow be connected to

Earth Mothers plan for this world. A plan I do not know the final outcome of myself. All I know is earth mother has tasked me with placing the pieces together for my right to be on the throne.

"Ellamight" I turn so she faces me too. Taking her hand, I grip hard my big hands eloping her gentle looking fingers. "I hear the fear simmering under your guarded shell. I know your quest means so much to you and I will not ask on this day what you are tasked with for we have something to important to work with first. I do ask you however- Why will you not touch Spitfire?" Looking startled I see there is a reason she is hiding from the world" She is your best friend, your companion. Spitfire is your tanned skinned fairy who's destiny is intertwined with your own yet the two of you wish not accept it. What stops you both for taking a leap like Nerdiver and Cyth? Your quest may need it of you both for its completion" Saying it straight, I cannot play coy like I have with Flighty who still needs to find his Souliune or Nerdiver who had already been falling for hers.

Brushing off the world around us waiting with a held breath like me, Ellamight shakes her white hair, the slight glow it gives off twinkling in the setting sun that streak through the branches of the trees around us. Not as tall as the trees grown by us in Nerdiver's grove, I wonder secretly if these ginormous trees are descendants from the great first elf tree so long ago.

Pulling her hands free from my own, I see I have pushed too hard, Ellamight's blazing navy blue eyes just like her fairies dust, turns from hurt to direct concentration on the spell we need to perform.

"We have a protection spell to weave. This discussion is for another day, and not with me alone. I will not talk about anything to do with me and Spitfire unless she is here. We have both been spoken about behind our backs to much in our lives. Our destiny has been decided by others who wish not consult us on it first" Making a clear stance that she will speak no more of this, she huffs at me. "Are you ready to do this spell or shall I come back?" Marching over to the base of the Chifferen Tree, the guarded stairway makes the protector in my feel sick. How Cyth ever thought having an entrance to his castle with not gate or protection at all astounds me. Yes, him and Nerdiver are very powerful but anyone could wonder in. Though maybe until now, we are the first creatures apart from them to venture this far into the forest.

"I apologise if I have made you uncomfortable or if it seems like you are betraying Spitfire. We shall do the spell of course. We are after all in dire need of it."

"Good"

"I must warn you though; I am not done with this conversation. I will bring it to you again."

"Right you are. Now let us begin"

Talking through quickly how we are to do this, we both move away from the steps and out past the line of guards. The circumference they have created is about two giant trees away from the Palace of Chifferen. Splitting up, we head in opposite direction. Walking around once, we circle where we are going to perform our spell, planning out the route so this works perfectly on the first go. All our lives count on this going without a hitch.

Thinking my legs would have wanted to have dropped off by now, I walk slowly, taking in certain points of my surroundings, working out the beat our spell. The moments where I will raise the power flowing from Earth Mother, I make marks in my head. Wanting so desperately to fall into her embrace and sleep, I do not know why but my mind wonders to where Master is now.

Will he know where we are. He is overly cleaver so I'm sure with his logic he will assume we have come here but what if he doesn't. The magic he is falling upon may be dark, however I know there is light in him still. If I can teach him, mould him in the right direction, the power in him would match mine greatly in bringing the next generation into our world. Only girls, that's is what I need to start with, for four males I have let to help repopulate with my girls, well two because two need to wait to match with the third generation so our bloodline has enough mixing to it. Oh how I love Zeit and Thadus but there love for each other really does make bringing our kind back harder. If only we were like the fairies and could merge our sparks together to create children. There would be millions of us rolling around by now.

Comparing the two front runners Leach and Master is an easy thing to do. One is so calm, casual, and in no rush for me to pick them. The other needs an answer now, he feels it's his goddess given right to be my match. Unlike Nerdiver however I do not feel love to either, I am not sure if I have the true capacity for true love. I wonder if that is why I push for everyone to find there Souliune so deeply. At least they can have a life filled with such deep love; mine I know will come from the love I give to my girls once they are here.

Meeting Ellamight at our starting position, I give her a meaningful smile, the spell we are about to perform will put us out of action for a few days. Each time you perform a high level elven incantation it's drains all the magic out of you. We are creatures born from magic, made so purely from it, that it takes a while for the goddess too flow it back into us. The groves spell had all four of us working together so we shouldered the burden but today the two of us will shoulder it alone. The night I performed the spell to give Nerdiver her legs, I was in Earth Mothers embrace for days. Using elf magic for small things does nothing to you but huge spells have a consequence. If they didn't they wouldn't work so powerfully.

"Ancestors great and small, Earth Mother mighty and powerful, I ask you to help us bind this place in protection. Your families and chosen are inside this Palace of Chifferen. Help Ellamight and I guard them, protect them, grow them. I call upon the lines of queens in my ancestry and I call upon the mystics in Ellamight's to grant us the power and energy to cast this next spell!" Moving my hands up on either side, Ellamight does the same our hands pressing into one another to begin our casting.

"Ancient lines flowing in our blood, I ask you to fill us with your wisdom, to make this protection spell work first time. For once is all we have and shall need. I ask you mystics, alive and well, dead and gone to sing us your chant, so we may sing along" Singing the last part of what she says, Ellamight's crystal clear voice could give Nerdiver a run for her money against her siren call.

Starting the spell this way is how I always begin when I perform elven magic for a big incantation. Ellamight doing the same in the grove, I knew then she was my casting partner for this me. Feeling our palms warm with the sign that the ancients are with us, we begin.

"Tracoon" We both call out, pushing away from each other, the beat of our spell joining with our heartbeats.

"Gurrat" I sing, walking along the route we have planned out.

"Lethin"

"Tracoon" Slow and Steady, each word comes out one after another to help the beat of my heart. The calming sensation I feel tingling through my hands as I float them up and down around me, flows through me, Ellamight I'm certain is doing the same walking the opposite way to me.

"Gurrat"

"Forine" Stopping after every third word for a silent beat, I sing the next word.

"Tracoon"

"Gurrat"

"Lethin"

"Tracoon"

"Gurrat"

"Forine"

Singing each word with each beat, I slowly pick up my pace, the points I picked out in my first walk around, signalling for each of my steps to gain in speed. My words following suit as I repeat and repeat and repeat, everything flows faster as the spell forms.

Power flowing around me, I do not look behind, knowing full well that this spell is working. Seeing my next point I picked out, I am now skipping hard, the speed in which I am moving means Ellamight and I will meet again very soon.

The trees all around mixing in tune with us, I hear the patter of rain drops hitting a thousand leafs overhead, the strong droplets coming from the power we are bringing to this place. The sky becoming heavy, whenever an amount of power like this is performed using elven magic a signal is shown. Needing to complete this before any attack comes our way, the swirling clouds up above that I cannot see will tell any dark army wanting Knollica where we are.

My words speeding up out of my lips, the spells sizzles away from me, projecting up, my body creating a line for where the protection spell will come to life.

My arms weaving back and forth, I hear a crunch in the earth, not knowing exactly what the outcome of our spell will be, I know no protection spell like this has ever been called upon. In the long line of mystics, the elven community do not usually create barriers against the world, which in favour of us will help when we move to attack and free the mirror Queendom from Kia's suffocating hold.

Ellamight coming into view, a direct line to where we began, the position which will bring us opposite the entrance to Chifferen marks the end of this call we sing to our ancestors of old. A warming wave heading in my direction, I know the same is headed for Ellamight, a build-up of what looks like thick maroon looking vines bursting out of the ground behind us.

Concentrating on my words, I click my fingers, inviting the rock troll ancestors to join in on our spell. Feeling a pull in my chest, it signals to me that I am about to sing our final words. The magic's in me letting me know I am moments away from Ellamight and sealing this Palace in peace, I put everything into it. Calling up the goddess's magic so the barrier will hold for eternity, I let the last of my energy free.

"Tracoon"

"Gurrat" I sing, Ellamight's voice bouncing off of mine as we spin closer together, our flowing movements egging on the weave of this spell.

"Lethin"

"Tracoon" My final four words leaving my lips, each word comes out as each footprint I make in the grassland under me appears, the speed Ellamight and I are moving putting so much pressure on the earth.

"Gurrat"

"Forine" My arms flowing so they aim in front of me, the elven goddess before me does the same. One step away from each other and I see the effort of this happening to Ellamight, an elf who has not received all of her Mystics training. From my point of view though these past few days shows she is way beyond a normal mystic level, her glowing form radiating more power than any elf I've ever seen use magic.

"Ethial" Our hands smashing together, ethial is the final word we utter, its meaning is forever. Power blasting out around us pain shoots up my arms and down my back as vines break out of the earth beneath us. The thick tree like defence aims to seal us both in the new shield we have created.

Without thinking, I phase into Tylimantrica, taking Ellamight with me to protect her. Yes we have created the barrier for Chifferen but never does it say in elven magic history that the spell will not harm the weavers in the process.

Vines growing up fast around us, thin tiny spiked ones swivel passed aiming for the space above while thicker chunkier vines just miss us as they squeeze around our forms. Calling to Earth Mother to move us out of harm's way, I'm instantly heard. Pulled in the direction of the safety of Chifferen, we are spat back up onto the earths top, mine and Ellamight's visions sliding to black as the rain we have crafted finally breaks past the tree line and onto our burning up skin.

Master

Sent away by your own queen, a troll who you worship more than anything else in this world, what an embarrassment. If it happened like that with anyone else I would be long gone by now, leaving this world to crumble. But to save our race, to be its saviour I need to take the underground way. Move on and wait for your opportunity.

Coming straight here, my home is the only place my darkness is appreciated. Deep in the heart of Earth Mother, my cave welcomed demon and I with its stale warmness and cosy confinement. The only way to make it to this place is through the goddess and for the rest of my kind Tylimantrica will not allow them here. If they want to find me, mother will tell me.

Made up into one huge low ceiled area, my cave has one section of to the side which I have carved into to create my laboratory. Demons home, anything I wish to work on lies there. My next task awaits me patiently, demons dark presence swallowing any chance of light making its way to my corner.

Before I give my newest task a thought I concentrate on the mini structure I have before me. Working on it for the longest of times, it started out with how the ruins of our previous Kingdom actually looked. Rotten and abandoned our once powerful castle and fortress shows me the weakness it's had instantly. No underground defences or quarters whatsoever existed. How could my ancestors believe they were untouchable. One small break in its armour from the heavenly creatures and my race crumbled.

Starting a recreation was at first for my own loneliness to be squished. Earth Mothers idea, she gave me the recreation as a present once my parents decided to let themselves turn cold and hard upon a hill and leave me with no one and nothing. Once I found out about Nimfa, her need to bring back our race and that she had a plan to do it, I knew she would be mine. After the gift I am planning to give her, the second of my gifts to her will be the beginning of this recreation. Eighty stories, thirty above ground making the castle stronger and harder than our previous home of power, my new design has fifty stories deep into the heart of Tylimantrica. The building devilling so deep into the core of power ready to feed us whenever we require it, the fact my ancestor didn't have the strong connection to Tylimantrica was there downfall for the get go.

Unlike my useless race that came before me, this structure will be a presence in this world that will crush all others. I gave the fairies a chance to join me and the burning orange circle on my chest burns with the pack I sealed with Flighty. I will make sure he is on my side when this battle is done but for the rest of his kind, they can burn with the elven monsters that control them.

Stroking the flat top of the squared structure I have created off to the left, this castle has so many different shapes and angles to it; I hope it hurts anyone's brain trying to look upon it while seeing if they can find out the best place of weakness. For my castle and future domain will have no weakness that even a rock troll could try to hurt. The earth is the strongest entity on this planet, and I will harness its power to shape my dark structure onto my people.

Tapping the squared off roof that will be the home where our races children will learn how to harness the dark power I have created, grown and crafted, I pick up my burning orange flame. Started with just one spark of my skin in the palm of my hand I move to the other side of my cave. Light being an issue for most creatures in our world, the one thing my kind did think to learn quickly was to harness our sparks and turn them into the flames to light darkness growing in around us. Not yet learning to see in the dark, I welcome the darkness, but ask it to let me see in its void so I can create and bring it forth as I do on a regular basis.

My last task I completed, I used the darkening part of the forest near Nerdiver's pond to grow the small creatures there into monsters nearly as big as me. What they went to do I am not sure, but deep down I feel a hidden figure guiding my actions. I once thought it was the goddess, but I feel the guiding hand hides in the void of darkness that I can create. I am certain in fact that Earth Mother is not aware of my demons presence. Knowing I do all this for her my need to let this guiding hand tell me what to do, to gain the gifts needed to achieve Earth Mothers plans outweigh the fear that could develop. For I am the one true dark rock troll and the future of our race lies in us winning at all costs. I am certain Earth Mother knows the price that is needed to pay for our goal to be achieved, the falsehoods in my own mind send strength to help me continue the work I bring into this world.

Moving over to my lab, the walls reflect my firelight here. Unlike the rest of my cave which is bland and subdued with the walls looking like black fresh soil. The walls on my lab have harden. Harder than anything else on Tylimantrica, the walls here have been imbued with the darkness I create, the rock surface giving off little black lightning bolts whenever my fingers graze them.

A table is not needed here for I am the only tool or machine I will ever need. Demon hunched in the corner, I do not even look his way, his need is only for when I fight. Anything else and he is useless to me. Considering he has so much darkness inside him that you cannot see his face or features even slightly, I see no point in giving him any time. What is the point in looking upon something you have created so darkly that you cannot use him all the time. Hoping to siphon some of that darkness away, not to weaken him but to make him more useful I concentrate on my next task.

Wanting a stead for both me and my queen, I feel it is only right the new rulers of this world should have something above anyone else in our world. Creatures who can carry us but also protect us if needed. I will have to be particularly careful with this task for to give one to Nimfa she needs not to be able to see or feel the darkness that will have formed our steads.

Standing before me are two cages, one has a small placid fur ball inside and the other, an overexcited ball of joy. Crying out to me, the overexcited ones face has huge eyes that for anyone else would cast a spell on and make them want to squish it. I on the other hand is repulsed by its cuteness. Why does everything or anything have to be cute in this world. My one feature I hate so strongly is the cute orchids that grow on my cheek, changing colour depending on how I am acting to the world. Turning pink when I was trying to seem friendly and calm to Flighty on our first encounter, it mainly stays black now, my true self refusing to hide as much.

Choosing the calm creature for myself, I feel Nimfa would enjoy the company of a stead that is a ball of energy. With all the children we will have one day and overexcited one will not hurt her.

Sizing to half the length of my leg, these creatures are far too small at the moment. The calm one being a feline of some sort, its fur is so long and pristine anyone would think a magical creature brushes it daily. Holding it down here for weeks I know that is not the case, the only time it decides to call out loud is when it wants food. Feeding both the feline and canine which the other one is regularly, I have been putting a tiny amount of my spark readying their bodies for the oncoming transformations.

Needing to able to hold the weight of my kind, they also need to be twice the size of us. A normal horse or stag which the elves ride would never work for us with their easily breakable bodies. No for us, we need feral beast that command attention and are feared by those that look upon them.

Choosing them first because they are a white colour, both creatures have a beige line running down the back of them, seeming even though they are different species that they are brother and sister. The boy being the calm golden eyed feline, its sister is the overexcited amber eyed pup.

Moving to the gates, I leave my ball of flame floating behind me, the feline giving me a side eye while the canine bounds against the cage door wanting me to let her out to play.

"All in good time little canine. After what I am about to do, you shall never be caged up again. Your mother awaits you but first we must have you looking your best!" Me glee at what I'm about to do feeling like a mistake, talking to the canine directly only gains me more excited cries from the ball of energy.

Questioning if I should have chooses another canine for this task, the feline moves so he is pushed up against his sister's cage. The excited canine calming so she can snuggle into the fur of her brother. I see the feline can calm her like no one else ever will, but thinking of my strong willed queen I know Nimfa will have no trouble.

Readying myself, I hold my hands out by my sides, letting my head lean backwards so I can stare up at the ceiling, the reflecting darkness crawling down into my opening mouth. Letting the darkness seep into me, the shine on the walls give of a cold touch, the iciness needed to perform dark magic. The drug darkness has become for me must be what Nimfa feels when using elven magic, though this is so raw and divine I do not know how anyone else doesn't use it like me. Flighty giving his partly up, I know deep down the darkness begs him to use it rightly, and when the time comes my pack will make sure of it.

Prepared, I drop my head back down, both animal creatures now sit patiently at the front of their gates, there need to escape their cages at any cost allowing them to let me do whatever I want.

Taking my index fingers on both hands, I reach up on both of my sides and place them on either shoulder. Our skin being the key to any and all power for a rock troll, I scratch down, the natural spark coming off my stonework lets me create anything I want. Only using it to form objects or weapons and armour in the past, Nimfa and I along with what is left of my kind have found out we can mix our sparks together to form greater magic's. Alone out of our race, Nimfa and I mix it with otherworldly power, our will then becoming reality.

My sparks bounding off my body, they spin around the lengths of my arm as I make my fingers work themselves down to one another. Creating as much sparks as I think I need and will want to balance out the darkness unlike when demon was created; I reach my left arm out to the wall, the black lighting sizzling against my skin before getting trapped by my sparks surrounding that arm. Holding it close to me, the lightning is like my own personal supply of darkness, numbing my arm as I hold it there.

The guiding hand still in the back of my mind, I reach out with my right hand, still not looking at him, I grasp the shoulder of demon, his vibrating skin buzzing under me as I listen to the guiding hand telling me how best to siphon demons darkness without taking his raw power away. Drawing it out of him, I feel the dark power numbing my right arm two, my sparks barley keeping all the darkness caged into me.

Putting my two arms together, I aim with intention at the two curious yet slightly fearful creatures looking at me, their giant coloured eyes seeing everything. Not wanting the colour of their eyes to change, I put as much of my spark into this transformation that I can. Grounding myself in Earth Mother, I call on her for a little light magic, the kind she is truly made of. The darkness I am using now hidden by my sparks, guiding hand has taught me to make it so the goddess only see's light she wants for this land.

Healing and warm, a small burst of glowing light rises up from the bases of my feet, my connecting part of her feeling like this so the only thing I am using to change these creatures. With me every step of the way now, Earth Mother helps me as I release all the built up power and fire it at the two baby creatures.

Splitting in two, the sparks, darkness and light smash through the cage doors blasting them open, only to fully envelope the two animals to the sound of their cries and smell of burning flesh.

Growing quickly, so quickly in fact that the cave walls expand with them, the two creatures become bigger than I had even wanted them to be. Morphing first, the canines shoulders burst out, her whole body becoming a mould of muscles ready to hold any heavy weighted creature on her back. Her tail which use to twirl up onto her back so it arched over her spine, now hangs heavy behind her, the only other difference to it is now it has a spike at the end like a scorpion. Clam and gentle her tail looks heavy, my hope it is something she can use to protect my Nimfa when the time comes.

Her feet no longer looking like cute little pads they are now instead heavy face sized paws with daggers for claws which scratch at my stone floor. Her face changing the most, instead of the cute hanging ears, tiny buttoned nose and droopy checks that hang down from her eyes. Her face is the only part of her coloured fur to change having turned completely black. Four razor sharp fangs now hang out her mouth, her cheeks only slightly drooping from her eyes, my best at keeping some of her cuteness working, for Nimfa needs to want to love her is she's going to be her protector. Keeping her button nose, yet expanding it to the size with the rest of her face, her ears now stand up, and are longer and wider than they were before. Growling at me her amber eyes now glow with power, her hunger to fight burning out at me.

Looking next to my calm feline, the creature has taken in much more light than I had anticipated. Glowing everywhere, the fur on my feline is not as long as it once was but is shines like the moon on the blackest of nights. Finding it hard to look upon it, the feline's features have morphed into the look of hate. Its nose now pitch black rather than the pretty pink it use to be, a suspicious look seems to be fixed on his face.

Just underneath its nose, its mouth has widened to double its size. The feline's cheeks are puffier than before to fit in millions of teeth. A creature trying to come at that beasts face will be torn apart before they even see the teeth from the light coming off it. Hoping the glow is something it can control, sneaking up on someone will be impossible if it's always as bright as this.

Its golden eyes turning to slits as it analysis me. The feline's ears have also grown in size. As well as its paws which look like they will give an even stronger hit than my own punches do. Buzzing with power just like its sister, I walk up to touch its fur; I hope the glow coming off of it is because it is happy that I did this.

Reaching out, the feline holds its head up as my fat stoned fingers touch the fur. Soft and hard at the same time, the fur seems to now be a kind of metal, yet completely comfortable for the new beast to have. Looking down at me, the golden eyes glow as the feline quickly licks a bright pink tongue against my face, making me laugh out loud at the un-expectancy of this move. Its glow dying, I feel a breeze reflect off the wall behind us as my feline swooshes it's magnificently ginormous tail.

"Well aren't you two the most Beautiful and fiercest creatures anyone could create. Nimfa is going to love you!" I shout, gaining two roars from my two new creations.

Moving them out of the broken cages, I move to stand in-between them, a feed definitely being on the cards before I bring Nimfa her new gift. Stopping before I have to chance to call out to Earth Mother to lift us to the surface, Demon's consequence to the siphoning I put into these new creations is clearer than I could ever have intend.

Start of a new world order

Nimfa

A gathering of the most powerful creatures in the world is taking place right now. Only a few are missing and that is solely on the account of this meeting needing to happen.

The room which reaches up higher than I think the sky even is a grand like hall and from the look on Nerdiver's face is a brand new purpose built room which didn't exist until we all ventured here. Working around the clock while Ellamight and myself had been past our for five days, the protection spell we weaved worked like a treat and every attack that has come our way has not even met the border. The vines that burst out of the ground not only show a physical ring of where a wall of invisible magic holds around the palace right up into the air but the vines also seem to be alive.

Telling me upon reawakening, Nerdiver has ventured out to the vines to see if she could open the pair of grand gates that hold the barrier line. Working with just her thoughts, Ellamight's and our hope that the queen and king of this place would have rule over the spell worked wonders. Of course the moment she had opened them an attack was waiting, hidden elves following us from the grove made an attempt to get into Chifferen but Nerdiver signal handily disposed of them all.

Explaining to me that the vines also act as a living being, from how she saw the vines had already stopped creatures unwelcome to us from getting close to the barrier. Some clearly slipping through in its early stages of growth, the vine does it job and more for stopping darkness creeping here uninvited.

The hall we are now in though let's in so much sunlight, I feel any creature that manages to get past the powerful protection spell with burn up from the light in the sky. Beige in colour, the walls have fine archways on all three sides of the hall, the only one that's doesn't is the main door of entrance. Two archways reveal elaborate stairways up into other parts of the castle while the one opposite the detailed carved doors opens onto a huge balcony that a whole army could stand up on.

Etchings with scenes of our past battle sit in between the panelled walls, the ceiling itself being an image of Nerdiver's grove after our uniting. Helping to remind us all of the fight that has brought us together, I live for the fact that Cyth wants memories of him and his loves life shown to everyone. The entry stairway to the palace shows the mellifine's transition from the beginning of their Souliune. When I finally regain my land and reform the Queendom of my ancestors, I know I will want our history proudly shown to anyone who comes to view us.

Split up into our categories, I sit on a throne like chair, the first I have truly had the honour of having since my life has begun. Wide set for my big hips and body, the chair has been personally created for me. The design in the woodwork has been made so the throne is a slight pink colour, the main piece of the throne matching my stone colour while the arms have moss growing out from where I sit curving over them and draping onto the floor, hanging like an overzealous curtain. Whoever designed it wanting to honour me and my kind by gifting eight seats around me, each matching the colour of one of my subjects, a personal place for each to sit on. The only one without a seat and presence here is Master, my guilt that he cannot be included in these discussions making me think that he is not the one to help me bring our race back. Even his pure and weltering devotion to me may not be enough.

The category next to the rock trolls is the fairies, the three tiny entities float in the air, there need to be seen by us in full means the seats that have be made especially for them are forgotten down below them. The crafter clearly understanding each of our kinds, they have made their seats all joint together on a platform of a tree log. The log reaching up to our height, the seats all sit equally, not one fairy up any higher than the other unlike my seat which makes it clear I am queen. Hoping they will sit in there leaf carved seating that are placed delicately on the log once we begin, at this moment in time all three look agitated as they whisper in a heated debate.

Moving around the room next, Ellamight sits uncomfortably in front of two of her own kind. A perfect leader in battle and in the day to day of running's of things but here as a mystic who hasn't fully completed the test and found what she is truly meant to be, she looks almost alone and awkward. Her eyes stuck on Spitfire and her family's forms, I can see clear as day how she wishes to be with them. Her choice would have her sitting on the log with the fairies all over her, her real family who care about her buzzing away with secrets she clearly wants to know of.

Instead sitting so upright and statuesque Ellamight could be made of stone herself, even the elves on either side of her locking into a stonework position looking like frozen in time. My own kind made of the stuff, the elves moving all over the world will always look much colder than we rock trolls ever could.

The elves seats are simple yet classic, with swirling designs covering the arms and backs of the seats. In contrast to the rigidness of the elves chairs, the final category in the hall is the queen and king of this castle. Clearly having been on a Souliune quest while I have been asleep, every time I see the mellifine's they have changed more and more.

There colours staying the same, Cyth and Nerdiver look taller, so there presence takes up more of the room than they use too. A feeling in my gut telling me there are nearing the end of their Souliune journey I believe deep down most of the drastic changes have already come. Their features both representing their new race and the power they hold with a fire droplet and a water droplet in the centre of their eyes, I know this is the future Earth Mother wants for our world. What there children will look like will be the true beginning of the new race, a feat I am excited to see.

Souliune which pretty much means true love is out there for everyone but just some creatures have been gifted by the higher beings to create a new. World shifters are what Nerdiver called us and I have no trouble seeing how this is very true. Never in our era of the world has a collection of creatures met together, so if we are to shift the world we better begin.

Our hosts thrones carve up from the tree base itself, two objects that I am sure will never move from the position they are in. Linked together by the back the new thrones are an entity of power in the room, the big curve at the back of the thrones surrounds both off them. Showing the mellifine's are equal in power and in rule, the curve haves a detailed carving embedded into it of Nerdiver and Cyth staring deep into each other's eyes, deep within a Souliune state. Matching the rest of their castle with tales of the world they have and will face I cannot wait to return here in a thousand years and see how there tales have grown into the memory of this tree.

A pool of water floating next to Nerdiver, Knollica is now alone in it, his all-knowing eyes staring deeply into the hearts of each and every one of us. Nerdiver's long arm is stretch out inside the pool of water, having already told us she well translate all of which Knollica wishes to say to us. One of his tentacles wrapped around the hand in his pool, I guess Nerdiver can hear his thoughts even when she isn't underwater. The physical-ness of their touch being enough to use their psychic connection, I still wish to have private conversation with him; maybe he can give me some advice on which troll to choose.

"I am amazed this is truly happening" Zeit pipes up next to me, my focus on Knollica taken away. "I know we have wanted this for a long time but for a meeting of this status to be coming true. You must be so proud my queen"

"I am proud. All the effort I have put into every moment has been working towards this. All of us fighting together, the elves who are true joining us and then Nerdiver's grove. Oh Zeit it is more than I could have imagined"

"And it's only the beginning"

"It surely is. I promised you the first time we met in that tiny cave you had taken up residence in that I would bring back out race. I promised we would not fade away any longer and Zeit I will need all of your help to achieve it. This discussion must go how we planned. We cannot leave this room until a strategy is in place for an attack. If we want the peaceful life all of us crave, we must work together to achieve it." Keeping my voice to a low hush, Zeit does the same as what he says next cannot be heard even by our people.

"You know Thadus and I want nothing more than a peaceful life but surely that is a long way off. You haven't even chosen a mate yet"

A shudder running through me, my hate at being rushed for a decision on such a topic flares in me. Knowing my people wait impatiently for me to decide who will Father the rebirth of our kind, I chide myself to calm down. "Now is not the moment for me to make that decision. I cannot hibernate now of all moments to form the youngling trolls. I am needed here to rule, to make sure my Queendom is ready to be ruled." I snap, the decision on who will be my mate is a decision decided when I am ready. When we have the strength of our land back, a place where we can deal with protecting the younglings without worry.

"I do not mean to tell you to choose now and create the younglings. I only we wish to find out who out of the five are eligible are in the running. I feel in my toes you have two front runners and I know one of them definitely is not Floouq for his immaturity shines whenever he speaks to any of us. Look at him now my queen, screeching like a baby bear at my hearts not so funny humour"

"He can be charming, and given time he may well mature enough by the time I have made my decision. Though do not put down your Thadus's humour, I myself have had a belly laugh or two on his account" I chuckle gaining a glance from Nerdiver who looks so heavy in thought.

"It's silly but we both love this place. There is so much light. The walls display scenes so enchanting that I do not wish to leave. Will our home be like this? I know it's the rock troll way to have dark and harden structures but I wouldn't mind having a bright place, one where I could teach all that is good in our world." Clear that his and Thadus's home is somewhere they will not return to, I think of how I have never really had a home. A nomad in soul, something has kept me moving off all my life, never letting me settle down in one place. Maybe it's because I await the time for our home to be saved or maybe I wish not to settle, because if I settle then I have to make a decision.

"Our Queendom can be whatever we wish it." Smiling at me, I couldn't ask for a better troll to be the one to teach my younglings one day. Bright and wholesome, Zeit is first and foremost my friend. The first of my kind that I found after Earth Mothers training, he has been there every step of the way with me. My closest friend, I know after this meeting and when we are not able to be heard by anyone else I will tell him who I am thinking of to be at my side. His reflective cream stonework gleaming like the buildings he wishes our homeland to be filled with, shades of bronze and mud scatter over him giving a layer texture to his skin. Wanting the same as him for our future home, I look into his bright green eyes, a complete contrast to his stonework, you cannot help be drawn into them.

"I think your younglings should be able to see the world as I teach it to them. High enough vantage points that Tylimantrica is completely open for them to see. The brightness of our world needs to be explained to them just as strongly as the darkness" He tells me sternly, like he is teaching me.

"If you want a view of the world and a huge enough tower that you feel the king of it, it shall be done" I say patting his bronze hand.

"Thank you my queen" He says leaning his head so I can put my forehead against his. An ancient offering of respect in our race, our stonework makes a tapping noise as we do it.

"Where shall we begin?" Cyth calls out to us all, the fairies all dropping down to their seats upon Cyth's way of beginning this discussion.

"Where indeed" I say, the rock trolls around me sitting to attention at my voice. Flicking my hand for Zeit to find his seat, I ready myself for the discussion I have wanted for so long with Knollica.

"I must first say to know you are all here after listening to the true tale of our world warms my stone fingers. To see everyone so willing to accept the truth and understand what has to be done." Smiling my wide mouth at them all, I am greeted with the same all around.

Making sure to thank everyone first is all I've wanted to do since I've woken up. If it wasn't for each and every creature in this room coming to my call or turning on their superior Kia then Nerdiver's grove would not be a place of healing it now is today. What awaits us moving forward would not be possible if everyone here didn't share my goal of healing Tylimantrica all over.

"Thank you for coming to our aid in the grove Nimfa. Without you all of us would be dead and Knollica would be captured for certain. Only giving information when he feels it is important or useful without changing the world's future too much, the elves would not have been happy with his attitude to not helping them." Nerdiver says, her hand tightening in Knollica's tentacle as he forwards words into her mind I am sure.

"I have been working for so long to get to this point. Prilance has been at this game as long as I have. Finding true fairy power so many years ago, it has been harder on you staying away from the colonies and not teaching them what you know." I say looking to one of my oldest friends.

"The elves would have tried to crush you the moment it was discovered you knew the power you fairies hold" Ellamight says to her real family.

"They could have tried." Flighty fires at the elves sitting behind his sister's future Souliune.

"Calm grandson" Prilance places a hand on her grandchild. "I knew from the moment I met Nimfa my life was going to change. How it changed was not what I expected. Fairies are more powerful than we ever thought yet I do not believe all of my kind should possess this power. I know Nimfa that it should all be fair and equal but just like the elves only certain are trained in the mystic arts are they not?" She directs her question to Ellamight.

"They are-" She begins cut off from quickly by Cyth.

"Most elves do not have or hold the ability to call upon the ancient arts. Elven magic is controlled and developed over time which many elves cannot grasp the first idea of. I myself being one of those elves" He tells truthfully, the mystic's arts only being a woman's power and not male in the elven world.

"Males can have the potential" Ellamight tells Cyth some truth I think has always been hidden from him. "However the mystics of old do not think the male ego can handle the power that we possess. They lied thinking you could use it for the wrong reasons."

"And elves have only ever done things for our world that benefit the creatures of this world. Never would they put other down and make them useless to what power lay dormant. Rock trolls have nearly disappeared because of the lies elves have told our ancestors." Xen, a usually quiet deep green rock troll says in a cold turn of the conversation.

"Like I just said to Cyth, the elves do lie. But Mystics live away from the Queendom. Only warriors like myself and the queen are allowed in the mirror Queendom of Horndon." Ellamight counters.

"Why do they live separately from the rest of your Queendom?" Flighty asks curiously, his interest sparking into more information that most of us have heard about the elves.

"Apart from warriors or the queen and her heirs, the mystics are not for the day to day workings in the Queendom. They have a higher purpose." Cyth says.

"What purpose would that be?" Nerdiver quizzes next to him.

"Only the mystics know." Ellamight answers truthfully.

"And you are not a full mystic of yet." I inform the room.

"But the power you have performed in front of us all. How can a mystic not completed of her training be out of the confides of the mystic community and be able to perform two such powerful magic's so easily." Demich, a ruby red coloured rock troll of mine asks behind my back.

"Warriors trained from birth who are found with the mystic ability are lessoned by the queen. Only when they have completed the final task do they go to the mystic community and find out the true reason for their power." Cyth answers for her, there long friendship still holding strong even though he is no longer an elf.

"Why did you and others of your kind have tasks then? You are not a mystic but you and Ellamight have tasks to be completed given by the queen. Yours was to imprison me as Knollica's protector which you did over hundreds of years ago. Why has Ellamight not completed hers?" Nerdiver asks harshly at her partner.

"My quest and final task for completing my mystics training is one in the same. But every highborn and high ranking warrior must complete a quest to show there worth. Mine has been finding a location of where I need to go over the last hundreds of years to complete my personal task. Only meeting Spitfire has my location become apparent." Ellamight says pushing her chest out at the fact that she could be soon finishing her quest and training, a small light shining from within her. "The reason we are here is to take back the mirror Queendom for the good of our queen and world. It is why I am not on my quest right now. My natural ability to use elven magic has always been heightened but for the reason we started this conversation. Prilance, more elves could potentially use the ancient arts but not everyone should. Take Cyth's father for instance or Kia; if they had the ability what we would be facing could be so much worse"

"Worse?" Leach hisses out directly behind me. "Hasn't she got mystics on her side or under her control? She may not have the magic herself but she has the soldiers who can do it for her." Making a fair point, I wait for Ellamight to reply.

"That is why we are all here today to discuss the next step moving forward. Not just in how races and world are changing but also the fight ahead we have awaiting us. The soldiers have already attack the border and it is clear they know where we are. Your border spell will keep them out for eternity but as elves they have the ability to wait an eternity." Cyth once again answers for Ellamight, a protective older brother vibe standing behind her at all times. "Mystics report straight to the queen but a few may have swayed from her leadership just like the army that attacked the grove."

"We did not sway, we were under orders, and orders commanded by the head of the Horndon Guard put in position by the queen. It is the queen we follow direct order from, and her orders were to follow Kia. We did, until the few of us that saw that was not what was right my prince. The queen is the one who commands the army. I am sorry to admit this but your mother is the one that sent us to attack the grove. Under her command were we meant to bring Knollica back to the Queendom." The elf to Ellamight's left pipes up, his words seeming to crush every ounce of Cyth in the throne he sits upon.

Nerdiver's free hand grasping her loves, she squeezes it hard before looking out at the gathered creatures around us.

"It is not possible what you say" Ellamight finally counters, her own eyes flicking to and throw on the floor as she seems to be working something out in her mind.

"It is the truth I speak"

"It is, I swear commander" The second elf agreeing with his fellow brethren.

"Did the queen speak to the army directly?" She snaps, the thought that this is the queens wish breaking her soul. Her eyes still flashing side to side on the ground, I feel she is trying to work a way out of this for the queen; this truth cannot be possible to her.

"Well..." The second elf stutters, unsure if he ever did see the queen putting the command forward herself. Looking to his comrade for confirmation, they both seem to think hard.

"Well what?" Prilance asks, her need to keep her fairy power to herself justified if this is how powerful creatures could overthrow. I understand her worry, and I have seen first-hand the selfishness of their kind with the treatment of Flighty and others can be. Maybe she can test the fairies she wishes to train, like the mystics do. It may be unfair but me as queen; I have elven magic and the strongest spark in my race. It is needed as ruler and head of a race to be the leader with power. Enough to protect us all. I will have to choose with the help of the goddess which of my girls will take over, a test that will tell me the one to carry on the legacy I am creating.

"I am sure I saw the queen." The first elf says his eyes un-focusing as he tries to think back. "The army was a small quadrant of our kind but it was still a big crowd to be a part of when someone spoke to us."

The two elves looking at each other behind Ellamight's back, I see fear raging between them that they have been fooled by someone other in their queen's place.

"The mystics Calendar" Cyth whispers from his side of the room.

"I know. That's what I am trying to sort through in my head. I am not bond to it as I have not completed my training. Memorising it hasn't been my first priority" Ellamight sighs, her clear honesty of wishing she was a full mystic shining through.

"What is the mystic's calendar?" Nerdiver ask what the rest of us are thinking.

"It is moments in our planned year in which all mystics have to take part in rituals, prayer, summoning, calling and so on and so forth" Ellamight tells her. "Warrior mystics are exempt from many occasions as they are key to the defence, protection and daily lives of our people. I am just trying to figure out where we are in the calendar for if-"

Speaking over her, Nerdiver's voice doesn't sing like it usually does instead she speaks as if she is reading to us. "Nevite untete takes place every fifty years to help find the source of all elven magic. Using all you have spoken of at one time, this time is one of seclusion away from any elf not included. A perfect time for an usurper to take full control of a city or Queendom." Knollica's knowledge clearly flowing through to Nerdiver so freely is spoken directly to us all.

"Would the other high elves not stop that happening?" Spitfire asks sounding surprised a Queendom could so easily be taken over.

"The higher elves are usually asked to be involved even if they do not hold elven magic's, they still hold powerful elven essence." Cyth answers, Ellamight still working something out in her mind. "Mother usually places one high elf in power to look after the Queendom while she is in a mystic's communion. I wondered how my father had a hand at gaining a small army to follow him to Nerdiver's grove. I knew he was crafty, but to be in bed with the person mother would think was worthy to look after everything was very sly."

"Your mother hated you father did she not?" Nerdiver seems to remember.

"Not hate... that was me. He just fell out of favour from mother, it happened a lot."

"Nevite untete begins at the rising sun on the day of the sun festival." Ellamight thinks aloud.

"That's a fairy tradition that they do five times a year. The last one happened weeks ago." Spitfire joins in her own thoughts.

"The fairies celebrate it five times yes but the elves only celebrate it once a year. Two weeks ago to be exact" Ellamight agrees "The event should end with the setting sun on at the beginning of moon festival. Which isn't for another three weeks"

"So if queen Glassadena and higher elves are locked away in prayer, Kia is the one who gave us the order. I'm sure I saw the queen!" The first elf puffs out in the stress of this new discovery.

"A glamour?" I ask. "Or if she was away from the crowd up above maybe? It would probably be very easy for her to paint herself in the queens light. She must have been planning the attack on the grove for the longest of times. This nevite ritual gave her the command and time she needed to find and secure Knollica. She clearly hoped the answers she would need to destroy Glassadena's reign and power, would be easily answered."

"I cannot believe Kia wanted to do this. She was but a strong willed good hearted leader up until now" The second elf comments, a history I feel with the usurper connecting them somewhere.

"She was a strong leader. One who feel in with my father and the lies he told. I would love to say he changed her, clouding anything she may have been in his eyes. A person able to change back but I do not believe so. If anything, my father pretended he wanted all the power and control himself yet he always feel under powerful women. An elven man who listened to the wills of them. Kia unfortunately is now only showing her true colours and we must do what we can in a short amount of time to stop her. It would be best to take back Horndon before the moon festival." Cyth says to the second elf but ended with his attention on the rest of the hall.

"The Queen is in need of our help. We must do what we can to make sure we can show her the power the mystics are looking for in the nevite untete is waiting below for us all to form as one. On that day the secrets the elves crave can finally flow to them" I say, looking at each warrior before me for a sign that what we are about to discuss will be invaluable.

"We need to have three groups when we attack." Ellamight commands "The first needs to be with the main armada that takes the focus of Kia and the guarded city. The second needs to be a special group with the aim to take out Kia, with it ending with her death or capture." Taking strategy control very easily, Ellamight's stern voice takes everyone's attention. "The last-"

"We must protect your mother. Any sign that Kia is the intended target and the queen will be in danger" I say locking eyes with Ellamight as we seem to have a plan that is identical.

"Who will be in which groups?" Flighty asks, he eyes looking with his best friend across the hall.

"We must stay with our queen. Her protection is our first priority" Nack a teal coloured looking troll says. His skin seconded roughest to Master, I remember finding him on the floor of a cave when he was a youngling, Earth Mother had tried many times to connect with him however his aim was to solely bury deeper into the earth thinking he was the last of his kind.

"Your loyalty and oath stand true and wise Nack. But it's the bigger picture we are working towards here. We must sacrifice our own needs of pure survival if we wish to make it out on the right side of this. Tell me, would elves switch to our side like you did at the grove if they see Cyth fighting?" I ask the elves across the room, Ellamight's timid position long gone now we are in full planning mood.

"If we did. I am certain of it" The second elf says.

"I believe anyone seeing all of us fighting together, just like when I saw all of you, will sway anyone. The truly brave enough to make a stand for what is right will choose our side. Kia would not have told many of the real truth behind her commands just like with us. We knew we were going to the grove to fight for our Queendom on Queen Glassadena's behalf but the reason was left out. Our blind faith was excepted until I saw Cyth and Ellamight, two of the highest elves in our race. When others shifted to what was true, so did I" The first elf answers me truthfully.

"In that case, my Souliune you and Ellamight must fight from the front lines. You must show the rest of your kind what battle they are in and which side they would be choosing." Nerdiver answers wisely, knowing Cyth is more powerful now than he ever was but his blur is and will always make him the fasted of his kind. Only the best of shots can ever hurt him.

"I will stand with you Ellamight" Spitfire calls from her side of the room "Always" My need to talk to them together sparking inside as I see them both smile at one another.

"Then our training to get your correctly powered for the harsh fight ahead must begin at once" Prilance says, her eyes flashing her deep purple colour, at the idea she can finally pass on her secrets she has kept to herself for so long.

"My rock trolls, most of you should fight alongside Cyth and Ellamight." Grumbles behind me, I stop them instantly with the flick of my hand. "My own protection has and will always be in my own hands. You shall do as I command. You will need to train with the elves to make sure they are ready and strong enough to penetrate the Queendoms walls."

"My queen. I ask that you allow me to be at your side at least" Zeit pleads. Him being my closest confidant, I wish to allow him by my side even to just make sure I protect him. I nod my head in a dip, my explanation as to why he won't be the only one to come with me will come when we are alone. "Thank you"

"Who will be part of the special unit to find and apprehend Kia?" Flighty says in a way that suggest he wishes to be a part of it.

"Master is to be the one who finds Queen Glassadena" Nerdiver's voice sounds, quizzing her own words as she says them.

"Why Master?" Leach fully questions the order that has come from Knollica.

"I agree. Master should be the one to find and protect Glassadena." I say my own need for Master to be away from the battle and put in a place where he cannot hurt any elves being key. Assuming the queen and mystics can one look after themselves and two have a no entry protection spell around the ritual, I feel this will make sure Master cannot do any drastic harm. Still fifty fifty on who shall be my mate to bring my children into the world I feel it's only fair to try my best at giving Master the opportunity to not destroy the world in darkness before I have a chance to heal it.

"I will go with Master" Flighty states his mind now changing from wanting to get Kia to controlling Master.

"No!" Nerdiver shouts as she leans forward in her chair. "He was the reason for your darkness! I won't allow him to taint you again" The protective best friend coming out, I see Nerdiver views Flighty as the little brother she has always had to protect still.

"That's precisely the reason I have to. I will not watch him taint anyone else." Flighty fires back.

"Master will not ta-" I begin but am cut off by Flighty's rage.

"Do not pretend to tell me what Master will and will not do!" He seethes, even though he is now more than he was because of Master, Master is the one who darkened him to a point he will not fully come back from. "I will watch him like a hawk. Any sign of his dark deeds and I will not hold back"

"I was about to say..." I stop, giving Flighty a stern look as Prilance puts a calming hand on her grandchild's back. "Master will not taint anything if!" I shout the last word before Flighty's heckles rise up. "You are there to make sure he doesn't. Your suggestion was going to be the same as mine young fairy. So calm yourself please"

Buzzing down, we quickly work out the rest of who will go after Kia and who will go with Flighty and Master. Bringing the meeting to a close, each group will reconvene and work out the details of our plans. They must all work together if they are to work at all. Moving to Flighty once the meeting is adjourned we both apologise for the miss interpretation of our positions on Master.

"I wish for you to control him while I am not there Flighty" I say with truth, my own curiosity of why Knollica wants Master to be the one to find the queen sparking. However taking him straight from the hall, I know I will only be granted talks with Knollica when he wishes it.

"I will ask for you"

Looking confused at the young ball of dust, Flighty smiles at me before explaining.

"I will ask why he wants Master to protect the queen. Give me time and I will return an answer to you" Flying out of the room after Nerdiver, I am left alone to work through my thoughts on how we shall pull this battle off. Hopefully we can before this becomes an all-out war.

Master

Desolate crumbled place of weakness. That is all these rubbles make me see of my kind. How they decided to create a castle that could crumble so easily, so effortlessly as their own need to survive, it makes me ashamed.

Knowing that this cannot happen again, this land needs to be whole. Healed, strengthened and masterful. It's Master has just arrived and I will make sure it will be impenetrable by the time I bring my queen home here to see what the rock trolls are truly about.

Wondering through the broken down entrance, every stone that use to be whole and strong now lays destroyed. Elves, knowing for a fact it was them, there magic resonate in the air over any stonework that hasn't been crushed to dust. Nothing still standing, no walls or fixtures have made it through whatever was finally done to this place.

Our history gone from us, I do wonder what stronghold my people were before they let it crumble to nothing like this. If only one statue, one past memory of a strong emperor of my kind survived, I feel I could pretend to be proud of our race. Looking around at this emptiness, I see that is something that cannot happen.

The rock trolls fleeing this palace before the only ones of us alive where born; none of us know what it was like. When all that is left is a pile of rubble, I know that if they were left long enough and Earth Mothers power bloomed again these ruins would be formed into new creatures like us. I will not let that happen, today I will use the ruins around me to begin the rebuild of the strongest castle in the land. My plan fixed in my mind, I walk with my beast's one and two to find the first location.

Finally thinking I should name them if I am going to gift them to Nimfa, the feline, my beast I have named Blaz for bright light he brings into the world. The canine who will be Nimfa's steed and protector is Cerene meaning calm for since I have performed the spell she has become beyond calmness and her immaturity gone.

Following me without even saying a word, I have left demon back in my cave, his presences will not be called upon now until we go to battle. He sight sickening me since I siphoned of the darkness keeping him blurred from the world, I know I needed to do it but to see what he truly looks like, who he truly is, angers me.

When Nimfa or I need to finally get in contact, Earth Mother will signal to us, taking us where ever we need to go. In that moment I shall retrieve demon, he pure darkness needed for the battle ahead. Assuming my rock troll goddess Nimfa is planning the attack on the elves as we speak, I ready our home for a place we shall need once we have won the war that has been raging silently for all this time.

Weaving in and out of the rubble, I scratch my fingers against stones as I pass them, my orange sparks flaring in the air as I make the presence of a returning rock troll known. My kind would have etched these rocks out of the earth moulding them over a millennia ago with their hands and feet. I only have until the elven Queen is defeated so tapping into my rock trolls ancestors past mouldings using the echo that fills this place, I shall build faster than any rock troll ever has. Doing it in a different way to my ancestors, I shall use my powerful spark to do a lot of the work while asking the goddess for a helping hand.

My darkness not to be used, I know I must make sure the only building I tap into the darkness for will be the dark school and lab where I will show my kind what powers I have tapped into. I know deep down the beginning of this process must be rock troll only, the looming presences guiding my hand in everything I do , must ignored for the duration of my time here. My hands and sparks being the only thing I can use, I walk up to a huge rock off to the fair right side of the ruins.

Today I shall start with three main pieces. The underground levels need to be warped out with Earth Mothers blessing which I know I already have, feeling her warming touch as I have moulded the small structured design out over the years. The first true place I will plan out under me will be mine and Nimfa's children's room, one for them all to start there small balls of life in.

Next I plan to reconstruct a grand throne room for my queen to rule upon, a place of strikingly clear brilliance that any wondering creature will cower in her presence. Lastly I will build a bedroom beyond any Nimfa could dream of for us, it including a perfectly secluded office for Nimfa to do her thinking, while working out how our race will grow. Our room will solely be more for her than me as it will be built as one of the tallest buildings in our castle so she can have the best view of the world all around us. The pinnacle point of the ruins, I look over to where I can already see in my mind which rock I will is for that. A granite stone the same pinkish peachy colour that her skin is made from.

Placing my hands on the rock in front of me, it's is long and flat, coming up so it is just higher than me. My creatures falling in on either side of me, I feel there light entity's emanating the fresh spell thrown into their bodies. Knowing it will slowly fade, the echo of my power will relax in them but right now the ebbing power coming off them helps me see the fine elder echoes of my people's presence here. The echo I need to tap into with building our future back up.

Tapping into it, I reach out scraping my index fingers from left to right in a slow concession along the rock face before me. The widest one I could see in the land, its need to be picked is obvious as it is perfect for making the shell face of the levels below. Fifty floors each will be crafted from the same gleaming colour that this rich green stone before me is made from. Ancient yet shiny, I want the underground world to reflect back our sparks as we walking the halls of our kingdom. Yes a queen will sit on the throne but this place will be my masterpiece, my secret kingdom which only rock trolls can enter.

With only one part going to be made of my blackest of night stonework back at my cave, most of the castle and kingdom will be made of multi-coloured readiness. Knowing more than anything that Nimfa loves bright colourful places, in her nomad way of life, any place I have hunted her down too is full of life and colour. I must make sure that the parts of this kingdom I am remaking has this in it for her. For if this is to be the one place she settles, it needs to have more hidden secrets and colours in it to keep her excited for the rest of our time.

Scrapping my index fingers they spark and spark again, my intent flowing against the rock face as I make sure I put no darkness into this creation at all. Hard work, I feel every scratch I make, each of my movements feeling like they are taking years with the fight of holding back the power that waits for me to use it. Too reliant on the darkness, I push through, my feet sinking into Earth Mother as my sparks grow, circling the whole stone before me its reflective smoothed off rock face ready to drop into the earth with me.

On my instruction as I place the full weight of my hands on to the rock in front of me, my sparks splitting into two groups moving to the left and right. Breaking up into fifty fine fire lines, my orange sparks burn fiercely as they glow brighter, turning into such a high heat they could cut anything on the planet. On my command, my sparks cut into the rock face on either side cutting in deeply as they serve the gleaming rock into perfectly divided sections.

My sparks dispersing after they do their work, I phase my feet out of Earth Mother and boost myself up onto the stone. Different to how I will be building my other two projects today I jump up into the air, the weight of my body landing down hard on the stone beneath me. Breaking any normal rock face, the green stone budgies how I want it to, digging into the goddess easily. Fifty times I jump on the stonework, for Earth Mother has to absorb each level separately, each one growing out into the expanse of the land each time the rock dips into the earth. Phasing the rock down into the secret underworld, I hope it looks just how I imagined it in my head.

The last stone slab waiting on me, its embedded sheet holding the top level perfectly still just above the ground to give me time to jump one last time. I see in my head how I want to earth to bend, form and break into the design in my mind. Jumping up again, I clap my hands mind jump while bending so my hands and feet meet the stonework in the same instance. My sparks bursting off my feet and hands all around me and the overgrown grass and weeds, I and the

stone slab are swallowed by our goddess. My finished
kingdom still a long way off, I get to work leaving my steed's
to relax up in the windless sun.

When hard work pays off

Nimfa

Pulling me aside now that they are ready to talk, Ellamight has brought me to see Spitfire. Clearly both so afraid of what is deeply between them I can understand just by looking at them, that they know something deeper is waiting to connect. Such a contrast in their biological figures, how could anyone think it be possible that these two are Souliune. Or at least that's clearly what these two are thinking.

Finally getting Ellamight and Spitfire alone and away from everybody else, this section of the castle we are in is enclosed within a full branch of the tree so there are no windows. Lucky at the opposite side to the door a balcony is possible. With a smell of freshly carved wood, I see once again I am in a newly created room, this castle growing so fast I do not think any part of the tree will be left to grow into.

With a simple desk, bed and wash space, I assume I must be in Ellamight's bedroom. No carvings on the wall, it is clear she has not made herself at home; the mirror Queendom still being her place of residence, I wonder where these two will have a castle of their own once there Souliune is complete. Mellifine is the word I have created for the moment for Nerdiver and Cyth but what will we call these two when they are no longer just and a fairy and an elf.

Dragging me through the simple looking door, I wait silently for one of them to speak. Spitfire sits at the corner of Ellamight's desk, her feet hanging over its edge. Papers are scorn out on top of the wooden surface, Ellamight's plan of how best to raid her home switching as much as my own theories of how we can gain access to the inner circle of the walls surrounding the elven stronghold without being seen.

Just as small as her grandmother and brother, Spitfire has none of Flighty's bulk in muscles, her body made solely for flight. Same dark hair, hers is recently cropped to a pixie cut, easier I imagine to maintain while her feature are strikingly similar to Prilance. If I didn't know they were grandmother and granddaughter, you would assume they were twins, Prilance stopped aging the moment we unlocked her powers. Wearing a grey waist coat on top of a long white dress that has a split down the side so she can sit easily, her face is with a soft button nose looks ready to crack.

Spending the last two days with Nerdiver and Prilance myself, we have been going through all and any avenue that is clear to us to break into the inside of Horndon. Cyth having drawn out as detailed a plan as he can, so far the best way we think we might find at gaining access will be of course, a combination of all of our talents. Now communing with Knollica to see if he can give us any clue that our proposed plans may work, these two creatures have taken the opportunity to bring me here.

Ellamight standing statuesque once again but against the wall so she can stare at Spitfire and me, I feel I am the one that will have to even begin the conversation. Ellamight's face powered with concern, I look deeper into her features. Her cheeks are high and pointed, cutting just under her blazing eyes, her dark skin making her ears pop out more as the break through the long white hair that covers her head.

Growing down to her hips, her hair looks like it could attack an enemy just as Nerdiver's does. Wearing warrior's leather, Ellamight is ready to fight whenever the need arises. Her little fairy looking like a fire cracker, I wonder how powers are growing.

"How is your training with your grandmother going?" I ask Spitfire a question that has nothing to do with why we are here, hoping I can at least just get these girls talking to me, period.

"Very well actually!" The small fairy sparkles "It's weird because before I never knew I had this extra power. All I thought in my life is I had a talent for helping the forest be healthy and grow a little extra when it needs it. But now the flood gates are open, it's maddening how much untapped power I held deep down." Saying this she looks down at her palms to check her newly found power is still inside.

"Have you tried using your new power?" I ask, very intrigued to see what Prilance may have got her to try for the first time. I know that Flighty created Nerdiver's powerful weapon and I remember way back in the old days when Prilance was about Spitfires age. She formed, knowing that her kind where not ready to know of her power and the elves would attack her if they knew of her gifts, a pocket of an Invisible home. Even to this day I do not know where Prilance takes up residence. How she did it or how she got away with sneaky back to the fairy colony one day to have her children before vanishing to be ageless and alone I am not sure either. I am certain Flighty and Spitfires family knows of her immortality but I feel up until what happened to Flighty they always assumed it was just an old wise tale.

"After I got it under control because I basically couldn't stop it pouring out of me at first. I did do something. I can see now how Flighty cursed half the forest on his way to Nerdiver's grove"

"Which is all healed now thanks to our joint effort Ellamight" I but in, my joy at the grove still shines from me.

"Which is so great! I wonder what would happen if I did the same thing and flew all over the forest while mine poured out of me. Yet that did not happen. Instead a pile of my sapphire navy dust sat in the middle of a randomly chosen room in this castle."

"If it is where you discovered your true gift then it is not a random room anymore. We must get Cyth to carve into the walls. Your family's history and self-discovery maybe?" Ellamight offers, her soul meaning to clearly help Spitfire feel loved.

"That would be a nice. Though we have already claimed the room now you see. The dust pile I formed, Flighty and my grandmother made me use that for my first time using my new power. The originally simple looking room much like this one except for the balcony is now cover head to two in a wild mini forest. Three trees stand in the centre all connecting at the roots as they branch out into a home for each of us. With a tinge of blue in every dark bark that covers the place, my power on first try changed the wooden items in the room into living breathing plants. My gift, the fairies gift is that powerful." Spitfire calls out in awe at how fairies can have so much power. How Earth Mother gave us all so much is a wonder but it is a wonder we must embrace and not throw away.

"It sounds beautiful" Ellamight whispers from her position against the wall cleverly hurt that she has not been invited to come see the feat Spitfire is capable of.

"Oh it is Ella! I cannot believe I have not made you come see it yet. Only when I arrived here you were so engrossed in your planning I wished not to disturb you and then you wanted to call Nimfa here." Her uncertainty for why I have been asked to come is clear, yet I want to make one last point to Spitfire before I begin pushing there Souliune in their faces.

"Spitfire, you're fairy ability is a very strong one. Though I have a theory your family... and by family I just mean the three of you, not any other of your siblings. I believe you are and will be the strongest of your kind. The kind of power you all possess is going to be unique. I know the fairies have untapped power but I believe it will not be in such feats as you growing new life from inanimate objects or Prilance and her invisible home. I believe your kind will just be far stronger than they are, strong enough to hold off against any other kind in our world but not as strong as the creatures in this castle." I say, informing not just Spitfire but Ellamight too.

"What makes you think that?" Ellamight asks what both of them are thinking.

"Nerdiver gave me the word of what we are on the march here. We are world shifters, created to shift the world in a new way. Our power needs to be great for this to happen."

"So the up and coming battle, this is what we are destined to do. Fight so we can shift the world?" Spitfire asks me.

"Yes and no"

"Huh?" The little fairy gives me a dry look, clearly a little confused by that answer.

"We are destined for this up and coming battle but as world shifters are destiny clearly lie's further ahead. There is more to our story awaiting us ahead. Who knows what that is, maybe Knollica. But for now the first step in us achieving this would be for you two to finally embrace your Souliune and begin your journey as Nerdiver and Cyth have."

Looking utterly stunned, Spitfire sits with her mouth wide open, making it clear no one has been this honest and blatant about the Souliune the two of them possess.

"What makes you so certain we have this deep connection that you say we have?" Ellamight quizzes me. Hoping it is to help Spitfire understand what they have inside them; Spitfire asks her own questions before I have time to speak.

"Yeah. We have touched each other's skins so many times over the years. Ellamight saved my life the first time we met by holding me in her hands. If we have this thing you say why did it not happen then? Like when Nerdiver and Cyth met. Flighty told me all about their history and how it works. As much as I love Ellamight, our races are two different for us to be together. For goddess sake she is bigger than my house back in the fairy colony." Spitfire sags, flapping her hands up in the air as she strops about idea that this could even be true.

"You have to be willing to allow it Spitfire. As horrible as the truth of it is, your Souliune could not have happened until the events that have transpired recently have transpired." I say breathing out a slow breath. "Without Flighty gaining his dust, Nerdiver her legs, this battle becoming a truth, you may never have had a chance to be the true Souliune's you are meant to be. You are special, so special that the goddess has chosen you two to change and became something new. You are able to start a new race, form an empire of your own. This is a gift you must embrace"

"Why must we?" Spitfire whispers, her worry that if it isn't true shining through. What if they try and it doesn't work. What if they feelings they both clearly have for each other are feelings that are just that, feelings. Nothing deeper which I promise them it is. "What if we try and it doesn't work. What if you are wrong?"

"Then I am sorry if that happens. I know deep deep in my rock skin that I am not wrong. Though...." I begin.

"There is only one way to find out" Ellamight finishes for me, standing as she motions for us to move out of the small room and onto the long balcony that curves up as does the branches arm of the tree.

Walking out first, I stride right up to the edge of the branch, a cluster of smaller branches are bunch here together. A cluster of birds nest has found sanctuary in the thick leaves, my first thought wondering if they are trapped here in our protection shield. Chirping and bouncing, I can't help but envy their innocence of the world we live in; clearly they are not upset if they are trapped here.

With no worries except to make sure whatever is able to eat them doesn't or that they find worms for their children, I envy them. If only I have to do that for my soon to be children. Instead here I am, pushing creatures to worry to embrace who they are for a future of a destiny that includes them for goddess only knows what.

Turning, I lean back against the balcony wall, my whole attention set on the two creatures slowly coming out themselves. Each so worried this will not work they won't even touch, spitfire walking out rather than flying just to make the build-up even slower.

"You both have to be willing for this to work. You must be open to this like Nerdiver and Cyth were open to the love that was waiting for each other. You are perfectly your others half's soul. Let them call out to one another and find the piece it is missing. Look deep into each other's eyes and let the world shift you into what it wants you to be, what your souls know you truly are" I press, waiting as the two scared creatures slowly look into one another's eyes, Spitfire pushing up off the ground so she hangs high in the air level with Ellamight's face.

"I'm sacred Ella" Spitfire whisper her own truth, Ellamight's hands coming up to hold Spitfire in them.

"So am I. What if we change so much I cannot complete my quest? What if we admit that what we feel deep down is true and it is all for nothing? I feel I cannot take it back one I let you fully in." Ellamight's own worries firing at her best friend are so raw I feel my chest ache. Ache for the feeling they have, ache for what if Spitfire could be right and I am wrong. What if Earth Mother isn't right about these two.

With no soul mate in sight for me, all I feel is a duty, a need to do things for my race. Love or a deep connection is not on the cards for me and I know it. My Souliune dos not exist, for in this life I have a higher calling than that of a lover. My next life, that's what waits for my soul, that's what will give me that gift, for this one. I have too many important things to do for my own wants to get in the way.

"Please just try girls. Just for me." I call out; both of them clocking me in a kind of shock, this impossibly private moment making them forget I am here. "If it works and you know it works, you can stop for now, complete this battle, this quest that awaits you and then finish you Souliune. But at least you will know. At least you will feel the beginnings of being whole." I push again, my patience growing a little thin that they won't just try.

"Okay. We shall try" Spitfire says.

"We will?" Ellamight asks her, them both staring back at each other.

"We need to know. I need to know" Spitfires honesty comes through, before she make Ellamight raise her closer to her face.

Reaching her tiny hand out to the strongly angled face of the elf before her, the two creatures lock eyes, Spitfires soft touch awaking something within them as they connect. Tiny but there, they freeze in place, their souls reaching out as a small amount of silvery glow resonates from Ellamight's dark cheek and Spitfires tanned skin.

Frozen in time, I stand watching for a long time, the Souliune reaching deep down into the centre of both these creatures. With how Nerdiver explained it, a world of white light guides you, the other half of your soul calling out to you through it. The goal, to reach the centre where the true embodiment of whom you both are awaits.

My body as solid as my own pinkish rock, I watch them, this Souliune not broken like Nerdiver and Cyth's first one was when they were attacked. Curious to see if they shall shift in anyway even at this point, I can't take my gaze off them. One so tall and giantess compared to the other, I knew they were Souliune however what they shall become is so interesting I feel my eyes may burn into the both of them while I wait for them to change.

A simple nock at the door shuffles my attention, my eyes which I didn't realise are so sore from just starting without blinking, leak with water as they try their best to refresh themselves. The trance these two creatures have drawn me into with them, does it's best to bring me back in as another light knock sounds on the door again. Not breaking there connection, the knocks are lucky just light enough for me to hear but not for them.

Swaying gentle past them so I do not disturb or intervene, I make my way to the door, it's softness to the touch confusing me but explains the light knocks as I pull it open to see who is there.

"Your majesty" Floouq nods to me, his dark purple stonework looking beautiful as it stands out from the palace's green walls behind him.

"Floouq. Are you okay?"

"Sorry to disturb you my queen. Master is at the main gate." He sniffs his manner of respect convulsing as he talks about Master. Most of our kind not liking him much I wonder how they will feel if I do choose him as my mate. Will they accept it or fight it until we are all gone.

"I see" I glance back behind me. This is their journey to take, I have started them on it but me leaving now will only be a blessing. Coming out of the Souliune I feel will be something they will welcome being in peace. "Bring him to my room" I begin to say as I exit the room, the soft door not even making a sound as I close it.

"He has asked for you to come see him. He wishes to take you somewhere" Acid falling from his teeth as he spits the words out, I feel a buzz of excitement that Master wants to take me somewhere. Never has he been so bold as to do anything directly before me. Maybe this is why I have waited so long to pick a mate. I want them to truly do things to impress me, not just the underhanded tainting he has done so far.

"Take me to him. This may be interesting" I laugh a slight chuckle, gaining a worried look from my subject. Just like Zeit said, this rock troll would never have been a choice for me. He is but a youngling who will hopefully be ready when my girls become of age.

"I must say though your majesty. Ready yourself"

"For what young one" I asked puzzled.

"The gates to this castle have started to become another graveyard. Kia is clearly sending a lot of attacks our way" Floouq says, a worrying sign we knew might come. "But at least we know your protection spell has definitely worked."

"I'm certain Master and I can handle a few elves but thank you for your concern" I send warmth to my subject, the fact my spell has worked, is a good sign for the battle ahead.

Master

"Why have you brought me here?" Nimfa's voice is filled with surprise, the crumbled stonework of our ancestor being in clear view at the angle the land makes.

"I have a few unexpected things for you" Wanting to give away nothing, I swing my arm wide as Nimfa walks on ahead of me.

A first few broken stones representing where the watchtowers of our old kingdom use to lay are piled here, the land muddy and dissolute of life. Ancient outer towers would have stood here, my first priority not being these, the ruins here help to keep what I recreated a secret. Hoping deep down it will still be an utter shock to my queen what I have been up to while they have been plotting, I move us on ahead. A burning ache coming from my forearm where a well-placed hit from a surprised attack the elves hit me with when I arrived where Earth Mother told me Nimfa would be, it didn't take me long to deal with them, though the hit is annoying to my ego.

Walking on, the land under us begins to steep upwards slightly, the ground hardening up as the muddy surface we have just trek is left behind. Hiding over the small hill before us, my newly build grand entrance waits patiently for its reveal. My hands crusty and raw after all the work I have been putting in for over a week, I never thought I was truly physically strong until I rebuild by hand the outer courtyard of my design.

Yes my kind are strong and our spark gives us the ability to form object we wish for but what I have already begun to achieve in such a small amount of time. If only my ancestors knew how much push we have inside of us, the feet we could have achieved on this world. I know deep down Nimfa believes the highly powered and over charged gifts all of us have is nature's way for fighting the extinction of our race, however I cannot wait to see in a few generations time the power our kind uses. The achievement I have already crafted in this time alone, the earth and stone listening to me, bending to my will.

This is more than just a fight for survival. The guiding hand hovering over me fills me with the knowledge that this is more. My dark power will give us all so much more.

Suddenly taking her breath in harshly I watch from behind her as Nimfa sees her newly built castle walls. Her feet doing what they always do when she needs to hold herself up, turning so they sink slightly into earth, I see her sway a little. Her fists clenching, her big pile of moss her even looks to curl at the ends she stares at the begging of our forever home.

Giving her time to take it all in herself, I finally step up next to her, looking out at the entrance I have made.

Classic looking, the entrance is broad, stretching out on either side of its drawbridge, held down over the extending drop down into earth, the moat I have dug falls so far into the earth that before it the brightly lit burnt red stonework fire's straight into anyone eyes. Finding the stone deep within what was the rock troll city, I move it to the edge of the land that now houses the inner fifty levels deep within the ground which has its contrasting marble looking green stonework.

Counteracting to the flashy green grassland under it, the high walled surround of our kingdom stretches up four stories, making sure any creatures thinking they could invade us will find it impossible to reach the top. The dip in the land before the wall was in need of Earth Mother's help, I found it completed once I hand stopped smashing my ruff hands onto the stone that now gleams before me.

Turrets stand out along the wall, places where I feel it is best for the future guards of our home to stand watch. The archway where the drawbridge comes from sits so high, I wanted to make sure when any creature actually walks into our kingdom the full stunning architecture fills the retinas straight away.

"Master... it's just so"

"Beyond anything you could have imagined?" I ask her

"I... I don't think I have full words." Moving ahead, she holds out her hands as she meets the drawbridge, her knees giving out as she leans down to place her hands on the rock, wood will never be a part of the rock troll design in architecture if I have anything to say about it. Everything will be made of stone, even the complex working that my sparks have already started to pull off.

"Are you ready to enter?" I whisper to her as her head leans down to touch the red stonework in an ancient rock troll greeting.

"There's more?" She sounds incredulous, as she shuffled to her flat feet "When did you start this build?"

"After the battle at the pond. I came here wanting to make sure we had a place to grow. We need our castle of strength to show every creature in our world we are serious and we are back. We cannot show what is rightfully ours if we have nothing to show"

"Nerdiver's grove" She says sounding as if she is correcting automatically.

"I'm sorry" I puzzle confused.

"The pond is now Nerdiver's grove. Oh Master you missed it. My dreams came true when four of us worked magic together. We healed the land and made it a place of healing and light. If only you saw it!" She gleans, nearly burning as bright as the sun as she ignores what I have said to her about our newly reformed home "Nerdiver's grove now represents the proof of what I have been saying all along of what could happen if we of all races work together. But what you have done here!" She shines grabbing my hand and flies us over the bridge, taking me into the work I have done without any other race. "I must see everything" Her true excitement to see what I have done, making me easily forget the first snub she had at my work.

A tunnelled archway, the thick walls of our castle stretch back like any true good defence. Entryways half way down, they allow easy access for the future soldiers of our kind to get on and in the walls. My wonder of what would even think to attack this place when we shall be the only power in the world by the end of this month astounds me.

Opening up just how the earth does when mother phases us up out of the ground, the tunnel unveils a huge open space mainly still filled with broken stones ready to be made into what my design is ready for. Reaching out before us is the biggest stretch of stone-tiled floor anyone will ever have on the planet. Simple designs can easily be shaded into the tiled floor but for now only one colour files under our toes.

Thinking ahead of how we shall grow in size and population very quickly once this battle is over with, I have expanded the circumference of our land, taking more than we may ever need. Cream in colour, the cobbles under our feet allow the outer walls behind me to burn as a warning to anyone thinking to approach our land. Off in the distance, the land is flat in our castle, the throne building and Nimfa's tower look small from where we have entered.

Moving in, I see Nimfa's eyes are alive with hope and the blinding future she can see just as clearly as I. Our outcomes may be a little different but once she see what I have created, what I plan to finish creating, I am certain she will join my side on how we must take out all the other races. Ours should be the lone survivor of the battle to come, but of right now it is time for a little happiness in our lives.

"It is not even slightly complete my queen but it is truly on its way."

"Master. How you have rebuilt this is such a short amount of time. I mean... I just cannot... I don't know... how have you done it?" She gasps, the throne hall becoming viewable the closer we make to it.

"Remember when we were young and Earth Mother explained to us how rock trolls only used there spark for mainly fire and had no connection to her?" I say moving us further into the courtyard.

"Of course, how could I not. Our kind we're pretty much like the fairies. We have agreed many times we may have well let ourselves vanish from the world. For if it was not for Tylimantrica's invention in our lives we could all be gone by now" Speaking of this many time's, it's in these moments I see my queen deep down does have the same goal as me.

"Well I have taken what Earth Mother explained and connected our power with it. That tree you were in is nothing compared to what this castle will be like when we are finished. I am trying my best to have it complete for when we have won the world" My pride puffs out, the work I have put in will be honoured, I will make sure of that.

"Oh Master you must stop saying that. Our goal is to unite the world; we just need to claim our part of it back." Her hand resting on my forearm as we step up to the clear view of the best creation I have made in the last few days, her touch soothes the ache coming of my scar as the throne hall fully comes into view. "You have already started our claim by what you are creating here, though how have you come up with all this? It is like you have taken my hopes and dreams for our home and made it more than true. I feel this place, it's alive like us"

"I have been planning our home from the moment Earth Mother found me" Signalling to something standing before the throne hall, I have brought my design of our future here so she can see it first-hand. Before she looks deeper into the giant building before us, I want her to see what our finished kingdom will look like. "What I have begun to form, what I have planned out here in this mould is a stronghold that no other race could even conjure up. We shall be unbeatable, and safe. My dreams of our castle our Queendom" I say through gritted gums "has been one of a lifetime, one I knew you would share"

"It's breath-taking. How you have come up with this is a miracle. Look at it all, so many different shapes and designs; it looks like something that could never work but works more than anything else in the world." Her fingers stroking particular buildings, I see she somehow keeps making her way back to the biggest building on the design, the throne hall that we are standing in front of.

"I have made it so our castle has more levels below, and the only way to enter it is as one of our kind. The best defence I could think of."

"A genius defence!" Her voice echoes up into the curved archways circling above us. "Are the levels ready to be seen?"

"Absolutely my queen" I say moving to pull her around the design of our new home so she is fully standing to stare at the building ahead. "But first would you like to have a look into your new throne hall?"

Giving me a smile that could break the world in half, Nimfa truly takes in the master piece I have created. My goddess and light, my biggest aim will be to craft a symbol of her grace and alluring power for all of our ancestors to worship. She may be the only female of my kind; however her shining heart is what makes her more than just another queen in our race. Her flawless stonework makes me want to reach out and take her whole.

Her sparkling two different coloured eyes glaze over as she stares at every part she can of her new ruling seat. The new building only freshly finish, I get transfixed myself. In a position of such power that if creatures make it in here, they shall know Nimfa is one untouchable monarch who will crush any who defy her reign, this stonework makes your brain stop just by looking at it.

No doors, the throne hall has spire after spire all interconnecting at the top with detailed shapes cut into the light cream stonework so from the inside the hall is lights up from all the natural light I could get to aim in there. Grooving Archways into every wall I made, only the front where we stand now has an entryway. Steps that swim around the whole structure, circle with a soft cover I know Nimfa would adore. Purposely putting no other kind of exit or passageways once you are inside only a deeply insert of a hallway takes you into the grand space. A hallway circling the outer rim of the building so anyone can walk under the archways leading the spot we are now in, I slowly take Nimfa through the elaborate stone so she can take in every detail she can get.

The entryway opening up, stairways move up on either side as you first walk in, upper seating high in the sky sit on the left and right. Wanting to make it possible that enough of our kind can fit in here when we have them, my aim is that all of our race no matter who you are will be able to watch Nimfa on the throne. I think I've managed to pull it off without taking away any of the light you see when looking up at the higher than possible ceiling. Taking a leaf from Cyth and Nerdiver's tree, I thought it only correct that our throne hall be as tall and surprising as there little tree is.

Clearly the work of Nimfa, the gates that now guard their home which gave me a little trouble when I first arrived, though thanks to my spark running through my veins and the darkness that anything in this world fears, they pretty much left me alone. Hoping Nimfa will make her mark on this kingdom too, we stop walking as we make it two thirds of a way in. The beaming green throne I have built for Nimfa alone calls out to us, its crystallized gemstone colour making sure it the draws eyes in the room straight to it.

"Your throne my queen" I give a sweep of my arm so she can feel the need to walk up to the powerful seat.

"Master your craftsmanship is a credit to you. This hall is so powerful; I can feel that underlining ancient residue of our race here. The passion you have flowed into this place will make sure any creature who enters will feel the light of us all." Grazing her finger tips on the inside of my hand as she passes, Nimfa walks up and surprising to me she moves around the throne. Her hands holding off from touching it, I see her reserve, the want in her is clear, but something holds her back.

"What is it my queen. I have crafted this for you. Once you claim it, no one shall take it away from you" I whisper in my kindest voice. My want for her to take this seat of power straight away drives me on, but my fear that her nomad status will hold her off from claiming a true home forever, all my work will be for nothing if she chooses Leach and to never take the seat.

"I cannot claim it" She utters the truth hidden deep within her, my head feeling as if it's cracking in two. Her small rounded feet stumbling away from the hard rock work as she moves back down the hall, in any other race the rounded heavy weighted body would jiggle. In us the stonework holds strong, the shape of us needed for us to be alive.

"And why not" I say harshly, feeling as though this entire feat I have pulled off is for me alone.

"I cannot claim anything until we have defeated Kia. I know it will seem absurd to you Master but to claim the throne would mean to claim our land. I will not do such a thing until I know it is mine without another fight brought to our boarders. These lands must be cleansed by my pack with the elven queen."

"Pack!" I bark, the audacity that we need a pack to have our land at all boils my blood. "We need no such tripe to claim our home. This is your true land, this is the reason you move around so much. This throne right here is for you to claim, and I am the rock troll who has created it for you. I am the rock troll that should be at your side my queen. We should bring the new era of our race in together. Your light and my..." Trailing off I leave the obvious hanging there, knowing Nimfa likes to pretend I am not as filled with darkness as I truly am. Yes when we were younglings I had only light in me like her, but I was never me until the guiding hand found me, if only she could see that. If I grew with the light, neither of us would be standing here right now.

"Master... I cannot" My Queen cowers, moving off to leave the hall.

"Nimfa do not leave me now. We must make our own pack. You know as clearly as I that I am the one to rule at your side. We are the ones to carve out the new world. Our world. Do not walk away and leave it all behind. We must choose this moment, seize it by the horns and form the path our race will take for generations to come." I beg her, my patience at waiting for her to decide which rock troll she will pick running out. It is clear it is meant to be me, I know it and so does she.

Rolling to her, I come up only to my knees, my hands outstretched for her to take.

"Master. Now is not the time" She sighs, the clear sign that this is not how she thought this was going to go.

"Please give me your hands." Doing as I ask, her smoothed off stone fingers fit into my ruffed fists perfectly, our destiny being so clear to me it cuts deep that she doesn't see it.

"I wish to pledge to you, my queen. I will eradicate every being who would stand against us. Every creature who would choose to think they are higher than us. I plead to you my queen that if you choose me, I shall wipe out all other kinds all over this land and gift that land to you. I pledge to gift you with more children than anything other creature to re-populate our race. I pledge to teach them, mould then into the rulers of this world. My queen I pledge to make our empire the most cut throat and powerful empire this world will ever see" Feeling my chest burn slightly as the ring I have created to bind me and Flighty is clouded in darkness, the darkness deep within me burns on as it wants what I say to become truth.

Pulling her hands free, Nimfa looks hurt, my need for her to make a decision clearly weighing hard on her. "I ask you not to. I ask you not to destroy the world as the humanoids once did, as the elves are now doing. You know as well I Master the balance the world needs. I ask you to help me with that. I ask you to help me bring the good in all the races together. Not drag us apart in world domination." Stepping back from me, I feel my chances of Nimfa picking me slipping away. My own need to destroy all, breaking the chances of her picking me, the guiding hand clouding my words I know could have convinced her with. Pushing it down, the hand's truth will have to wait, my own fear of not being chosen flaring brightly.

Knowing deep down more than anything that I need to be the father of our kind, I swallow the darkness bubbling up inside. I ignore the guiding hand helping me with my awful pledges. I see now I must do what is against everything I have become, I must mould myself to Nimfa's ideals to gain her trust. I must do what I must to become her chosen mate.

"Tell me my queen. What is it you ask me to do? What is it I must do for you to choose me?" Hearing the weakness in my voice, I see that it is what she wants, her eyes blazing with light as she sees I am willing to follow her orders wholeheartedly, even if it goes against my own gains for our race.

"We will be invading the elven Queendom within weeks. I ask you, to do as I ask. To not harm one elf who does not deserve it and on the order of your queen to move and guard Queen Glassadena from harm. I ask you to help me gain the footing we deserve in the world but by doing no harm" My gut flipping over and over inside as she speaks, my eyes burn into her two different coloured ones as her request asking me to be all I am not, flaring my soul alight.

"Master" She says stepping back up to me, grasping my chin by her hand so she holds my life force in her grip. "If you do as I ask. If you protect the elven queen. If you help me free her and gain the equality our race deserves. If you let your darkness go with the goal of world domination. I will choose you as my mate." My chest soaring as I feel every word I have ever wanted Nimfa to say to me hits my ears. I smile at her, my long elongated mouth looking as if it could fall off with how wide it has become, the guiding hand, clawing at my mind pointlessly for every word I have ever wanted Nimfa to stay to me fills me with the truth I have always wanted. To be picked. To be her mate.

"Is that a pledge to my cause? Is that your agreement for my plan?" Nimfa ask sternly, the softness that first coated her when we arrived here has completely fallen away. Left by the hard cut throat ruler I know I can help her be once we are side by side, I swallow my own plan; swallow my own wants for the goddess before me. One day she will let me shift this world, one day she will let our children help me.

"It is my queen." I agree, stepping up and back as she lets my now sore face go. "As a sign to my pledge, I wish to gift you with something else." I tell her before calling out to Earth Mother to bring our creatures here.

"More gifts? But you have crafted this place so beautifully it is all the gifts I could wish for." She bemuses, her softness creeping back in.

"I have much more to show you here. But first..." I leave the words hanging in the air as Earth Mother rises the stead's up on either side of me. "A stead, one for each of us"

Her orange and pink eyes blooming, Nimfa is in true shock as I introduce her two the beasts that will help us win our land back to full strength. A strength that will make her finally take that blazing green throne behind us.

Queens Choice

Master

Nimfa's tower truly has the view I had imagined for it. High up, with a hefty balcony that circles all around, I cannot lie that I was beyond ecstatic when my queen yelped at how beautiful her own space is.

The stonework outside matching her skin colour, the pink granite will stand out forever against the buildings I will eventually build down below. An array of three different types of stone rubble await be at the bottom of the tower ready for me to carry on with my construction work.

First wanting to take in her room and office alone, imagining her curled up in a perfect circle on the platform in the centre of the room, it begins to help me accept that I said I will not harm any unjust elf in the up and coming battle. Pressing my hands and then my head against the deep sea blue walls of this place, I take breath after breath for the fact I pledged that I will not harm the queen. How I have said that I will protect the evil creature that helped nearly be the reason we never existed anymore.

How could I pledge this, me the dark retribution wave coming for the rest of the world on behalf of our dead race. I feel as though I have betrayed all of our ancestors, thrown away who I am for a promise from my queen who could die in the battle to come. If standing guard for the elven queen is the only way for Nimfa to finally choose me and me alone, it is the right thing to do.

My queen, my goddess, wants this of me. She needs this feat performed by me and goddess it will take every ounce of my deprived soul to do it. Already I feel my fingers twitch at wanting to smash some elven monsters. I want to go home, take my newly acquired axes from Nerdiver's grove and chop some fast moving, life long, angelic pointed tall creatures that I am honestly surprised have managed to convince every creature in our world they are the beings of pure power and brilliance.

Taking another set of long over-due breaths, I concentrate on the orchid on my cheek. Black is not the colour it can be while I do my best to stow the darkness flowing through me. The fight ahead needs me to be light. It needs me to present the creature Nimfa wants me to be.

Taking the room into my soul, I breathe all my thoughts into making my orchid a light blue. Blue is the colour of the sky, the colour of the sea, two pinnacles we have need of in our world. If I am to be strong and stand next to my queen, I also need to be pinnacle in everything that happens here on out.

The change in instantaneous, and I feel it ripple all along my rounded ruff skin. Showing the world inside what I am feeling inside, the times I have forced colour into my orchid has helped me believe I can be the creature I'm needed to be. As of right now, pushing off the wall and strolling out onto the balcony to take in the bright blue sky of a new day is a must. The sky around Nimfa's tower is so clear and beautiful, if nothing can help me change the darkness set inside me, maybe her towers view of the world, of the kingdom may help me get through the one thing I have been dreaming about since I was a youngling rock.

This battle we face has now become to me a guarding post. My soul in mourning, I have hope too many elves behave in aggression while I stand guard to the queen in hate, giving me the position I need to kill a few. If not I know I will regret the day I could even get my chance to give some kind of payback to that race. They destroyed our home, destroyed the rock trolls. I deserve to make some of them pay for what they have done to us. Even if Nimfa doesn't think so.

Looking down over the balconies border, I see my feline stead far below, curled up in a ball just like how I look when I sleep. Resting for a while as it is too big to make any way up onto the tower, my fluffy steads calmness may also be what I need right now. My hands gripping the stone edge in front of me, the stonework soothes me as I scrap it under my fingers. Another wave of panic and pain that I cannot hurt one more elf, my reason of existence, burns through me deep, the guiding hand trying to break but in.

My eyes on Blaz I stand up straight as he calming presences shifts, something in the distance putting him on guard. Some kind of entity has entered my ruling lands, and if I am lucky enough, they might have a death wish.

Looking up, I see figures dotting up out of the ground, Nimfa's tower being so high in the sky I can see out of my kingdom's exterior walls. My stead clearly having a sixth sense for anything near us, I watch as nine figures erupt out of the earth, my kind, or unfortunately what is left of it comes walking through the archway to enter our lands. My idea of the rest of our race not seeing our home until it is completed, I feel let down as I watch Nimfa waltzing her subjects over the courtyard after I told her I wanted to finishes our palace first.

How could she do it. Yes she has her gift with her, her stead following at the back of the small crowd yet why would she lie to me and say she won't bring our kind here if that's exactly what she's done. If she lies so easily about this, what else may she lie about. What about the promise she has made me to make me her mate after the battle. So I promise to not attack any elves not deserving of it and she still goes and picks Leach, the ugly small faced troll waddling next to her.

Anger setting a light inside fiercely, I watch as Nimfa brings all of our kind to my design, each of them looking to take turns in touching the buildings I have taken so many years to craft. There dirty fingers rubbing my stonework, I hear on the whisper of the wind there laughter springing up to my ears as I hear my feline growl for me down below.

Turning away, I move down the towers steps, my first thought of making sure Blaz doesn't move to attack my kind out of loyalty for me. Yes he could destroy a few but all of them against my one stead. He has no chance.

My small feet slapping against the cool inner steps of Nimfa's tower, the extra rooms I have managed to fit in here lay empty for the day she decided what else she wants in this bright lit home for herself.

Thudding out next to Blaz I place my huge hand against he's his spine. His body relaxing instantly, he turns his razor sharp face to look at me, only to give a push off the side of his soft face into my raised hand. How could I know such a calming creature could end up loving me so much. His presence once upon a time would have irritated me, nevertheless now gives me the relief I am not alone in the angered feelings I have for my kind being in this land before I have had the chance to finish it.

Watching them all gather without being seen, I am truly invisible to my kind as I have always been. An outsider, a nuisance, my kind have never and will never want to make the time to get to really know me. All clouded in the queens perfect image she has for them all, seven of my race walk up in awe to my throne hall, my architectural feet clearly impressing them. However before I have the chance to feel joy about this, it instantly disappears in one gulp of a breath as Nimfa drops into the earth with Leach, there two bodies moving down into the goddesses embrace as Nimfa takes Leach alone to see the levels I have mapped out below.

The girls room, huge and cosy, I tried to make it how any young group of children would want it. Fun, spacious and perfect for anywhere they want to fall asleep they can. Leach won't understand why I have designed it how I have. The force of my hate on why should he even get to see it pulsing through me. If I hold up my end of the bargain, the queen's hand is mine. Why is she even showing him where our children will live. Searing hate for Leach biking in my mouth, hate for this situation that has gone on way to long cracks down into my core as I impatiently wait for them to return to the surface.

Why I am left out. All of my kind are here to see my work, see our land moving on to a brighter future because of me, yet I am not asked to show them. Am I a fool for believing Nimfa. If she playing me until after the battle is won, our land fully restored to us and Leach is then stood next to the throne making changes to the building I have so perfectly planned out for so long.

The guiding hand hovering over my heart, I feel the darkness deep within me squeeze at my heart. My deep breaths, my battle up in my queen's tower beginning again, my fight will not be over unless I become her mate and find a way of getting rid of this darkness. Helping the darkness out two figures pop back up into the courtyard, I watch in revulsion as Leach takes Nimfa by the hand gently before silently passing my design plan and begin walking off in the direction I have planned to build next. Completely ignored, I do not even try to hide myself, Nimfa's stead staring directly as me before it does as I had commanded of it and follows its queen.

A gift from me, she doesn't even notice it's there. My powerful magic's crafting her something Leach couldn't even imagine forming and they both ignore it. So off in the land of bliss that I have made, they move off to a space in our castle filled with rubble. Rubble I plan on using for certain things.

Following slowly, I give them a perfectly wide birth, Nimfa's stead clearly seeing my agitation as it stops walking to wait for my feline and I to catch up. Giving me a look of unbreakable love and my feline a side rub, we keep walking, my own design undoing in my head as I try my best to work out what they both think they are walking towards.

Voices echoing behind me, I skirt around a boulder far bigger than me, one that will eventually house the storehouse for extra food we will be in need of when our race is back to full strength. The seven slower moving trolls who entered the throne hall alone waltz past to meet Nimfa and Leach, my eyes scrutinising every single one of them.

To relaxed, to happy, is all I can see. How can the rest of my kind be so calm when we are nearly wiped out. I forever have wondered why they do not want to rule the whole world like me. It is our right, our true revenge to the world that has nearly let us be wipe for the face of Tylimantrica.

Hand in hand, two of my kind are in a pair, walking as though there infuriation for the same sex doesn't hinder our race clawing back from annihilation. Happy for then to be in love, I only know loyalty, the need deep in my soul for Nimfa could be one of love. Yet it is of survival, of wanting to be the most important person of my race. If I am the father of the new line of girls, I will forever be known. If I can bring this world to its knees, all of these rock trolls I despise will beg for my favour.

Each a different colour, except for me with the traditional grey stone work, when the men meet with the couple still holding hands, my gut screams for me to burrow down into the ground and burst up ripping Leach in two. Even in front of our kind Nimfa is making it clear that she has chosen Leach. To me this says our deal is void. To me this is the sign that my promise not to hurt and bring this world to its knees is over before I even had the chance to contemplate choosing it as an option.

"My brothers! For our queen, for our fight! We must build a blacksmith and armoury. Today we as a race and a group of craftsman need to build armour for the rest of our battalion. The elves as we all know are weakened by their feeble weapons and armour. We shall craft the best for our comrades helping us in the up and coming battle. Today we shall help Nimfa in her vision of what the future holds. Every creature helping us invade the Mirror Queendom of Horndon will be gifted with a piece of us. Because of us, every creature invading will have the highest percentage that they can of surviving this fight!" Shouting out at the troll like he's speaking to a viewing army before him, my own laugh is snuffled out by the cheers he receives.

"Are you choosing Leach my queen?" Thadus asks outright. My hard fist pressing against the boulder, crunches slightly as I hold myself back.

"My choice is not yet made" She says giving Leach a smile she has never tried to even give me.

Seeing what I see, the trolls before the two still willing to hold hands, kneel down, my chest caving in as it is clear she has made her decision. My heart no longer squeezed by the darkness, I drop into the ground taking my two steads back as I demand Earth Mother to take me to my home.

Dropping from the ceiling, I feel darkness echoing off me. The stead's moving to the opposite side of my cave, Demon does the same as my pain ebbs out around me. Throwing myself into my lab, this time the object I want to change is me. Having enough of this pretending with no outcome, I will fully embrace the darkness. I will let the guiding hand fill me with everything it can. Nimfa has made her choice. It is time the guiding hand shows me what I can fully be.

Unbeknownst to Nimfa and everyone else, I know who she has chosen. I will now just to pretend to play the game until I find the elven queen. Then all I am about will come to light. On this day, I pledged truly and honestly to the darkness that it is my one aim to bring about the rule of the dark. The light has had its day, now it is time for me.

Punching my fists into my reflective dark cave walls of my lab, my knuckles crack the pain I should feel does not exist. Pouring all my hate, my shame at believing Nimfa. I push my anger at my kind into this, my own hands beginning to break away as the marble wall before me cracks open. The reflective stone oozing now, I watch closely as the soul shifting darkness of my walls envelop all of my arms. My cave starting to collapses down on me, all of my home oozes into a dark ice cold mud which solely aims for me.

Earth Mother taking my three creatures away to safety, I relax feeling the emotions I manipulated Flighty into using to embrace the darkness so long ago now, wash out of me as I feel a peace. My peace with this being my destiny, I open my mouth the oozing substance taking over my old home as it fills everything up, even my own throat as I am no longer am able to breath.

My eyes covered, I surrender to the nothingness circling around me. My old being now gone, I feel only the guiding hand fully, my body dissolved as I fully and wholeheartedly connect to the black my soul has always been. The goddess leaving me like everyone else always has, I known my rock troll body is still here somewhere, yet now I am bound to something else. I am something else, something darker more sinister and more uncontrollable than anyone would wish me to be. I was the invisible one. Now I will now be the only one.

Nimfa

"My queen!" Zeit bursts out calling me over in excitement. "I forget how easily my hands can make things without me even knowing how. Our blood really does remember talents for us!"

"The goddess has always told us that. Yet I have to admit, until I saw the walls of this castle I couldn't believe it was true. Master has gifted us with this incredible home, one designed right down to the tiniest detail." Moving to Zeit's left side; he pushes his hand into a dusty brown looking stone we have been making the blacksmiths out of. Denting the rock face, Zeit moulds the rock into a perfect furnace finishing off the last piece in the building that we need.

Everything made of the same stone; I made certain we stuck to Master's plan and used the stones that he would have wanted for this place. Only hoping he is happy and not anger that the rest of us have wanted to help move our home along, something simmering inside tells me it will not matter when the rock troll I think I have chosen for the good of our race becomes clear to him. Taking my thoughts straight from my own head Zeit says to me.

"So Leach..."

"What about him?" I brush off moving back into the biggest smithery I think any castle in any place in the world will ever see. Having a whole armada to create weapons and armour for, we all agreed this kind of space will circulate the air and give us all our space as we work on pieces individually. Using the stones from our pasts soothes me. Master's whole design and idea has taken my heart away, his talent and real gifts lie in this. The darkness I could see when he was speaking of world domination makes him a mate not ready to be by my side, let alone the father of my children.

"Do not pretend to play coy with me lady. You were holding his hand, in front of every one of us trolls. How long have you been doing that?"

"That was the first time. And you see I haven't made my final decision. Master is still in the running"

"I would hope so after this masterpiece he has solely created for you. Who knew that dark drool had this much talent. I suspect if we didn't have his design, this building wouldn't be standing right now" Smashing his hand down on the work surface in front of himself, I smile feeling slightly more relaxed that I am not wrong for wondering if Master is the right choice for moving our race forward.

"The darkness that circles his essence though. I feel it growing." Placing my hand on top of my friends, I feel the need to ground myself pounding in my head. The weakness of making mistakes and not knowing every answer is something I can show to Zeit. Any other creature in our world looks to me for guidance, answers and the way everything should be. Yes I am queen but I am also at time's just a rock troll trying to find my place in the world.

"I believe you are the only one that will be able to stop that darkness. To take that essence out of him. Something has reached for him, grabbing hold of his soul before any of us even met him. You say yourself all the time this battle is only the beginning. Something bigger awaits us out there. Our race is in need of its next generation, but what is it Nerdiver called you" The intellectual mind of my subject has always been so true that anything you say to him he absorbs up. Knowing we have a higher purpose than just what is about to happen with us and the elves, Zeit always seems to be ready to help me understand what I am doing is right.

"World shifters" I answer, the words feeling as they are sticking in my mouth with what already lies ahead before whatever Knollica's believes we will have to do.

"An entity or existence has clearly tapped into Masters loneliness before we all found each other. Even when we had, you and him were the only ones who saw each other, the rest of us have always been kept away from him. If there is something in him that is saveable it is through you my queen."

"What of Leach? He has been so patient and understanding of me not just making a rash decision. He only held my hand this day because of this epic castle Master has formed for us all. I believe it was out of friendship he did that. Though all he has ever done is wait for me. The kind of mate I need is someone who is willing to step up when needed. Like making us build this magnificent place together, bringing us all together and not just by me saying it. The future of this world demands of us to bring every creature together in unity." I cast out of my mouth, the words freeing themselves from the argument I have been having about who I am to choose for so many years. "I need a father for my children who will guide them in the best direction for our race. Someone I can trust to be with me on everything I choose is right for us all. The queens of old demand this of me, they tell me so far inside that I already know who I want. But is it the right decision for our people if my decision could have consequences?" I ask my friend, my confident, my children's future master of knowledge.

"Nimfa you know me and our people will follow you till the end of time with whatever decision you trust is the correct one. We are here for you no matter what and I tell you now. I am going to take all of us back to Chifferen for a rest before we come back here to work even harder than we already were. We have an army to be weaponised and protect." His commanding tone showing me what a hard teacher he surely will be for our future generations, I already am aware that he will have soft touches of kindness hidden for the right moments. "You and Leach are going to stay here and have some real alone time. I do not think you ever truly spent any true amount of time with your two final suitors, and something tells me seeing Leach in his element of crafting armour will help you in your decision making"

Moving of before I have the chance to say anything, I laugh out loud hard when I hear him screaming at everyone to stop what they are doing and move with him.

Silence following this, I wait a few moments before I exit the room I am in to have a look around our new overly sized improved blacksmith building.

Separated into sections the building has two levels. One for moulding and creating amour and weapons and the second for storing and design work or that's what Xen has decided as this will mainly be his play ground. Obviously gone with the rest of the trolls, the smith has been let for me to search alone. Thinking Leach was meant to stay behind, I feel like a mini troll as I cue around the building in search of a crush.

Popping my head into a few rooms that hopefully one day will be teaming with our race, I only find empty spaces. Leach maybe hiding from me as I try my best to not call out for him. Wanting our time alone to feel natural, I first want to stumble upon him without him realising I'm there. Seeing one work alone tells you so much more about a creature than what front they always feel they should put on.

Pushing at a newly build stone door, I do my best to be silent as to my happy surprise I find the little tinker. A subtle noise at first, I stand by the doorway as Leach taps his forefinger lightly into something metal before him.

His spark blazing in the hearth behind him, the colour of his spark embarrassingly I have never noticed before is a pale pink colour. Light and happy, his spark gives the viewer hope. What our sparks mean of who we are is something I am hoping to discover when I birth my own children. Maybe seeing your child grow will explain why we have different colours like fairies do with their dusts. If only for my Zeit's behalf I wish our children could be formed just as fairies are.

Two loving creatures no matter who you are bringing your love to a point of creation. The tuff substance our race is formed from makes this impossible, however what it does give us is the position to create many many things with just the strength of our own skin.

Leach as a troll is completely different to Master. Where Masters face is wide and rounded with every scratch and crack a troll could have, Leach has smooth and shiny skin, to the point where a drop of water could easily be seen falling down his face. Small in size, his face is more of a ball, than the rest of our kind's faces are shaped. His mouth also smaller, it's now a jagged line as she concentrates so hard on what he is making. His eyes are like pools of pale cream that glow out at what he sees while a lighting strike of the same cream shatters out all over his navy blue marbled skin.

A round old belly, his hands are thicker than the rest of our kind perfectly sized for a baby troll to sit in while he tells them a story. His height slightly smaller than me like all of the males of my kind, he is the only one that could nearly reach my height if he tried. Rubbing my ball of a belly as I watch him tinker, I cannot help the small snicker that escapes my long mouth as he squints his eyes to try his best to look at the intricate design he is hitting.

His head shifting upwards so fast I think his head may snap off, I stumble fully into the room as his eyes blaze to life. Wild and wanting, I feel exposed as he glares at me, the single item that binds him and Master being the matching orchids they both have growing out of their one cheeks. Moss sprouting out life all over a rock trolls bodies naturally;

Master and Leach have this extra plant because of the family ties in their blood.

Always forgetting myself that they are cousins, I wait for him to move or say something while we both just stare at each other. His orchid petals turning from the bright green colour it was while he was concentrating so hard, it has now slowly crawled to the same colour as my stonework.

"Do you happen to be thinking about me Leach?" I ask sweetly, my voice breaking slightly as I move further into the room being the first to break our eye contact.

"What makes you say that my queen?" He smirks returning his gaze to his work. "I thought it best to work out the design for our troops before we all start crafting armour for the army. No one wants us all questioning that when most of the work is done. Now is the best time to get this kind of thing planned" So certain of the need we have to make a banner for our battle, I now realises I never really thought about us needing a sigil for my Queendom.

Nomad in nature solely because of how all our parents decided to leave us all and let our race die; I have never had the priority of needing a house sigil for us until now. Understanding Leach's logic that now is the best time to make one, seeing as our home is not yet finished and completed on Tylimantrica, I cannot think what our banner could be of.

"Your orchid gives you away." I signal at his face as I move to meet him on his side of the work slab his sits behind. "What kind of sigil idea do you have for us? As much as I wish I knew what we should have... I have to admit I am blank for ideas. I have way too many other things to deal with at the moment than to-"

"My queen please... calm your mind." Leach soothes me; my need to take all the burdens I am beginning to feel weighting me down and let them all go vanishing when his creams eyes lock onto mine. Calming and relaxed, the key attraction Leach has over me is his need to never pressure or make a pushy decision. Only wanting what's best for our race and us, I wonder if all I need is him. Him to help me make it through this last part of this plan I have been working on since I first felt Earth Mother's true presence and first saw Prilance's true gift.

"I ask you now to join me my queen. The other trolls have travelled back to the Mellifine's Queendom"

"You call them Mellifine too!" I beam, our synchronised minds linking as I hop down next to my subject. How it must feel to not have the weight of your entire race on your shoulders. Your own future made with only with a few options, options you've been far too afraid to truly connect with encase you connect with none of them.

"I do call them mellifine's. That is what they are, are they not. Part elf, part mermaid. The future as you so perfectly point out. However that is not why we are now here, alone, together. No. We are here" He says moving ever so to the left as he takes both my hands under his and pulls them towards the work slab. "To make sure the future of our race will forever know that one day the reason they are even alive on Tylimantrica is because of the sacrifices our queen had to make to get us here. Close your eyes. I want you to feel the sigil by your fingertips."

Doing as I'm told I wiggle my fingers against Leach's as my body turns cold, the tips of my fingers burn hot as they are placed on the metal surface now invisible to my eyes.

"Nimfa. You tell me you wonder what our sigil could possibly be. There is no other options than" Swaying my hands over the metal of a breast plate, I feel the raised pattern before me, my own crowned head naturally always attached to my own skull is laid out before me. Born as a queen, I and whoever of my girls are next to be in line will have a head like mine. One showing the world we are the queens of our race and no one can pretend different.

"You" Finishing his sentence I open my eyes to view the masterpiece that I do not think could represent us any better.

"Leach…" I stop my breath, the image of my own crowned face and mossy hair being the sigil has me speechless. Classic in its swirls that it's made of, the shining grey metal plate sings to me of the powerful message our armour will call to our enemy. My face being the sign, I only hope I can pull of my part of this up and coming battle for equality. Nerves and doubts cloud us all, especially those in power.

"My queen. You are our future and past. Our armour and banner should shine by you alone. For yes you shall choose a mate eventually but only you wear the crown. Only you can handle the burden of ruling our land. You know I am ready for you if you decide to go with me. Although until the day you make your final choice, I will hold your hand tighter and tighter, until you do not need me anymore" Clasping his hands gently around mine, his thick slabs of fingers engross mine, my want for a better life may have already begun with a single act of spending some time with one creature.

Last of the preparations

Nimfa

"Nerdiver my darling!" I half scream as I wonder over the foyer of my mellifine friend's castle. Water trickling down from the grand pool way above, Nerdiver looks so much like a goddess with the sunlight blazing light around her whole body in a halo.

About to be armour ready, we embrace hard, her slim webbed hand taking mine as she pulls me off into her home. Being at my own castle making armour and weapons shows me the contrast in nature of my rocky world at the moment. Not complete I have a vision of my new homeland connecting nature with every building but alas for now I have returned ready to start final battle preparations. With only one last piece of armour to make when I left, my people will soon follow me here, our last strategies are left to me to discuss before we march.

Master not showing his face since the smith has been built, I know I will have to send a message through the goddess to get him to meet us. Taking my stead back I am certain, I haven't seen the cute chunky wolf since I have shown my home to the rest of my subjects. Crossing my fingers Master's got her and not that she's ran off, I know for a fact I need Master to still do as he has pledged and protect the elven queen for our plan to work. The fact that I am certain who I will choose to be my mate, my tingling stomach wants more than anything to get a tiny bit of advice from my fish friend about more than just our up and coming battle.

"How are the preparations going? Do the elves feel ready for the attack?" I ask as we slip into a room with a wide circular table chairs dotting all around it.

"The soldiers are prepared to do what is necessary. Ellamight has informed me that her people were struggling with coming to terms with having to attack there home at first but now we have a plan in place they all seem pretty confident in it." Both of us falling into seats, I don't realise until my bum hits the wood how tired I am.

Working day and night to get armour and weapons ready for every creature who is joining us has taken its toll. Marching tomorrow as soon as our discussion is done I need to get as much rest as I can before we leave. Knowing I need to be alert for what needs to be done, I catch the glimpse that Nerdiver is as tired as I feel, her own focus having been on getting Knollica and the colony of fish settled in her home which was meant to be only filled with her and Cyth a lot longer than it was.

"Leach was just finishing the last piece of breast plate as I left. My people will then bring everything here. I think we should stick to the plan of marching from here as getting to my home first without the ability to travel underground will just be a waste of time." I say, knowing the way to my home from here means skirting round the land so you pass the mirror Queendom. If the Kia's spies are still hoovering out there they will spot us a mile away. Giving away our ability of a semi surprise attack will reduce our chances for success I have no doubt.

"Everyone is willing and prepared for what we need to do. The main armada will be our cover until we split off to gain access passed the outer wall. Cyth believes Kia will be in the main tower on the wall once our army attacks. He thinks she will want to see everything while commanding the people. That is where we shall go but like you Ellamight says the mystics will have produced protective magic on the land main times over the years. We will have quite a few barriers to pass before we make it to the wall itself."

"It's a good thing they may not have thought of using a barrier on the water running under the left side of the Queendoms walls. I have made sure that your armour flows down from your middle and does not create trousers." I inform my friend, when we swim under the wall like the plan has us do, her tail will return meaning trouser armour for her is definitely not an option.

"Good thinking, thank you. What of Master in all of this? Is he going to keep up his part of the plan?"

"Master has made a pledge to me that will not be broken. He may be changing as darkness grips him but he is always true to his word"

"Not that I do not believe the words you clearly think are so binding but I saw what he did to my best friend. Can we really trust him?" Nerdiver's pain for what had to happen to Flighty being valid; I know her part in it makes her feel guilty, though without it none of us would be here now if Flighty hadn't been tricked by Master. Explaining to her what I have told Master he will get in return, I see it doesn't soothe any worries she has.

"I knew this would be the only way to make sure Master does protect the queen and not try to kill her"

"Like he did to every elf at my grove. He relished in destruction of every creature he turned to dust. I understand the anger he has at the race, I've felt it myself but Master gives off something else from inside him. There is a rot about him Nimfa. Any creature that is near him can feel it... see it. Think of how you had to send him away so he didn't scare or hurt any more elves. How on Tylimantrica did you manage to get him to pledge to not hurt the head of the race that have nearly brought you all to extinction" Worried for me, I smile at my long-time friend. My memories of her as a tiny tadpole when she first found herself trapped in her pond flashes before my eyes. So young and so bright was her need to see the world, the fact that I was the one to give her the ability she now has of walking means she is someone who will forever be in my life. Knowing that fact I tell her the truth.

The truth of the pact I have promised Master, the truth of how I have decided deep down that I will be choosing Leach to be my mate. Masters darkness is a cloud that cannot be passed onto my next queen. One day he may be able to mate with one of my descendants making our bloodline more diverse, but I am not the creature to fully change him. We do not have the love that is needed to heal him. No all I can do is blackmail him into not ruining this invasion. I only hope it is one that will stick until everything is done.

"What do you think he will do when he finds out that you've chosen Leach? Surely it's better to tell him the truth now"

Nerdiver questions me, her concerns so clear that it match's every concern I have asked myself.

"If I tell him the truth all of our planning will be for nothing. We haven't waited for the moon festival all this time so Master can go on a crazed killing spree" I contest

"Of course we don't want him to go on a killing spree. What if we don't involve him at all? Flighty can handle protecting the queen. Prilance can join him"

"He already knows when we are to attack. Ignoring him and going ahead without him could end with him killing anyone on both sides of the battle not just the elves"

"That's my exact point!" Nerdiver stiffens in her seat, the realisation that Master being on our side will always have ended badly. "When he finds out you are not going choose him even after he pledged to harm no elves directly. What do you think he's going to do then? You said you can feel the rot that I spoke of building inside him. This may be the exact thing that realises it. He is not a good soul Nimfa"

"You don't think I've worked that out. Maybe if I actually loved him, he may change. Earth Mother has always protected him. She has made it more than clear to me that he's special. Why would she do that if he wasn't worth trying to change? Something must have control of him. The reason we are world shifters are not for the invasion tomorrow. Something bigger is coming; something the goddess has had me trying to prepare us all for all these years." I push back at the ethereal creature telling me everything I've already told myself.

"Master is a liability. We cannot trust him to be part of this invasion let alone the world once we have done all we can to equalise it." Her words only telling me everything I fear, the same thought I know every creature has when they see him.

"You don't think I know that!" I push to my feet; the window letting the only light into the room begs me to jump from it. Aim myself at the land below and let Earth Mother hug me tight until all this is over. "What am I meant to do? Everything I have done up until this point, even letting master pledge to me. It was meant to help him. Nerdiver Master was a scared Little Rock troll once. Just like me he is one of only ten left when we found each other. All he has done, does do… is try and make the world fair, his heart is in the right place though something has tainted him. Something has told him the world should be at our feet. He needs help; I cannot just throw him out"

"I know all you want to do is help him. Just like you helped me, helped Prilance. Even how you are trying to help Ellamight and Spitfire. Nevertheless you cannot help everyone. Your people must come before Master. Yes he is your subject too, but he cannot be the father of your future. If you loved him it would be understandable that you would try everything to help him but he cannot be helped. Not by you, not by anyone here." Taking the longest breath I think either of us has had since we entered the room, I know we are now both deflated. Talking about this is all well and good but the fact still remains what are we going to do.

"Unfortunately for us our only option is to rest and I mean rest Nimfa" Nerdiver tells me moving over to the window so I can do nothing but look at her. "Master is a problem that we shall have to solve another time. The invasion has to come first."

"Why do you think Knollica wanted Master to be the one to protect the queen? Does he see something we do not" I ask hoping he has given her a tiny bit of insight into what could be lurking around the corner.

"He told me no more than what he said in the meeting. Only Flighty has spoken with him since and from what I gather Master is a topic Knollica is keeping quiet about. From my own history with Knollica if he doesn't tell you outright then it is something he sees that we have to deal with ourselves or the correct path will not be open to us. Whatever we do Master is now part and key to our plan in succeeding against Horndon. All we can do is hope that the repercussions of Masters rage when he finds out Leach is your chosen mate won't be as devastating as we think"

"The craftsmanship he has brought to the architecture of our queendom Ner. It's such a waste if he cannot get through the rot building in him. I know you have said I can do nothing of it, I just wish it was in my power... my destiny to stop it taking over him." Reaching out for my huge hand, Nerdiver's slender fingers hold onto me tight, as I feel the weight I feel of letting Master down wash over me like Nerdiver is controlling the wave herself. Getting this out now is what I need, for tomorrow all our heads have to be firmly set into winning equality for us all without the complete annihilation of the elven race.

"Come on now. It's time for us both to get some well needed rest." Pulling me from the room, I let the dazed rush flowing through me take my mind away with it. Tomorrow is a day we shall hopefully win with much less death than the battle at Nerdiver's grove.

Master

I am different. Nothing inside or out of me is the same though I feel like I am finally truly myself. Scrapping myself up and out of the ground, Earth Mother could not help me move as I dug out of what was left of the black ooze that surrounded me, absorbed into my entire being.

Shivering as I entered the night world, shadows covered me, even in the light of the moon I call every shadow down around me. Darkness in full, I am who I was always meant to be, black, cold yet something else. I feel like I'm shivering, or something in me continues to shiver but not from a cold breeze. Instead something inside shivers against with what pulses in me, the tiniest light the toddler troll of me had once is slowly disappearing forever.

Backing off when they first saw me, my stead's and demon stepped away; even demon whose own darkness could match mine didn't want to be next to me. Telling me it worked, that all the power and hate I have held and wanted has finally come to this. My skin now looks to move like the ooze that swallowed me whole, never settling. Dropping down from my being, I am solid yet not, it is as if I am now made of the glistening ooze.

No longer am I standard grey, my body is now reflective and soulless. Showing the world what darkness was hidden deep down inside, my skin is now what it should have always been. Growing in size, I also feel as if I am bigger than I was. Bigger than what Nimfa stands out. I deserve this change, this shift in what I have always needed.

Sitting cross legged on the floor, I slowly move my hand over my face and shoulders feeling the ooze that is now my body solidify whenever I need it to. My punch or hit to any creature that comes near me will regret the pathway that connects with me. The moss and orchid that have been a part of me for my whole entire life are gone, destroyed by the darkness that I am now. Wanting this, needing this, I feel the best I ever could.

Knowing this is who I was always meant to be, I reach to my left and right picking up the two axes I stole from the battle weeks ago. My oozing skin melting down onto them so they look like that have become a part of me, I am ready.

Ready for our invasion to happen, I call out through Earth Mother to any rock troll willing to hear me. The goddess may longer connect with me but she needs me for the fight ahead. I know it and so does she. Nimfa not on my radar anymore, I don't let mother send the message to her. Not needing to see her again, the elves await me, the battle calling in my depths for their blood. Wanting to see them change into the godly statues Nimfa loves so much, I will then destroy the statues into pieces. Any sign that the elves even existed is no longer an option. Burning inside, I clock eyes with the golden gaze of my demon opposite, the dirty forest floor we have ended up in hiding the rest of his dark body as my control over him feels stronger than ever before.

"We will kill every last one of them!" I shout at him, my vile hate spitting out of my mouth.

Grinning at me, demons two long horns stretch up and out of his head, his deep thangs dripping saliva as he imagines the joy I speak of. Two long claws at the end of each of his arms, demons body is still humanoid in nature, his black skinned chest, rising up to his beautifully angled face giving away something it didn't before.

His feet panther like, they explain clearly how he blurs so fast, weaving through an army and only looking like a black line as he kills everything in his sight.

Small and petit, demon is the size of a small baby tree, the size he has become from the transformation he was put through. Curly hair, his arms, legs, head and face have long curls trailing out of him, his blazing eyes and thick lips being the only thing to give away who he once was.

"Do you think Flighty will recognise you now your buzzing facade has worn off?" I ask him, receiving only a deep growl quickly followed by his feet scuffing in the dirt.

"Come on Psyc! Reunions are a blast. I can't wait to see what he thinks of what his dust did to you all that time ago. But don't worry. We won't introduce you until it's just us in our group" I smile deeply my love for the moment I have been waiting to hurt Flighty since he healed himself about to come to light.

None of the fairy that was once there still living, Psyc is now what I call him, a demon. A monster made not by me but controlled by me. The darkness even more mine to wiled now is inside this creature, his being made up of the thing I am sole controller of. Flighty my first victim will once again by under my rule, our packed over our hearts making it a destined fact even he can't get past.

Feeling the pull from mother, I signal to my stead's to come, our time for the battle to begin is near and I want my creatures to be a part of it. Holding my hand up to demon, I will call for him when the time is right, his features being clear as day now had me worried but knowing it will be me and Flighty who are to protect the queen, I cannot wait to feel the rush of killing every single elf and the queen herself while Flighty panics over what he has done to demon.

Stead's at my side, we drop into Earth Mother for I am sure is one of the last times. Her fast pace propelling us through the undersoil so fast we make it to the rock troll kingdom in unprecedented time. Rising up, I pull shadows down around me quickly, the twilight hour making it easy as Zeit stands alone in the new smithery building, my race having decided to build themselves.

Not doing a bad job, I take it all in, the choice of stone being what I had planned. Not completely angering me now I only notice that the inside is laid out different to how I imagined, yet the separate rooms make it far easier to hide my oozing skin as I make conversation with one of my weaker kind.

"Zeit!" I say as he stares openly at my two stead's near to me, there bright white figures taking all the attention easily off of me.

"Master. I knew you made one of this for the queen but they are both so beautiful." He says with such amazement anyone would think another of our kind has built the foundations of our kingdom alone and not me.

"It is so shocking when the place you stand in is of my design. The land we hold ourselves on would still be nothing if it was not for my talent and gifts. You are all welcome for the beginning of our home by the way. I just hoped Nimfa could have followed my wishes and waited until it was completed before bringing you all here. Though when has anyone every listened to me" I seethe, doing my best to hold down my new growing hate for Nimfa and the lies I have allowed her to get away with all these years. Telling me I was in the running to stand by her side. Obviously not.

"Master! Our queen was so taken back by the feat you have crafted that she couldn't wait to show us our home. What you have forged and planned will make any creature weak at the knees when they see it. Our home is now one of strength and a stronghold only open to us. The queen couldn't wait for us all to see it." Protecting her just like he always has, I feel myself bore instantly of talk of Nimfa, of the home I put all my time into. No longer wanting any of it, I look at the stone slab next to him, litters of metal covering it all.

"What is all of this then?" Seeing my need to change the subject, the bronzed handed rock troll obliges me and turns to the armour by his side.

"We have spent considerable time in make armour for every creature and weaponry too. Nevertheless I see you already have axes in your hands, at least in the shadow that's what they look like" He scuffs as he runs his hands over the mounds before him, clearly my race have been working very hard.

"They are axes yes. Taken from the dead elves that thought they would try and defeat me." I scold their memory into the fire burning in the hearth to the side of the room.

"Yes I see" Zeit ignores my hate and carries on. "Every creature working with us will have armour if needed and a chest plate to show our sigil newly designed by Leach"

Making a hissing noise even without meaning to, Zeit stops mid-sentence as he looks at me, trying his best to see through the shadows which hug me tighter as he lingers in my direction.

"This one before me is yours if you still wish to wear it. We move on first light. Your team is made up of Flighty and an elf who knows the city well. You are tasked with finding and protecting the hall where queen Glassadena has been in ritual for the past month ending tomorrow on moon festival. Find the queen, hold off any elves trying to hurt her though under Nimfa's request she asks you to do your best and not kill any."

Scuffing a reply, I tell him I know the plan already. If he can just inform me on how I am getting into the mirror Queendom of Horndon and when I must be ready to leave, he can leave me in peace. My patience for this conversation has come to an end and I want to just get on with this invasion.

"Is your demon following you into battle?" He asks his eyes clearly looking for the creature I have not brought with me.

"He will be. Oh and on your way out, you can take Cerene to Nimfa. I'm assuming she will want her stead I took all the trouble in making for her." Whining as she goes with him, Zeit does not say another word as he leaves me to look upon the armour our Leach has so beautifully designed.

Nimfa's face, crown and all have been swirled onto the front piece of my armour. Doing my best to hold back, I do not smash it. In fact looking at each piece of the armour, my whole body will be covered making it easy to hide my oozing darkness until I want it revealed.

Slamming my axes down on the slab behind me, the drops of my blackness now wait on the rocks surface. Soaking slightly into the stone as I turn and do my best to put every piece of armour on I can without letting my oozing presence be clear to anyone who see me. I feel the begging of my ooze to take over this place. If my new plan is to work I must convince everyone until we are in the Queendom that I am just old me, so pulling at the dark ooze to return to my body, the need to consumes the home I spent so long designing will have to wait.

Blowing out a few deep breaths, my armour fits nicely, it's strong metal surface holding my oozy skin in tight as I grab hold of my axes once again. Somehow knowing I was bigger than I once was, Nimfa's face shines out from my chest, my round head squished into a helmet that could hide any dark creature in disguise. Needing one for demon so Flighty doesn't know who he is until I want him to. I look to my beast of a stead, the feline meowing at me, his voice being so soft I feel my heart break for it. How I have let this creature of light so into my heart.

"Ready for the battle of a lifetime?" I ask, gaining a purr before Blaz brushing its huge face against my whole body, his harden fur twinkling against the metal now holding me in.

"So am I" I agree with him.

The Battle begins

Nimfa

"I still do not agree this is the best idea" Cyth's concern is felt by all of us, most of all by the fairy staring daggers at the elf who is crazy enough to believe what she wants to do is right.

"It's crazy!" Spitfire burst out, her body having grown substantially since her and Ellamight's first and only Souliune trance.

"Spitfire." Ellamight sighs, her honest hope that this could holt everything before it begins comes with how she moves to place a hand by her love. "I have to try. My people deserve the chance to make the decision. If it doesn't work-"

"Doesn't work! Of course it isn't going to work. My brother and that evil little troll have already sneaked off to get into the Queendom. If anything you'll be a momentary distraction that gives them time to get in. That's what the invasion is meant to be for, Nimfa, grandmother and Nerdiver" Spitfire growls out her panic that Ellamight could die before any of us are there to help fight and protect her. "Why can't we just stick to the plan?"

"Because even in this moment. Even after the battle at Nerdiver's groove I still wish to believe my people have minds of their own. The army awaiting our orders are a sign that my kind are sane when they know the truth."

"Kia will not let you near the city" Nerdiver says trying her best to reason with our friend. Though I know Ellamight has already made up her mind on this matter.

"Kia will kill you way before you have time to tell your kind the truth." I say knowing it's falling on ears closed from all of our fears, but for my own sanity I have to try.

"Kia will know by now you are with us. If you were not, you would have arrived back in Horndon weeks ago. Ella please listen to us. Stick with the plan. If our kind see us fighting, see us battling for what is right the true hearted will join us. Just like in the first battle." Cyth pleads to his oldest friend, the brotherly love he has for her flashing over his perfectly chiselled face. The fire droplet in the centre of his forehead looking as if it is about to turn from the outline to a real life flame, I wonder if he will be able to control fire one day like Nerdiver does water.

Since he and Nerdiver have both been decorated with these beautiful patterns I wonder if the other Souliune's will end up with the same. Spitfire and Ellamight having changed far more than how Nerdiver and Cyth did after their first shift, the two new Souliune's having both grown in size. Rather than being as small as a daffodil Spitfire is now half the size of me, her new size making it obvious she doesn't know how to place herself in the world. Ellamight's change is different, her change coming from within, as every now and then her hand seems to sprinkle out a little bit of dust. No one else paying much attention to this, I lock eyes with Prilance over the group discussion, her interest in this being as big as mine.

"I'm not going to change my mind. Get on board or back off. I leave in few minutes so tell your army to prepare. If it doesn't go the way I want and I am not stupid I know it will not, get ready to join me."

"Join you. I'm not leaving your side. If you're going to run full into deaths arms I will be by your side." Spitfire rises into the air, her shining new armour glinting off all of us. The sound of rain pattering off the rest of the army behind us dotting out through the woods gives a calming sensation to everything. This may be the biggest battle this world has seen in a long time yet the weather will always carry on as it must. Today the sky cries for the lives that will be lost in it, I only hope we are able to end it before the queen tries and fails her moon ritual again. Us being here is to show them the truth the elves have searched for all their lives. If we do this right, I will be the beginning of a new world for us all.

"Fine. I can never refuse you. But stay hidden; what I have to say may not work if you are spotted first."

"Remember my fire. You are no longer the size you were, but your dust is more powerful than any of the elves in that Queendom will be expecting. So use it. And use it well" Giving her grandchild a kiss on the head, Prilance's tiny form shows how much Spitfire has grown, nevertheless the pride in her grandchild has clearly grown too.

Leaving everyone to say there last words, or commands I move to my own people. All crowded together, they stand in a small patch of the woods that is open, the sky's full power leaking down upon them, yet it has no effect. Water having always run straight off of our skin, my soldiers look broad and strong in there armour. Ready to fight and die for our future, my heart constricts that not all of us may make it out of this.

Yes the first battle was easy and we defeated the elf's like they were no more than snowflakes. Alas this time I am in no doubt Kia will have formed stronger weapons and armour just like us. The fleeing elves from our last fight will have told there leader of our power, our unbreakable skin. I may have talents in Elven magic yet my knowledge is still somewhat limited to what I want to create and old tales of what I can do. The elves not included with the queen, the mystics of the Horndon will no doubt be the only first defence except arrow and sword the elves have.

Cyth and Ellamight's own honesty has admitted the elves are so content in the power they hold that expect for the building defences and last minute defences they would have been building, the mirror Queendom is not prepared for an attack. They are or were the strongest place in the land. No one would dare attack them or could up until this point. The rule of Tylimantrica has been there's and as such they need not to train every elf unless out of an old tradition of honour. There weapons because of this are not as strong as they should be for the long need of them has vanished.

The only threat lying up north behind mountains so tall and treacherous only a single path leads through to us here. Border controlled with no threat of attack, the elves have become way too comfortable. Kia may want more power but on her grab to grasp it she has unleashed the only people able to stop her.

My wanting to connect with the queen, make our land equal and powerful together, I wonder what threat we unleash ourselves from the north. For now that is of no concern for first we need to make our land free. Earth Mother pressing a reassuring warmth up to me, I call out to my male subjects, bringing them to me for a final prayer.

"Is it time my queen?" Zeit asks, the battle ahead raging worry through his thoughts.

"Soon my friend" I give the best smile I can muster, our plan after plan running through my mind as I stare at my friends. "A last minute change of direction has become apparent. I will explain all, but first a prayer to our goddess." Stepping in to the centre of my race, they all circle in close as they make two rows moving around me. Standing before me, Leach gives a reassuring glance, his faith in me showing no bounds.

Dropping all our heads, I speak quickly and clearly to our goddess. "Our mother who has brought us to this point, this moment we have been destined for. We thank you. The moment to take back our right to be seen, our right to exist. Is now and we ask for your truth and guidance once again as the unknown fight awaiting us. Bless us be Tylimantrica"

"Bless us be Tylimantrica" My subjects echo my call.

Feeling mothers warmth flow up through the ground into us, all of our head rise in the same instance a relaxing calm coming to us all that we are doing as she wishes. Giving me time to explain the small change in our plan, I move over to my group that will infiltrate under the wall as the battle commences. Our goal is to capture Kia and stop this battle before to many deaths ensues.

Master and Flighty already having gone, they have moved on ahead with one elf of Ellamight's choosing to get to the queen and protect her at all costs. Flighty being able to breath underwater just like Nerdiver, it is his talent that will get them into Horndon. Or at least that was the plan if like Cyth's information the walls next to the lake do not reach the earth. Breaking what little protection spells the elves have had on this castle for generations that was the moment we created for them to sneak in. Giving my stead back to me but without a word or a glance my way, Master left us here as quickly as he came. Giving Cerene over to my people for the battle, stealth isn't really what my canine is able to do. Her excited buzzing will keep Leach safe while the all-out battle will be perfect in lessening her energy.

Zeit no longer coming with us on this stealth mission, I asked him how he would feel if Thadus died without him being there to protect him. His love being his weakness, I had to use it to make sure Zeit is with the main armada. They need all the help they can get if they are going to help keep the elves busy while we do our job. And I don't need the extra worry of trying to protect him while we sneak into the city.

With so much going on and so many armoured creatures behind me waiting to begin I move to with my group to the far left, giving us a clear view of Ellamight strolling up to speak with the grand glass like walls of the mirror Queendom.

Nerdiver on my left, her armour gleams as water trickles in through the branches above, the rain I feel will not halt until this day is over. Silver metal attached to all of us, our arms and bodies are so cocooned in armour you would think none of us would be able to move let alone breath. Instead thanks to the talents of my kind our armour feels more like a second skin, my men and the elves being the only ones with helmets to protect their heads. All of us females have opted to keep our heads uncovered, our hairs hopefully being long enough to protect us.

Unlike the rest of us, Nerdiver's armour doesn't attach to her legs; instead it falls into long metal layers creating a skirt for when her tail comes back in mere moments. Stopping at the forest edge we are in, Prilance lands on my shoulder; her own metal armour making a singing noise as her legs hits me.

Just the three of us, our battalion in made of just what we need. Strength yes, but undiscoverable. A small armada will not let us sneak through the Queendom to find Kia. Of course it would be more protection if we run into trouble but I think us three powerful world shifters can help ourselves when the time comes.

"Are we foolish for letting her go out there?" Nerdiver nods her head at the elf wondering alone out on a field muddy and desolate. Kia having clearly freshly cut down any trees paving the way to the mirror Queendom, the land is now open for all the glee to see anything approaching. According to Cyth and Ella, trees should have covered us all this to the gate. Instead Kia doesn't seem to be foolish or in the mood for a surprise attack. Ellamight's last ditch effort to bring her people on side may end her life before our battle even commences.

"She has to do this for her. Even though she knows it will not work, you have to give it to the girl for trying" Prilance says clearly proud of the elf.

"My people!" Ellamight's clear voice fills the empty air. For an elf alone in a field of dirt and mush Ellamight still manages to look assertive and powerful. If her people don't listen to her, today is going to be a cold day that will sweep this place for years to come. Kia has done an injustice to her kind and if only it wasn't for the moon ritual, Ellamight could commune with the queen first hand.

Looking up to the heavens, clouds like every day since the battle at Nerdiver's pond cover the sky. Two bright spots are all that give away something that should be happening today. The sun to one side, I know from what Ella has told me, the second spot is moon, today being a time when the moon shines its own full raise on the world filtering its power down to us. Tapping into this, queen Glassadena has tried for decades to tap into its power from the moment the sun festival begins and the first signs of the moon showing itself.

Hoping our plan works, too many deaths should not happen today, yet considering we can see nothing upon the top line of the mirror Queendoms outer wall, my gut doesn't tell me this is going to go Ellamight's way.

Usually connected to trees the Queendom of Horndon use to have trees growing right up against its shining walls. Made from a sort of rock that looks metal or glass from here, the

Queendom faces out to a lake, a moat circling around and under the left side of the building, it flows straight into the lake, our aimed entry point, we wait for our time to make our move.

Making the place look cold and perfectly clean, the walls of this Queendom look unclimbable. The broken carcasses of the trees that use to line it have left tiny debris in its wake. Hoping the inside of the city isn't as cold as the outside, my discussion with the fellow queen may now be as powerful if she's let her own city die already.

Only coming here once when I was a little troll this place has not changed, its unwelcome feeling coming at me in waves. Feeling every citizen should see the kind of home that they could make here, the queen in her own right Nerdiver by my side needs to show these elves the palace of Chifferen.

Listening closely, I feel like I should shout out to Ellamight to be more on guard. She knows the magic's and weaponry they have in her old home, yet she believes in her people to proudly to want to protect herself properly.

"My fellow elves listen to me. I am here before you to ask you to open the gates! Let me and my comrades inside, give us the time to meet with our queen and explain all she needs to know. Information all of you need to know. General Kia is lying to you! The queen did not send our fallen comrades to Nerdiver's Groove! The queen does not seek the great eye of Knollica to be our captive. She was the queen who tasked our prince to find protection for the underwater creature in the first place!"

"Lies" Screams fired back at our friend, the words she was speaking work more on the rest of us waiting in these woods, helping our moral build for the fight ahead. Kia will never let her people believe us and if she has them as convinced as the queen was to leave her in charge, Ellamight's words will be futile.

"No! Never lies! When have I lied to you! When have I not been by the sides of my sisters, by the sides of the mystics? Our highest order, a place I would be standing next to my queen and princess right now if it's wasn't for this! Sister mystics you must head my words Kia has and is manipulating you! Do not allow her to ruin our race! I am here to show you the power we have in our past of working equally with the others of this world! Join me and every dream of the truth we have had will come true! Join me and fight for what is right!" Shouting out her last few sentences, her voice reverberates down to my core. Her speech being one I know we shall have to show to the queen, a power we have all been a part of and witnessed in Nerdiver's grove will once again have to happen in this Queendom, a quiet castle wanting of its true life once again.

Silence ebbing back at her from the hard wall, Ellamight looks defeated, her head sagging down as I feel her heart breaking that her people are being so delusional. Poor elves dealing their own fate. Hopefully once they see us all working together and that there price is here to fight too. The true hearted elves will join us, just like the army waiting behind the position Ellamight is standing.

Fired out, a single arrow sings through the air, it's slicing of the wind screams alone as it aims true at Ellamight's stature.

Her hand flashings faster than I think even Cyth could move, Ellamight plucks the arrow out of the air with a glum look on her face. "So that is how it will be" A warning shot, Ellamight breaks the arrow in two, her hands flashing up behind her as she produces two long slick looking swords, a touch of Spitfires navy looking fairy dust sprinkled all over them.

Screaming out in one collective sound, arrows stream up and out of the queendoms walls, an army alone in the air of black lines. Stood on my other side Nerdiver intakes a breath at a sight no one in our lifetimes has ever seen. A true battle of land and power, even Ellamight is not fast enough to slash through all of those arrows alone.

With nothing to do but watch, I feel the whole forest pause, a roaming fox appearing out of a bush to the side, it's bright Viking blue eyes trapping themselves to Ellamight just as all of ours are. Looking up before her, Ellamight seems to embrace the arcane of arrows her chest reaching up to let the attack come. If her people will not listen, then she will sacrifice her life for the path we all wish to follow.

"She's not going to let herself die because her people are foolish and follow Kia is she?" Nerdiver panics, her grip moving to her sword even though she knows the range of her weapon would never stretch far enough to help her.

Movement behind her, Spitfire appears from nowhere seeming to come into existence from the air itself. Spinning to be in front of her Souliune and protect her love. Spitfire raises her ever growing hands, her body looking small from here yet I know she is not as small as her grandmother anymore. Power firing out of her, a circle of navy fairy dust blooms to protect the two lone creatures on the battlefield. Bouncing off harmlessly every arrow that would have destroyed Ellamight smashes on impact. Gassing the shield while the rest of the raining cloud of black sink in to the muddy field that now stands before Horndon, the battle has begun, there's no turning back now.

"I taught her that only this morning" Prilance gloats proudly.

"The swirls of dust you mean?" I ask as I hear the war cry go up for the army to press forward into the attack.

"No silly, my invisibility trick. And if you ladies are ready to be invisible yourselves, this is our que" The tiny fairy motions out into the field as arrows raining down on our army breaking the forests new boarder line.

Shining out in all its silver glory, my army's armour reflexes the bombardment of arrow easily. The wooden stakes flaking off harmlessly against our talented strong metal, if these are still the same weapons this battle will be over very quickly. Roaring as a tribe of wild beasts might do, the army runs full ahead to meet with Spitfire and Ellamight who are trying their best to keep the main arch of arrows off their bodies.

"We need to move before our chance to surprise them from inside is lost. Are we sure Kia will be where they said she will be" Prilance double checks our plan will even work as she gets to using her purple dust on us. Holding hands with Nerdiver I first forget her aquatic fingers don't have gaps in like us land creatures and readjust my hold.

"It's all we have to go on but I'm sure we can convince someone to run to her for help once we are inside" Nerdiver says before hissing as Prilance's dust sinks into her skin in a sizzle. Where the dust is absorbed, before my very eyes Nerdiver vanishes. If my own hand wasn't attached to hers I may think that the dust was casting her out of the world itself.

"The water will wash this dust off of us. I do not know why but this particular goal of the dust doesn't like it when you are submerged in water."

"How does your home stay hidden when it rains?" I ask, only ever seeing my old friends home once many years ago.

"That is a border and not what I'm doing to us. The air isn't alive as we are, not in the same way. Now I'm on your shoulder Nimfa so don't run like a mad man of legend." Her scolding voice comes like it is said from a teacher, my only reply being a humph before Nerdiver pulls us out into the scenery of the battle.

Our plan is a simple but effective one. Since the lake water that runs around the one side of the castle and deep under the walls of this reflective place, it give us the perfect opportunity to get inside quickly. With the cover of the battle at hand, the arrogance of the elves thinking no creature except mermaids who cannot cross land to get to the lake would be able to breathe underwater long enough to get inside. Means we have a perfect opening to get inside the Queendom.

Flighty taking Master and one of the elves who was at our war meeting earlier, I didn't even get the chance to look at my subject who promised me he would look after the queen. Hoping Master is still binding himself to our pack, I know we need to get to Kia as quickly as we can. The longer Master is protecting the queen, the longer he has to break his oath.

Moving ahead before any of us, the first team needed to be at the queens buildings before the battle began just in case Kia sent an order to kill her early on. Hoping not, Flighty's team snuck in when Ellamight and myself performed a spell to break down and through a much weaker protection spell that circled this land. When a protection spell is moved out further and further over time and the threat level to the land is majorly reduced each lifetime it is no surprise that the field was pretty much non-existent.

Looking to my right as we run to the water waiting before us, I see Ellamight is nearly at the gates, Cyth blurring next to her as Spitfire looks to be growing something out of the ground. Squinting my eyes, my body is yanks forward and down into a vat of icy cold water, my immediate reaction is to take in a breath just like when I am underground. Nerdiver's face springing before mine; her hand is covering my mouth as she indicates she hasn't brought air down for me and Prilance yet.

Correct on her dust being washed away immediately, Nerdiver's hair sparkles and gleams pure white brilliance around us, the water flowing down so deeply that you cannot see the bottom. Earth Mother making it very clear to me long ago when she set me the task of communing with the elves is that she would not help in anyway. Even my men out in the battle field have no pull into the ground, her stubbornness matching that of Master's that we must pull this fight of alone, twinging me with annoyance at my goddess.

Nerdiver's tail appearing where her legs use to be, her long skirt floats up to her waist, the armour on top of it looking more like layer of moss than arrow defying metal. Prilance's eyes bulging next to mine, I think she's signalling to Nerdiver that she needs to bring air down to us now.

Don't panic Prilance. The air is on its way.

Nerdiver's voice floating in my mind, I let out a giggle, the sensation of someone playing in your mind bringing another new experience to me in these ever changing times.

Moving her arms up above her head Nerdiver's power ebbs at the surface as she does her best to make sure nothing looks odd on land. Giving away our location just to have air will make the reason we have come this way pointless. My hair flowing like an anemone on a reef, air returns to my mouth and noise as a small bubble pops around my head. The sensation of having your body underwater and you head not when you're not at the top is very confusing on the brain.

Taking in a deep breath, we get moving, finding the wall which dives far deeper than we expected. Clearly more invested in there protection against underwater creatures than we thought, Cyth's information that the wall doesn't move into the ground is old news. Having done this long ago, the elven queen must have suspected this could happen one day.

Swimming down the wall quickly ahead of us, Nerdiver runs her hand along it until her fist finds the soil at the bottom. No way in, I wonder where Master and Flighty decide to go other than this route, or there would be six of us stuck down here.

We need to smash it. Nerdiver's voice feels my mind, the weird entry into my mind not being something I feel like I could get on board with long-term.

With my turn to do something, I swim with the help of Nerdiver, being a heavy weighted creature moving gracefully under water isn't as easy as moving underground. Punching out a couple of time, it takes me a few attempts to get the strength behind the movement. Water slowing you down, I am amazed at how graceful this mellifine swims through the water and at a speed. Mermaids are truly the opposite of my own race yet what a fish would be like underground I'm sure would make me look the graceful one.

Finally smashing through the bricks down here, a crack first appears running slightly up the walls surface. Worrying me the crack has flown to the top of the wall giving away our location. All I can do is hope not as the reflective substance the walls are made up of above water level is not something they thought to bring down into the depths.

Moving in the small hole I've made, I wish not to make it greater as this is the stealth mission after all. The three of us pushing up as one, our heads stop just at the water line. Listening for any sound, Nerdiver is the only one who has a chance at hearing something from down here. Prilance and I looking at one another, she summons a few specks of dust and pushes her hands together to create a small purple shield for herself. If they have managed to know our plan we shall be ready.

Indicating for us to break the water's edge, Nerdiver says how she hears no noise at all. On higher alert at the news of no noise we once again move up as one, our plan of not being discovered gone before we could even hope to get to one guard. Standing all around us with weapons glowing a harsh maroon haze, twenty guard's aim arrows and swords at our arriving faces.

"Ah I see you knew we were coming" I laugh out, two of the guard's dead ahead looking uneasy.

A blast sounding from behind the majority of the armour glad elves, one is obviously nervous and panicked as he lets his arrow slip, the dart shooting right down into the water where my feet hang. The marooned weapon burns with power as it slashes right through the centre of my right foot, a pain I have never thought I could feel arcane's through me. My skin being harder than any rock on this planet, that shouldn't have happened.

"The weapons are bewitched" I cry out, Nerdiver's scream reaching up and around all the walls that are in our line of sight.

Power bleeding off of her, the Mellifens voices screeches all of these elves to death in seconds, there bewitched weapons never standing a chance. Bodies all falling as a mass, mine and Prilance's hearing only hear a twinge of nuisances as before our war meeting, Nerdiver treated every creature in the room to a high pitch call of her voice. Wanting us to be able to speak with her without the allure of her power taking our minds over, a question I want answered is does this protect us forever. Still working even now, her killer scream doesn't affect us as it could.

Exiting the water onto the shore line, my foot bleeds through both sides as the perfect arrow shot has left me with a perfect hole. Orange blood, I've always wondered what lies beneath, a rock trolls skin being so hard hardly anyone of my kind have ever seen what is beneath it.

Prilance jumping to action, the tiny bud drops to the grey rubble like dirt around us, the closest buildings now watched by the siren for any creatures silly enough to think they can match her. My fairy friend's hands digging into the earth, my own natural magic tuning in as I feel her dust call out to any plant life that may have tried existing in this world of mirror. No greenery anywhere, I feel so surprised at the coldness this Elven castle gives off. Cyth's connection to trees is so great, even the elves that helped develop his home showed a natural affinity to them that I would think this place would be more in tune with nature than anywhere else in the world.

"I see now what the queen has been missing all these years for her moon festival. Life." I say before I scream out as Prilance grows a weed like stem up through the hole in my foot.

"The queen has lost her way, as has my love's whole race." Nerdiver says with solace coating her voice. "How was that arrow able to piece your skin?"

"Ellamight thought the reason the protection spell was so weak and that no new magical defences have been put in place is because the mystics not at the queen's ritual may be doing something else. I believe they are in communion even now holding a spell that imbued all of their kind of weapons with the anger of the world. The maroon colour of their metal is no work of a smith. We must find the mystics before we find Kia. Or all of our friends will be dead before we make it to her." I pant as Prilance grows the weed so its wraps around my foot like only a fairy bandage could.

"It's all I can do for now. I don't have time or the pull here to grow something that will heal your foot. The earth here is dying. Nothing natural can grow... why get fairies to keep the forests alive if they are letting their own homeland wither?" Knowing she knows the answer, her question is rhetorical. Being around as long as I have, Prilance knows elves have turned their back on the natural order of things, I just believe it and seeing it makes her so shocked she has to ask it out loud.

"Knollica will be able to heal you once we get back. He healed my head at the battle of my grove." Nerdiver indicates to my foot, asking if I will be able to walk okay. "Why is the world so dead here? I thought elves were above all races and more in tuned with nature, even more than the fairies. I thought that had a deep connection with plant life." Nerdiver asks as she brings me to my feet, a flash of pain going through me for I am sure not the first time today.

"Elves are not like fairies in we can make things literally grown into existence. Elves have a connection mostly with trees and how they mould with them. Here every tree must have been destroyed, the elves themselves not even realising the weakening they are bringing onto themselves and the world." Prilance explains, knowing just as much as I do about the history of our kinds.

"Let's get moving. Though let's try our best not to get cornered again. I have a feeling my scream won't work on every elf we find. Cyth isn't the first elf to think of putting blockers in his ears when he first came to see me as an adult." The smirk she gives for her love is a happiness I hope endures the rest of our fight ahead. "They clearly know we are here so let's move as quickly as we can."

Master

What a bleak place this is and that's saying something considering I am a rock troll and all we need in life are hardened areas... period. Nevertheless this mirror Queendom as they like to call it is cold and unforgiving.

A place laid out like an army unit, every building is squished together in a perfect order of seven. It seems no matter what is inside of them, seven is the perfect number. What this signifies is I do not know and I keep holding myself back from asking our little tour guide who if I utter a word too I will squeeze to death.

Silent in our decent into the city, this place's reflective surfacing makes it much harder to move around. Earth Mother allowing me zero help on getting to our goal, demon and I are hidden under armour that hides both of our true forms. Demons horns sticking out through the metal I quickly forged in the smith before we marched here, Flighty gave him one quick glance before hanging back behind us to watch all of our moves. The truth right before his eyes will hurt him as deeply as Nimfa has hurt me. Or at least I'm counting on it.

Taken a keen interest in him, feline keeps looking back, it seeming he either wants to eat him or cuddle up to the tiny body filled with dust. Either is good with me for as long as I can get on with this invasion quickly I don't care what any other creature does from now on.

Bringing us up and over a wall on the lakes side of the castle, only one guard was on duty. Knocking him out before I had been able to get my bearings, our guide seems to adapt to being fired with fairy dust into the air easily. More powerful that I thought the little spike would have become, Flighty's gifts thanks to me are one thing he definitely hasn't spoken to me about. Seeing him fight in Nerdiver's grove I know the darkness still lies within him, I just need a little incentive to bring it out.

Populated much more than I think I ever thought it could be, elves mill around everywhere. Many not in armour or ready to fight, you can see that these creatures think so highly of themselves that they do not even prepare to fight. Our army may be small but once I deal with the queen and Nimfa has dealt with Kia these creatures will be in bedlam for power. My goal has been the same since I managed to convince Flighty to make a binding oath with me. I still wish to destroy the elves and everything they stand for.

Looking at the design and emptiness in the castle, our world will be in ruins if I do not stop it. Reaching my hand out before me, my guiding hand subconsciously aims my power at a group of elves milling around a corner to our far left. My oozing black surface bugling together, I let a jet of my darkness fire at them, my goal simple. Eradicate every one of their kind that I can.

Buzzing like the bee I want to pluck the wings off of, Flighty dashes in the way of my fired kill shot. His own dark dust spinning out and around my shot before enveloping it into nothingness. My anger blasts as I grab the tiny creature daring to get in my way. Slamming the dammed maggot against the wall, I growl at him for getting involved.

"How dare you!" I seethe with rage. Who is this thing to think he knows better than me. A new born baby compared to my existence, his pack will never be complete, his oath never breakable for my control is only a single invasion away.

"Shhh!" Our guide of an elf whispers next to us both, a terrorised seizure panicking through his body.

My disgust that I even have to pretend to listen to this feeble creature echoing to my complete annoyance, the only thing I can do to him right now. A glance of hate. Stepping back quickly I see him relax slightly as the group of elves vanishes moving on in their deep discussion.

Letting Flighty go I stare at the elf in front of me, his lanky body doesn't have the usual regal-ness of the rest of his kind. Instead he's uncomfortable looking. Not a traditional beauty either, his armour is that of what he came to Nerdiver's grove in just in case anyone spots us. Reflective like all the buildings around us, I huff that we need to hurry. Our goal is to be at the ritual building before the battle begins.

"We are nearly there. Two more streets." How he can even tell the difference of this place, a big reason I designed the rock troll empire with every building looking different is so no matter where you are, you can also find the place you want to be. Shame my kind will only end up living there as slaves until I have the race that sees me for what I now am. A god.

"And don't do that again" Flighty spits in my direction, his hand motioning for me to carry on with our stealth march. Demon growling at him, I still cannot wait for their reunion, how gleeful it shall be.

"Don't get in my way next time" I fire back before letting the twink of an elf lead me to where we want to be.

Not in the centre as I would think it would be the chosen building for a ritual that takes the queen away from her people for nearly a month is very simple looking. Deeper in the city, the building is on a slight hill, the outer wall behind the buildings here dropping down as the land rises away from the lake water behind.

Reflective as is the rest of the city, this building is a two story high box with a sharp looking roof to the sky. One doorway, the wooden panels are the first of its kind here. The oldest thing I have seen, Flighty seems to have had the same quizzical thoughts as me as he asks our guide if this is the right building.

"Yes I know it looks to small and simple but this is the oldest building in the Queendom. The building is just big enough for the queen to squeeze in with all her nominated elves to get inside."

"Why does it take so long that they are inside for a month? Clearly the answer hasn't come about your origins so why bother performing it in the first place?" Flighty asks, my demon beginning to look fidgety now we are here.

"The queen still searches for answers. She's been doing so all her life and she will never give up. The ritual is a huge part of our lives now. Kia must have had enough of the waiting for answers and is taking it all into her own hands"

Having enough of this pointless discussion, I move up to the gates doing my best to open my hearing up to see if I can hear inside. The rising of the moons full bright gaze and setting of the sun will signal the end of this day and the end of the ritual inside. That is what this elf told us on our breaking into the city. If I want to get the element of surprise I need to act now.

Turning from the doors, the elf hasn't realised how close I have gotten to him, Flighty so interested in finishing out my pointless information about these elves we are about to wipe off the planet he doesn't even see my axe arching up and through the creature before him before until it's too late.

Crying out as my axe wedges up from his backside and through till his head is spilt in two; the elf I have just executed now lies in dual pieces on the front steps of his people oldest building. Pale green blood everywhere, his whole form turns into diamonds, break up slightly now that his body is no longer together in one piece. What a feat, his ancestors made these step for him and now he's died on them.

Looking more shocked that I think he could even try, Flight hoovers in the same place he was moments ago yet he cannot even fathom what I have just done. His brain not even catching up with my ease of a display, I play my next card so these gates can open up and the real fun can begin.

Flicking one of my axes towards demon, he rips his helmet off the use of it on his head being more of a nuisance that a guard. His golden eyes flashing bright as Flighty's slack face registers the fine features that Psyc still possess from his past. His horns look dangerous and weaponised, the memory of myself and how I was taken back the first time I truly saw him. Seeming to have grown extra spikes on his horns ready to help when ripping apart anyone who gets in our way, what Psyc now is and can do is a mystery, even to the guiding hand in my dark soul.

Looking back to Flighty, I hear him whisper Psyc's name the creature he has created from what use to be Psyc growling in reply.

"My friend Flighty!" I beam, the darkness under all this armour read to also relieve itself. But not until I have Flighty where I need him.

"What is this?!" Flighty flaps like an angry bee his wings buzzing aggressively behind him.

"Do you not recognise him? You're once and only confident that only wanted to be friends. To be more than that in fact.

I've brought your craftsmanship to see you once again. It's taken me sometime you see to get demon to where his body wasn't pulsing constantly with your darkness. No creature could have even seen who he was but look at him. Isn't he magnificent!" I echo everything I know he is not feeling.

Shame and sadness scolding him to the core I know this is not what Flighty believed would happen today. Yes he thought I would betray the cause and my oath but Psyc appearing. This is a nightmare he never thought would come try.

"He died... you died" Flighty gasps, his voice becoming quieter as he begins to float down to the ground. The darkness running inside him wanting to burst free I know it.

"Not death Flighty. No! Just like with the creatures that came to Nerdiver's Grove. Though yes many many where not yours, a few indeed where creature of the aftermath you wrought through our homeland. A disease that still festers. Today is the day we begin the cleansing of any wrongness in this world and you and Psyc are going to help me."

Turning to the gates before me, I rest my axe weirding hands on the wood. Demon and my Blaz approaching on both my sides ready to do what we are here for, I feel the glee of my guiding hand is pleased that we are finally here. I am finally going to eradicate elves from this world and begin my true purpose in life.

"I will never help you destroy the elves." Flighty sparks his rage at me, throwing some of his dust at my back as a warning. "We are here to protect the queen. Showing what I have done to Psyc only helps me see what darkness you cause to this world. It can no longer go on"

"Oh little bug." I say the nickname I gave him the first time we met. "Simple tiny fairy, whose anger always gets the best of him but doesn't realise the repercussions of his past actions on even himself. Unlike I who didn't seal my oath with the queen. You young fairy are oath bound to do as I say. Until Nimfa is my queen or the elves are destroyed forever, you have sworn to help me. Any breaking of that oath and..." I begin, Flighty's scream echoing in these cold streets as I feel the burn of our firing circles on our chests raking through his body to mine. The enjoyment of using what I must to get what I need flushing through me.

"I hope you're ready to win a war of a lifetime" I laugh as I push open the old gates.

Nimfa

Finding our way up and into the outer wall was far harder than I thought it would have been. No easy access, the first entrance we found was overflowing with elves all armoured upped waiting to enter the fight when needed. Only hoping our people are doing okay as I see this huge crowd, another echoing boom making its way through the city itself. Someone's winning; I just hope it's us.

Finding a side door, probably used for guard swaps, my first step on the stairs brought me face to face with an elf with a very long looking spear. Throwing it quickly out at me, I've never felt myself move faster as I hit out with my forearms on the spear moving it to one side before impaling the elf right through the chest.

The mystics may have been enhancing the weapons of their people but there armour is still as useless as it has always been. Flying up the stairs faster than me and Nerdiver could go, Prilance deals with four guards waiting at the top for any enemy's that manage to make it this far during battle. Roots growing through the ground and stabbing each elf all over, the fairies connection to the earth is just as strong as it is for her granddaughter.

Keeping one alive, dust begins to dot the ground as this elf has its arms held tightly against the wall, it's friends turning to ash on death.

"Where are the mystics?" I ask politely as I can.

"Pah! Good luck finding them" The elf tries laughing thinking it was in the position of power here, though the shuddering pain flashings through her body tells another story.

Stepping up to show her the opposite, Nerdiver moves to one of her ears, placing her mouth just by the tall arch this females white skins has. "Ready to tell us?"

Looking at me with a confused face at why Nerdiver is by her ear. The elf looks to wonder if she should be afraid. Wagging my fingers to left Nerdiver does what she needs to get the information we want. Screeching at such a high frequency even my own ears started to hurt again, the power wave she puts us all through in her hall to protect us from her voice does not even help with how powerful her voice truly is. A siren through and through, her voice scraps down to the core of this elf, her body shaking so rapidly without dying I was surprised she could be alive.

Prilance moving around so my body could protect her from Nerdiver's on-slate of an interrogation. She watches the pathways of the space we were in, while I do my best to feel out no footfalls on the stone we stand on. Our chosen location being perfect for this fact finding mission, this elf just needs to hurry and tell us what we want to know.

Finally succumbing to Nerdiver's voice and under thorough inhalation of anything the elf could take on her body, the creature spills everything we need to know. Somehow choosing the perfect elf to leave alive, this one knew where the mystics are, how many guards are stationed with them and how close Kia is to them.

Thanking her, we leave her hanging alive; her body going through enough that death seemed unfair to perform. We're not complete barbarians that we have to kill every elf we see. Her ears may never recover but something tells me I think she's learnt her lesson at following orders just because your told it's what's right rather than deciding what may be right yourself.

Finding the mystics location was fairly easy. Deciding to perform the ritual in the near middle turret of the outer wall so they are closet to the fighting elves they are embedding magical evil weapons for, we should have known they would be here. Kia our second goal happening to be exactly where they are too, Cyth's original thought proved correct on where Kia decided to be for the fight. Watching the fight from up above, our turret shows a newly grown tree having destroyed a huge chunk of the wall so both armies now fight in an open plain on the other side of the mystics turret.

My goal is a simple one. To keep Kia alive. As an offering to queen Glassadena I wish for her to be the one to pass judgment on the creature she chose to control her people while she tried finding there start in the world. If I did that and came back to this, let's just say living trapped in the goddesses womb for eternity would be a worthy alternative.

"How do we want to do this?" Nerdiver asks seriously as she stabs two more elf's in one clean extension of her morphable blade who came barging in the door. Most of the elves leaving there high posts to join the mass of the fighting down below, the team that was waiting for us on our entry to the city must have been the only ones assigned to the likes of us. Clearly thinking with their magically enhanced weapons we would have been easily handled.

Kia clearly being so arrogant that her people could deal with any situation, like a group on a secret mission, I call out one Elven magic word to check for any hidden spells surrounding the turret waiting before us. Echoing back a strong spell of protection, I smirk that of course she is the kind of leader who doesn't up the defences on the outer lands of the castle but puts a powerful spell around herself in time of war.

Wondering why this mastermind wasn't in the midst of the fight herself today or at Nerdiver's groove. I see now its self-preservation she is hunting for. She wants to be alive to rule this land once this is finished. Fighting herself against an enemy even one she's is certain she will win against is no option for her. Me on the other hand, I'm ready to fight until my own last breath if it's means creatures like her have no power left at all.

"There's a protection spell surrounding the turret. That why she hasn't moved further into the city or why that tree next to it has done anything to damage the glass or rock underneath."

"My child, look at how powerful my little Spitfire has become just from opening herself up to what's deep inside of herself." Prilance beams at the creation her blood has made, not what we should be concentrating on but I smirk alone with her.

"And opening herself up to love. You yourself know the extra boost you get after doing a Souliune Nerdiver" I hint as another elf screams bloody murder as she comes running through the archway behind us. Nerdiver sword making easy and quick work of her, the wet clay substance she turns into is true the worst mineral they can form into on death.

"I do yes. Though I would much rather hurry this along so Cyth isn't out there too much longer fighting this is pointless war. So what is the plan if they have a protection spell?" She moves us on quickly taking us back to the point we are here for.

"The guards out circling the turret on the balcony are not in the spell. Everything inside seems locked down so not even Kia will be certain what is happening right outside the door. She will be able to view the battle but not the close area around them; the turrets walls are too thick. If you two can take out the guards all around the sides I will work my best magic to break through the wall of protection." The turret having a balcony circling the whole thing, I see guard's back to back, weapons ready to attack any form of creature coming their way. This will be a very hard fight for my two companions and unfortunately from the looks of it, unlike at Nerdiver's grove hardly any of these elves have decided to join our side. Either it's a duty to protect their home no matter what or they are all tainted with no hope of redemption.

"Do you need to be close to break through or can you stay in here? I don't want you having to fight, defend yourself and use your magic if it's all too much at once. We won't break through without your help." Readying her sword in her hand, Prilance moves to the door readying her dust for an all-out attack on the elves before us.

"Nimfa stay here. Do the spell and we will take care of the guards or any waiting elves ready to help. Be quick about it so we can finish this battle before it goes on any longer than it needs to."

Nodding my head, I feel a deep shake in my body. Never have I had to go full on against Elven magic being performed as a constant and against high Elven mystics who are direct descendants to the powerful matriarchs who formed this language of power.

Starting simple, I clap my hands together using the one advantage I have over them. My rock troll magic.

Flickers of flame breaking at the creases of my hands, I speak the opposite to the spell Ellamight and I weaved at Chifferen. Not dancing this time, I direct my intention at the turret before me. Seeing it through my minds eyes than my real eyes, the girls flies out of our own turret and descend on the guards fifty feet away.

Arrows and cries to the others around them I hear the new battle begin. Sounds from the main battle echoing up from the deep ground behind Kia's centre turret. All the warring creatures fighting for what we believe in all beginning to weigh down on me in this moment. A creature myself who has boosted and claimed the magic I have had for decades, I feel it centring on this moment. This counter spell I weave, rubbing off the stone inner walls of this overly reflective castle, I push everything I have at that turret.

Sparks flying off me, my power reacts harshly to them waiting inside rock in front. I will break through. I do not know how many mystics work on the protection spell alone, but my power is greater. I am greater. Tylimantrica has put her faith in me to make us all equal in stature and life but in this moment and in any moment where I fight for the future of my people and against the evil that could wipe out the whole world. I am the most powerful. I am Nimfa queen of the rock trolls.

Closing my eyes, I forget the words I have been trying to use on the spell. Elven magic is not on my side here, today I need to be a rock troll. And a rock troll alone. Pinching the tips of my fingers together, I utter one single word. A word I feel that runs so true and free for any creature in this misguided battle I feel everyone stop dead with what they are doing.

Speaking in my own tongue I forget to use of Elven words. Instead this is the time for my hands to point out straight and I...

"Release!"

Blasting out of my mouth in a scream, the walls before me and far opposite vanish as my hands fire out a pure beam of light. White in bliss, the beams shatters everything in its path. Breaking what feels the world in two, my beam keeps going, breaking off into tiny streams of light each stream searching out for every creature in this place blasting down on them in one glowing white moment of the truth.

My beam letting me go as I see every creature now has glowing white eyes, a trance given over to them as I feel Earth Mothers pull to the ground. Letting her take me, I flow with the stone of the wall, in seconds I am brought back up, Kia's figure on her knees before me as her eyes glow with the truth I am showing everyone. Gripping the back of her neck in one swift move, her eyes stop glowing, her armour popping off in one quick pop of light.

Every creature around us following suit, the same happens to them as the elves of this land are released from this battle. My people the only ones with armour and weapons left; make point as they aim them at the elves all ready for surrender. Kia seeing her loss let's out a scream that could rival a banshee.

Master

So completely engrossed in there ritual not one creature hiding inside this building looks up to the sound of my laughter.

Far simpler than anything we have seen in this city so far this building feels old, much older than even the water running around the left side of this Queendom. No reflective surfaces sparkle in the inside of this building, no instead pure cornerstone is just one smooth elongated lane. Empty apart from four pillars holding up the extra height of the back part of the ceiling. The back wall is the only place light can filter through.

Stain glass like the humanoids of legend, the scene depicted is of the exact ritual that seems to be being performed. A crowd of elves all circle what looks like an ancient dead tree. No leaves are left as every ounce of life and water and been suck out of it. The tree has a huge thick base that stands slightly bent before hundreds of tiny branches break of searching for some kind of life around the top.

In the top centre of the stain glass window behind this is a hole, one designed just big enough for the sun or the moon depending at which festival these elves are performing depends on which light can shine through.

"They understand the tree is dead right?" I ask out loud my voice shattering the serine peacefulness the elves are trying to perform within.

Watching my voice skitter across the surface of the floor with the queendoms emblem fading from it, a smell of ash hits my face. Not only are they humming to a dead tree, they are burning what is left of the dammed thing.

Having waited enough in all of my life for this moment I call my creatures forward, darkness flooding the stain glass window on my command. No light will be filtering into this place today, no ritual will be completed. Able to finally let my ooze out now, my armour breaks off revealing my true nature to all.

Before any of the elves even have a chance to scream out, I rip two of my axes up and through one elf completely dividing the thing in two. Sounding my attack into action a fierce boom shakes through the building. Not like the smaller ones felt early I feel the difference in this one. Someone's performed some powerful magic tonight, and the moon is about to try its own. Killing these elves needs to happen now for the sun has set and the moon festival should be about to be completed.

Feline diving with its claws and teeth, none of the elves are battle ready; there time consuming magic is no match for the hard physical attack of me and my creatures. Turning to the next elf in line, I throw a huge amount of my ooze at her, its piling substance suffocating her into a silent death.

Demon blurring by me, his slashed and thumps like a rhino into his pray. Taken down three in one, I catch a glimpse of Flighty hoovering back looking at his hands as darkness once again trickles from it. Not actually calling him on his pack with me I wait to use it. Instead his own thoughts of hate and anger resurfacing on behalf of what he's done to Psyc is enough to start breaking him while we kill all these elves.

Slashing out with my axes, I hear as a unit they begin to summon a spell. Useless while I am here, all three of us growl low, stopping the majority of the elves dead in their speech. Never thinking this could happen to them, they don't even wear armour, our massacre flowing freely as my weapons and skin kill and kill.

White linen hanging on these creatures in a way most would find beautiful, I see only skeletons, thin creatures that don't deserve to have the fine things they think of in life. White no more, the different colours of their blood mix, shading this stone room as the dead turn to stone or dust. There true self's never hidden in death like it can be in life; these creatures note the end of the elves reign.

How many elves were in here I don't even know, but I do know is that my axe sticks in one on my left which I leave, it giving me the chance to really feel the pain I am causing to this creatures now. Dropping my other axe with a clang I see an elf hiding behind a pillar flinch. Relishing is the fear I am prejudicing I race at the elf meters away my arms ready to slam my hands down into the inside of this cowering elf.

Male, his clothes exude superiority, a higher status of his being. Pathetic in my book any cowering creature without the will to fight to the death doesn't deserve to live. Screams of pain advancing from behind, I leave a trail of bodies and bits as my darkness pulls this space ever closer to death.

Reaching the elf at the pillar I raise my hands as I dip them down and through the pillar before me. Getting to the elf, I see my ooze filling the pillars stonework, my ever growing darkness spreading out before me to taint this Elven place forever.

Searing heat biting me back I rip my hands free, the ooze on the tips of my fingers hardening for a moment. Confused I shuffle around the pillar to find the cowering elf is no longer there but no ash or diamond stands in his place either. No a few feet back from me; right next to the tree he stands with whom I can only assume is the elven queen. Three elves left next to her, she squint's her eyes alone with one other who looks the spitting image of her and her son Cyth combined.

Demon flying at them, I feel my own insides scorn as a powerful barrier only just put up and able to save four of the forty who were here, throws demon against a far wall double the speed that he threw himself at the elves. Crashing to the floor in a lump, Blaz moves to attack them too before I quickly call him into submission. I will not lose him in the frenzied attack I have got us all court up in.

Yes they have a protection spell, but I am not just a simple rock troll any longer. Raising my fingers into what would summon a spark and a flame; I stop dead in my tracks, my ooze self-defiling this ancient space as a only one creature could halted but only one possible thing.

My queen's cold hard voice cracking down my entire self as she and the waiting crowd behind her enter the ritual building. Nimfa gives off a presence I feel she has unlocked like a door while fighting on the front lines; she steps inside while dragging a prisoner who I assume is Kia by the scruff of the neck.

"Oh bug"

Last chance

Master

"Is this your version of keeping the Elven queen protected?" Nimfa's voice shakes down to my core as she throws a sacred looking elf to the floor in between the doors she stands at and the tree I hunt the queen from behind.

The elf's body covering the faded sigil of this once great queendom makes me laugh out loud. No longer afraid to impress my own queen my laugh is like a cold hard slap to Nimfa's face. Unlike the cowering creature lying between us I will not end up in the position she has found herself in.

I came here for a reason and that was not to do the bidding of a false queen who thinks to betray me behind my back while I carry out an oath which would gain me nothing. I am here to eradicate a different queen. Today I will cleanse this world of the dirt that has clouded our race in pity.

Initially thinking I was have been caught I now realise I don't care, what can Nimfa do to me. I am darkness personified, my demon is untouchable and my feline is unbreakable. Unlike the bodies or what is left of the bodies of the creatures in this hall, I am not feeble and I will not be stopped by Nimfa any longer.

"Actually this- " I say showing my hands all the darkness I have started to reign here. "Is the beginning of the rule of Master. Once I have dealt with the cowering queen, I will deal with the rest of you"

Completely turning my back on the crowd edging their way into the hall I move forward. Raising my arms ready to unleash the full might of darkness flowing through me, I see the feeble elf on the ground cower. Her eyes searching from the ground up to me, Kia the female who made this possible for me looks to be afraid. How after all she has achieved and was able to do could she be afraid.

More annoyed than anything that she couldn't have held back our invasion a little longer so I could have completed this before Nimfa had a voice in the matter; I clock my head in her direction. Demon answering my summons easily, the pile of what would have been a stunning elf in the Elven realms once ago holds herself defeated. Her eyes heavy and panicked, Kia naturally glowing skin hums the same slight glow that Cyth the Elven prince gives off.

Looking at my own targets again, the queen and her daughter mumbles words under their breaths, the two only surviving elves wrapped around there legs on either side cower like the weaklings Elven men are. A shame I killed all the females for a talent of magic, I am not surprised that the elves keep men down when they are this pathetic.

Letting my power free, black flares from my hands as I fire at the royal elves of Tylimantrica. Long having abandoned me just like everything else in the world I feel nothing of Earth Mother agreeing with what I am doing. My only companion now aiming a powerful slash of his claws at the neck of a pale green elf on the floor, I punch out my big oozing fists at the shield around my targets. I feel my day is completing, the guiding hand who has been with me nearly as long as the goddess has, it aids in my strength for this last push, as I pound black upon black against their pathetic barrier.

The elf's voices doing their best on working against me, I feel they are slipping with such a quickly and badly made protection spell. Raw power is always far better, Nimfa's cries for me to stop only spurring me on.

A flash of blue slipping past my right eye view as something crouches before Kia ruining everything for me. In a matter of mere seconds everything that could go wrong does go wrong.

The blue flash guiding into place perfectly to deflect Psyc's death strike is performed by none other than the creature who ran from me in the battle at Nerdiver's Grove. Her reappearance being that of an Oman, her beautifully carved sword made from what looks like the gods themselves pushes Demons claws back as she rises to her feet, somehow being the only creature in the whole universe to have stopped Psyc in his tracks since Flighty's curse.

Far taller than him but just as quick, the blue elf kicks out at Psyc sending him flying over the hall to a far wall in a loud crunch. His body slumped and lifeless, Flighty fears over to his body seeming to check if he's alive. Crying out I slam my fists harder against the barrier before me, my chance of winning this slips away further every few seconds.

Nimfa gliding forward in the same moment, she rest her thick firm hand onto that of my felines head. My ravenous creature only doing what I say ever, succumbs to the binding of his mother. Made for me and Nimfa alone, feline, relaxes as canine shuffles through the awaiting crowd to come and lie with her brother. All happening at once, my own power is disrupted by the only people who are left to truly betray me.

Popping up from the ground in a succession of twos, the males of my kind who have always hated me finally get the chance to unleash there flames upon me. All my focused power on trying to break through the queens barrier, I have nothing to defend myself with. In a practiced time order each of my kind clicks their fingers summoning their own personal coloured flames. Having spoken about what they have needed to do to me before, they work without words all burning there flames directly onto me, my darkness not powerful enough to fight of all of them alone at once.

A multitude of colour, I feel like I am suddenly in a rainbow as heat blast my power away. The guiding hand always hovering over me disappearing in the same second my kind betrays me, I am left alone as my magic fades to the inside of myself. The heat crisping up the ooze that has become my skin, I harden only my watching eyes left with the ability to move. Seeing everything else going wrong for me, I watch as the blue elf darts before her queen, a gloried smile spreading over her face that I have definitely lost this one. Like a kick to the teeth the worst of thing to see is Flighty receiving warm embraces from his family and Nerdiver helping him to instantly bring the darkness back under control. A pile of dust with a line to Demon, Spitfire and Prilance look to pour their own light dust over the substance containing any outbreak Flighty's power could cause.

The rock trolls flames still ablaze and fierce, I feel my own self wanting to break free yet held locked in a position I do not know if I will ever break from. Taking the opportunity of my hardened status to do the unthinkable Nimfa moves up to me ignoring the queen behind her for now.

Not seeming to use Elven magic which she usually does, Nimfa sparks her blazing white fire that courses through the tiny veins just barely visible on her stonework. Calling on true rock troll magic I have never witness before, her flame seems almost like a beam now it's light so raw it looks to have become a sort of moonlight. Not alone in my inner shock, I see the astonished look of the queen behind her as Nimfa binds me into a caged made of pure white.

Other creatures around us not looking as confused, I manage to gage out one sentence through my hardened state.

"How did you stop Kia and bring this queendom to its knees?" Thumberling over a few words, Nimfa looks to hear me clearly as the flames of the rock trolls around me stop instantly. Nimfa having trapped me for as long as she wants and I know it, my rigged body cracks slightly as I move my mouth.

"I followed my goddess destined path laid out before me Master. Unfortunately for you." She says her face giving me what I know is true sorrow at seeing what she has had to do to me. "This cage is your new home until judgment has time to be properly placed" Suddenly feeling the heavy presence of our goddess, I growl out in anger as I am pulled down into the earth, the one sheet of rock filling the halls floor ceils up perfectly behind me as I am taken, my aim for the invasion truly destroyed. As is my soul.

Nimfa

"Rock trolls?" The queen scolds out from behind us. "What is happening here, why did one of your kind attack us and on one of our most sacred days"

"My queen" Kia's voice rings out pulling the four elves in the protection spell to move their ring around the dead tree hiding them from the watching crowd.

Not letting Kia actually get a word out, Ellamight and Cyth dive forward into the centre of the hall there presence clearly taken all the attention of a mother and daughter.

"Brother?"

"Ellamight. Why are you covered in blood? Why are you covered in our kind's blood?" Queen Glassadena exclaims in panic. Unable to comprehend that her own child and highest student could be a part of the attack that has left most of the elves in this room dead, she locks her jaw giving them a harsh stare waiting for an answer.

"Mother. We have come here to save you" Cyth's tells the truth which from all the dead here will be slightly hard to believe.

"Save us from the beast of a rock troll that they just caged up. And its thing over there on the floor?" Cyth sister, next in line for the throne ask relaxing slightly that we were here to stop this attack.

"Actually. Master was meant to protect you while we dealt with Kia and the mystics she had manipulated into waging a war while you have been in ritual. Nimfa has brought us here to show you the truth" Ellamight informs them, the realisation that these deaths here are my fault the full force of the mirror queendoms royals turning on me.

"You did this." Queen Glassadena asks.

"I did. The elf you chose to help keep harmony while you performed a ritual that will never work decided to attack Nerdiver's grove and do her best to take the Seerer Knollica captive." I confess. Not holding back on the fact that the ritual she's been performing for decades will never work, she clearly ignores that comment.

"Knollica. The all seeing Henddropus!" She startles at me.

"Yes. The creature placed in mermaid Nerdiver's custody by you and your son was attacked. If I and my people did it step in to save them they would have been killed or captured. Your disciple was planning on overthrowing you, destroying our lands and learning the secrets only the goddess and the other gods should know. All you have to do is take a step outside your cold walls to see the destruction she has caused to your already dying land."

"Dying land?! Our land is not dying" Cyth's sister voice slices through anything else I have said which is important.

"I'm afraid it is sister" Cyth's agrees with me. Her brother probably being the best person to try and convince them of the truth I say, I step back into the hub of my subjects doing my best to check everyone is here.

"Brother is that really you? What has happened to you? Your face has changed; your whole being has in fact. Mother said you went to be with a mermaid. How that works I do not know but what has she done to you?" Leaning out behind him with his hand, Cyth's Souliune places her delicate hand into his, there bright skin and hair shining out on this ever darkening day as he presents his love to his family.

Looking to the sky outside I see night is descending, the window at the back of the hall preparing for the end of the ritual the elves perform. With so much to say and explain I hope we have time to prove our words to this sister queen of mine before the chance to finish her ritual properly vanishes.

"This is Nerdiver. My Souliune. My queen. My life."

"As are you my love." Nerdiver sings back to him her voice spelling anyone who hasn't been protected from it, the harmony the two of them seem to bring to the hall calming everyone.

"This is the elf you left to be with?" The queen questions sternly, her manner giving away nothing to show she may feel about the fact her son is changing into a new being and it is all because of a creature she agreed he could leave to be with.

"It is. She is my breath and I would have it no other way." He tells them, the betrayal of Kia almost forgotten about.

"It is good to meet you at last my child" The queen speaks dipping her head in a sign approval. Cyth looking to relax as does his sister and Ellamight, a sure sign the queen is still approving of her son leaving to make home with a creature of a different species, the room relaxes even more. "We shall have time for proper introductions, stories and glee another time. For now I want to know the truth. Everything and anything you can tell me. Ellamight I trust your word explicitly and know you will not lie to me. Start at the beginning, and if what you say is true..." Her eyes glowing gold in a single moment, she gazes upon Kia, golden chains appearing out of thing air binding her to the floor. Notting that the queen is able to perform Elven magic without even uttering a word, I know her, her daughter and the two Male elves next to them only live because of her quick ability to use the magic that flows through their veins.

Starting truly at the very beginning, Ellamight first explains how there kind has ruined our land. Much like the legend of the humanoids, elves has made the land of Tylimantrica out of balance. Leaving out the truth of our goddess who the land is named after I feel that she is leaving that but for me to explain. The explanation I know will be more of a show and tell like at Nerdiver grove. Our goddess sent me here convince the elves to help bring balance to our land and just like Nerdiver and Zeit have said, something far worse than Kia or Master are coming our way.

Explaining to her queen that before even she was born our ancestors seemed to have let the elves take over the land and convince us all that we are lessor than the elves. The creatures who do not commune with nature as they once did now rule this place. "For example my queen. Our home, this queendom." She circles her arms out around her for a punch "It is divulged of life. Seeing this only myself once I have lived out there in the world that is barley stable and hanging on. Cyth has found his connection to nature, to a way of life that brings new growth. He and his Souliune are forming a new race in a palace created from trees! We don't even have any living tree in our land. Kia has even killed every tree that has tried for centuries to grow back into our lives and renew us with the power and flow our kind should be connected too. My queen you pray on the sun and moon ritual to a dead tree." Looking shocked at the passion Ellamight let's slip from her, Cyth's sister looks to be understanding what has become of the elves better than the queen.

Stepping in, I explain the first discover of power in a second race that the elves told are lesser beings with my adventure with Prilance. A fairy first of her kind in only the goddess knows what that found the true power lying deep within. "You see sister queen, each of us are an equal part of destiny to keep a balance to this land. I hear you have been searching for the answers of your kind and its true origins. I have that truth; every elf battling just now has seen that truth shown to them by me. My journey has been a long one, one given to me by the goddess who you do not know of yet but you will. Do you know where the name Tylimantrica comes from?" I ask looking for a truly honest answer.

"I was told as a little girl that this tree was connected to the core." Turning from us the queen reaches up on her top toes as she moves her fingers up to find a wicked looking branch craning down to meet her. "Here long before this fortress. Our people. This tree symbolises the beginning of our race yet our kind let it die many moons ago. In one ritual I was told as a little girl, the elves let the moon and sun soak up what was left of the power in this tree letting them take it in return for rule of this land. The coating on our buildings outside is light, real light from the two gods in the sky. Keeping my people alive while I hunt for answers, for a way to bring life back to this tree, I see now you are that life. I do not know where the name Tylimantrica comes from but I hope you are here to educate me and bring back the life my kind is so desperately in need for" Dropping back from the tree, queen Glassadena looks dead at me, waiting for more of an explanation.

Between all of us with me starting at the beginning of life on our goddess after the humanoids destroyed the land, I explain who Tylimantrica is. Standing in silence, Cyth sister asks only one or two questions at intervolves, as the journey of Flighty, Nerdiver, Cyth, the grove, the palace of Chifferen, the lifelong sadness of the rock trolls is explained to the queen and her heir. Sugar coating nothing, or holding back, everyone's pain is laid out at the queen's feet. The pain of the first battle with Kia, the deaths, the tried kidnapping of Knollica. The death of Cyth's father who I see no sign of sadness from his sister is clearly not her father.

The true kicker to the queen and the three elves who were not blasted with my beam of truth is the Souliune discovery. World shifters as Knollica puts it, his knowledge is far greater than any of us here and I see wisdom in the queen as she understands truly that he know all, gifted with sight by gods unbeknownst to us. She is after all the queen who had Cyth hide and protect the creature in the first place.

Seeing that she has only ever done what she can to try and care for this world, unlike Kia who wants to control it, queen Glassadena is like me. She searches for answers, for a way her people can be saved. Now she knows the combination of our kinds could bring the answer she has always searched for, Nerdiver telling of the spell we all weaved together to respect the dead at her grove. The unique joining of our kinds which has never happened before brought new power to this world, light power which we all know is in great need of right now if our world is going to survive.

"Wait a second." Cyth's sister buts in only once Nerdiver has finished.

"Galnestia. Let them finish" The queen scolds her.

"Mother really." She says giving her a side look. "Why if all of this is true did one of your kind attack us here undefended? Why did that thing killed so many of my kind with no pretext. If you only want to solve the issues between us why send a creature who would attack us? That beast there might now look all cute but it's killed half the elves in here. The caged one you sent away... he was this master? Why was he here helping you if he cursed Flighty over there in the first place? A creature so strong he was meant to control him but it looks like he ended up broken in the corner cowering. My kind are dead because of you. And I mean what even is that thing over there" She cringes slightly as the soundless body of demon, only it's horns really being on display as Psyc lies unconscious against one wall. Flighty to my delight is hovering near him, protects him without meaning too.

"Master was my decision to be sent here. I take full responsibility and am truly sorry for the loss of your people" I answer honestly wishing I caged Master up long ago when my doubt about his intentions where clear.

"Knollica said Master needed to be here. Today was a sight I'm afraid you both needed to see. You are not invincible..." Nerdiver's words crash over the four elves before us. Her truth not holding back as she lets these creatures who are meant to be the rulers of this land have it. "Your kind have put down and discounted rock trolls and fairies for far too long. You are killing this land and every land over Tylimantrica. A land meant to be under your rule and protection. Your great power and status elevates you to a level even you cannot stand upon. Look at the tree your praying too! I'm sorry to tell you but its dead and while the month you have locked yourself in here for, the elf you chose to lead your race has conspired with an elf who was rotten. Sent an armada to kill me and take my charge for their own and destroyed the land trying to bring your castle back to life before trying to wipe us off the face of the land. Queen Glassadena I ask you..." holding his breath tightly next to his own queen Cyth looks pained but glad his true soul is able to say everything his has not managed all these years. "Are you ready to accept the events that lead to this day, these deaths are partly on your hands? On your ancestors hands? In this day are you willing to stand back and let each kind of creature this land has gifted work together to heal it? Will you be a part of it?"

Silence ebbing off everyone, I feel fingers lace into mind on both my sides. Looking left first Leach holds my gaze strong; signalling that he is always with me and this is now my turn.

To my right I come face to face with my best friend, his hard rock face clearly in pain as I realise one of our kind truly did not make it through the battle. Only seven of my male trolls left, Zeit's love is missing. "Thadus?" Shaking his head he lets my hand go before stepping back into to crowd of our kind.

One of mine gone. No longer ten, I feel a wrecking in my gut as the truth hits home that one if mine hasn't made it to this point with us. Harder than any weapon thrown at us, he must have died before I could stop the mystics. Surged on by this truth I step away from leach, my time having come to once more show the world the miracle all four of us creatures working together can create.

"Prilance, Ellamight, Nerdiver. Can you come with me please?" Moving past the queen and her people still holding the protection shield strong, all four of us circle the ancient tree at four different points. "Just like at your grove Nerdiver, let us come together and bring this tree... the beginning of the elves back to life."

"This is the first tree you mentioned when you described how my people came into the world?" Ellamight quizzes as she looks at the shrivelled hunch before us.

"Why do you think your people built a city around it? Your mystics knew to do a ritual here all these generations; they were just missing the one key ingredient." I soothe my own panics inside as Earth Mother feels me with warmth telling me I am right and this is the tree she first formed to bring the elves into this world. The sun and moon festivals and ritual is just, it is real and a true journey we have needed to take all these years. Only the elves where not meant to do it alone.

"What ingredient was missing?" Galnestia asks truly curious for what we are about to do.

"Union" Prilance answers for me.

Working as one, all four of us do not even say a word to each other as we all move to touch this broken ancient tree. Ellamight reaching up she lays her hand flat against the grain of the tree branch above her. Aiming for the highest point she can get, I feel a thrumming echo down through the trees interconnecting veins as I place both my hands on the base of the tree. Prilance floating up above us she sits on a branch, my oldest friend places her tiny hands onto the stick of wood underneath her, the thrumming echoing into mine and Ellamight's as Nerdiver moves down to one of the oldest roots that Tylimantrica will and has ever known.

Snaking out and through the tree, the thrumming scores through the bark of this dead tree, every vein switching on like it's been waiting dormant for us all to come along. Showing its wide connection to every inch under our feet, the roots of this tree quadruple out far further than this tree would ever be above ground. Unlike at Nerdiver's grove this time there is no light show, no fabulous display of magic. We are not making something anew; today we are bringing back life to something that should never have died in the first place.

Night time arriving just at the moment we have begun, this moment has been my destiny. This day was meant to always happen and on this day the moon and sun ritual will come together shifting a new world on Tylimantrica, connect us all with the gods in the sky.

Blinding light turning on behind me, I feel the moons full gaze suddenly fill the spot in the window behind me. Its light illuminating everything around this hall a hue shows that something is about to happen. Understanding how the elves for so long have though that the ritual they have performed all this time was doing something I look over to Flighty his face looking stunned at us four creatures holding onto the tree of life.

Knowing deep down in the roots of this tree, if we are to heal Psyc from the pollution rotting his core, it has to be now. Moving to call out to Flighty to bring Psyc here, my voice comes out instead as a siren call. Looking to my sister creatures, all three of my friends eyes blaze white, the moons light personified in us all. Opening their mouths the same noise comes out as all of our heads lean back calling this dormant tree to come back to its people. Something ancient waiting for this call I feel a stir deep within the depths of the bark under my palms, our siren call ebbing out in Tylimantrica calling not just the ancient tree home but more than we may be asking for.

My own mind wavering, I assume the girls feel the same, as my last ability to see the world around me brings, Cyth carrying Psyc's small body over to Nerdiver's lap, Flighty in a worried panic buzzes next to him. Reaching his tiny fingers out to graze Psyc head, the golden dust Flighty absorbed so long ago now given by Nerdiver bursts out of him and flows all over Psyc's body turning him into a ray of sunlight.

Light as bright as the sun, Nerdiver's body begins to take on the continuous glow from of the shape that was Psyc, both Flighty and Nerdiver turning into glowing Psyc gold forms. Cyth placing his hand on his Souliune shoulder he joins the golden forms as the light spreads into him, the white moonlight into Nerdiver's eyes now shining out of all four creatures locked into a siren call for life.

The simple non-display I thought was going to be this journey changes instantly as Spitfire flies to join her love, placing her hand on her own Souliune's hand touching the bark, her wings freezing her in place as she and Ellamight both turn sunlight gold. Leach borrowing under the ground, he comes up next to me, his hands rest gently on my shoulders as the light absorbing all the creature on the other side of the tree starts to flows directly into the deep veins of the ancient tree and comes at Prilance. Seeing how Nerdiver and we all are touching the bark, I watch as the queen lets down her shield, her and her daughter stepping forward to touch the tree adding their own light to this night.

Curling around and up, the light beaming off my friends and the trees veins looks so much like the beam escaping me earlier today, the power in this hall finally becoming what all the elves have wanted for such a long time. A truth of where they came from and a power to save this land.

Watching behind my own moon beam eyes as it completely takes over the tree, the sunlight then takes over Prilance, queen Glassadena and Galnestia's beings before at last the light looks to come for me. Starting with Leach who has leaned forward to touch the tree as well as me, three points of contact allows the sunlight to connect to the moon shine on my back and in my heart. With the sunlight given to Psyc to protect the day when his was born, his golden dust pours into all of us as the white light deep within my soul acts as the moons side to the harmony this tree needs for coming back to life.

My sight blazing brighter than a star, two circle form in my sight. One turning in on itself as it take the shape of the moon, its half curved self then leans onto the shape of the blazing sun to its right. A sign or a sigil I am not sure but this is the last thing I see before darkness takes me away from it all, a blankness which foretells of what is to come.

My mind going blank, it is only when I am lying on the ground leaning on Leach that I get to fully see the transformation our union has had on the land we have created. A place of pure brilliance and light, the Elven land is finally a place is was meant to be. One full of nature and life.

Destined for greatness

Master

They caged me. Bond me, and trapped me like a wild animal, fit for slaughter. My own kind stopping my act that was going to save us all. Just one more push was all I needed. I felt the weight of that shield under my fists breaking, I know just one last punch and the queen would have been mine to destroy. Mine to take away, just like how the elves took my entire race.

If only Kia had been better, more clever and direct with her assaults. Such a let-down of a creature after being able to control all of those elves, having the ability to warp there fickle minds into attacking anything she told them too. If only she was stronger, if only they were smart enough to use their time consuming magic to make it harder for Nimfa to reach them. And she reached them alright, far quicker than she ever should have.

Finishing our home in a meticulous fashion, my caged or bound white beams now sits atop one of the highest towers in the rock troll land. Unlike my original design, the tower that I should be in was meant to be made completely of darkness, a stone chosen from my own caved in hole in the ground.

Blacker than black, my tower was meant to be the school of dark magic a place I was going to teach my children the ways in which this world should be bent on their knees. Instead this mighty tower now holds my life alone, a prison made solely for me. Made of a white solid stone there is not one imperfection in the stone itself. Hollowed out in a way that I can see everything in the land, not one troll has come to see me except Zeit who brings me my food and water twice a day.

Time passing quickly, I have watched as my people have built each building I designed, and for some unknown reason actually built it the way I crafted it on my mini structure. My prison being the only one difference I am yet to see, I suppose it is only because my prison is for a different purpose now. Having watched the world unfold down below, I have to say how nice it is to not have hidden figures swaying over my thoughts anymore. No goddess trying her best to teach me what is right, no guiding hand telling how everything should be done. I am now truly alone and sadly I am pretty happy about it. My creation forming down around my birds eye view, the second to this building on difference is the way the rock troll land is being changed with the introduction of elves and fairies coming in.

Watching even way up here I see their kind mingling in the streets below, my stone clad courtyard with wide open spaces now altering into a natural paradise with tree and plants blooming everywhere. The fairies however do not come in drones like the more frequent elves, my guess being the ones I see are the precisely chosen creatures Prilance has granted to know the true power they possess. How she will keep it hidden from the rest of the little bugs I am not sure but such trivial thoughts are beyond me now. My hate for the elves now slowly dissipating for the time I have been locked up here, I do see the light they are helping to bring to our land.

My guiding hand vanishing the moment I was stopped from killing the queen, my skin has softened since I was hardened in place. Still made up of darkness, the power is now mine alone, nothing telling what I should do with it or how to make my next move. Happy enough to wait, I let my own body relax, solemn my kind now have a truly beautiful place to rule from. Watching today, I will see just from my vantage point Nimfa and Leach's wedding, the preparations buzzing as Nimfa has truly become a ruler of this queendom. My once beloved second goddess I would have done anything to be the one marrying her Instead of that Leach, though now I see I never loved her. I only loved the idea of being her consort, the last female of my kind I didn't have any other options than her. If she had loved me how I thought I loved her maybe I wouldn't be here right now trapped in this cage of light, but then maybe I would have ended killing not just the elves but everyone.

Preparations in the process, the grand hall I designed now has flowers growing all up and through the many holes I personally grooved out. Pink and Blue the flower represent the two of my kinds stones mixing to become one, a queen and her consort ready to finally bring the next race of our kind into this world. Months have passed since I was caged and I do wonder if Nimfa will ever come and give me her final judgment. Always having a soft spot for me, I have asked Zeit each time for when she will come even if she is ready or not but he never utters a word.

Only informing me that Kia's judgment was passed days ago and she will be rehabilitated on the bases that the our queen decided not to kill me, I laughed at the news that Kia gets to live. A sadness always coming off of him when he is about, I do not know what has happened to make Zeit so upset but something from our invasion must not have worked out for him. Saddened further when telling me of Kia's easy route out of a true punishment, I wonder if Zeit done something wrong in the battle for him to be the one to bring me and food and drink all the time.

Hearing footsteps tapping on the hearty stone steps now, he is right on time. Punctual as ever and with the wedding I would expected him to have forgotten about me today, I usually get a small width of food but today my noise is filled beyond anything other than fresh lilacs. His best friend is getting married, so I guess he's been around a lot of the flowers down below, but I can't help thinking surely he should be at the forefront of getting everything ready for today, not remembering to bring me substance.

My prison open on all sides, I spin slowly from the world outside, the whole top floor being mine, my cage unfortunately is the same size as it was when Nimfa and Earth Mother sent me blasting down through the earth, the goddess's earth never chipping off hard against my skin when I travelled underground like I did on that day. Waiting for my prison being made, it was the last time I saw Nimfa when she explained to the males of my kind what she wanted made. The complete opposite of me, I see why she when for this stone, yet it does mean I stand out like a saw thumb every minute of every day.

"Master...." A strong voice making me finishes my turn more quickly than expected.

"Nimfa!" I pipe up, utterly shocked that it is her voice that tickles my ears. "And what do I owe the pleasure of your company on your wedding day?" I say trying my best to push down the fact I am slightly shaken that she has come to see me today of all days.

"I thought it only correct that I finish our business before I make my oath in beginning a new era for our kind"

"I have heard already that Kia is to be rehabilitated on the basis that my life be spared. I assume I owe you a thank you" I say sarcastically before forgetting that I shouldn't lean against the bars of my prison.

Scolding me fiercely, I feel a hardened line appear starting down the side of my face before it traces down my shoulder to my side. Solidifying my ooze straight to the stone skin somewhere underneath, the ooze on either side of the hardened space pile over the line, warping my already funny physique even more. Putting me off from knowing I cannot do this, her presence is one thing I did not expect to see today. The Elven queen wondering through our gates with a battalion of elves I saw fighting us months ago, yes. Nimfa is a master communicator who can make anyone trust her. Look at every fool who is in her equality truce. However to see her here before me, I feel my soul sag at the monster I am.

"What have you allowed yourself to become?" Nimfa's eyes knit together, real concern taking over her being.

"Like you care. You have what you have always wanted. A consort to control, a queendom to rule and a binding agreement with the others of this land. Tylimantrica little pet all the way aren't you." Trying as I might to put as much venom into my voice, I feel I crack against her like a whip.

"You believe this is what I have always wanted. One of our kind dead? You... you a monster"

"Wait who's dead?" I ask before all the obvious pieces that have been slapping me in the face daily fit together. Zeit's depression, his role as my guard. He was always the nicest to me of our kind, if you can call it that but I guess not feeling the kind happy creature he was with the death of his love, bringing me food and being around my presence doesn't matter much when all you feel is sadness.

"Thadus did not make it through the invasion. If you had done as you promised you would have known that already. And let me guess you have fired horrible retort after horrible comment at Zeit when all he's done is his best to keep you alive. If not for him, the rest of our kind would have happily let you starve up here." Truth in her words, the only thing she has got wrong is that I wouldn't say anything horrible to a creature that has given me the only company I have received. Even if it was silent company.

"I have done no such thing. Like you said he is the only one to feed me and no matter what you think of me Nimfa I have felt his sadness everyday he has come up here. I just never knew the reason why. He doesn't speak. Instead he comes up with food and watches the world outside just like me. In fact I see your equality pack is working out very nicely for you. The only kind I do not see here are mermaids but that may be because no sea water has route to our land" My observations finally having a chance to be mentioned. Wondering just how this queen is going to get the complete opposite of our kind on side when she cannot go see them, we wait in silence for a while as she seems to think about what she wants to say next.

"Master I am not here to talk to you off the future I have planned"

"No?" I ask puzzled "Then what of my future? What has the magnificent Nimfa, queen of the rock trolls, bringer of equality, protector of the cold hearted!" I shout out, the loudest I've felt to be in a long time. "Who would have let me believe the oath I pledged would have come to pass if I had done what she said. Yet I saw you the day you brought our people here behind my back. I saw the day you had already chosen Leach, holding his hand showing him the castle I had made for you. Designed for you. What is the future for the monster who took his life into his own hands?"

"Banishment." Nimfa calls coldly.

Surprised once again today, I can't help but wonder why "Not death?"

"No not death Master. You are to be banished for the next ten thousand years after the moment you step foot over the borders of this land. Unable to step foot again on this soil or under it I might add until have shown your soul to be healed and whole. Never in the history of this world has anyone been banished for the trial of retribution. Your soul is black, darkness clouds your thoughts but this is your time to find a way out of it. This will be a time for you to do something right. I only hope I am making the right choice of course" Her judgement feeling final, I am not sure how she will be able to make sure I do not step foot here again. Ten thousand years is a long time even for our race, and putting a personal barrier around the land just for me seems like a lot of effort.

"Why I ask again, not death?"

"Death is a waste to a kind with hardly any of us left. Master you were not destined to be my consort. I see now you were never meant to help me bring back our race but your bloodline is too old to be wasteful. To not let you have the chance to change your actions and help us thrive again in the future would be a foolishness I will not make."

"I am to live so I can come back and breed like a caged animal one day. Thank you but no. I would rather you kill me"

"Master, this is not your choice. You will stay here until my first litter comes into this world. Zeit will inform you of when this happens and on that day Flighty will escort you to the end of our land. The goddess, helped by the Sun and Moon gods will watch over you for the duration of your banishment. If you have changed and are worthy you will be allowed back here to help bring our race even further forward into the world. If not, death will find you and not by my hands. By the goddess I hope you find the light some way, for I know the goddess will burn you up into crisp that your soul will burn with it. Master take this opportunity and make yourself great with it. You were destined for more than this, I just wish you could have seen it" A silent sob breaking her lower lip, it escapes for a lost baby rock troll I was when we first met. Already too late, the guiding hand had found me, though I wonder what would have happened if I hadn't started this with Flighty. If I hadn't been the darkness incarnate, what would have happened if I went to protect the queen. Would we even be standing in the new rock troll queendom or would we all be dead.

"Why do you give me this chance? Surely I have lost all chances of redemption" My curiousness spiking as Nimfa looks to leave.

"This is the last time you shall see me up close Master. If you are to return and change, one of my children who may choose you will decide if you are worthy to be in my presence. If not, this is goodbye Master. I only wish you had already been ready to choose the light."

"Choose the light? I was never given the chance to be part of the light!" I shout at my old queen, her back already turned on me as she begins to descend the stairs. "Unlike you I was chosen by something else! Darkness looks for the weak Nimfa!" My words making her stop dead on the stairs, I see her hand squeeze at her sides as her last words to me dig deeper than anything else she ever could say would.

"You should have been stronger"

Her cold as ice voice slashing at my heart, I fire words at her. "Watch your back my Queen because you will never know who the guiding hand will fall onto next!"

Seeing she wants to turn back to me and ask me who I am referring too, the rock troll queen stands strong, her crowned head showing she was always meant to be queen no matter who wished to rule us. Moving on from me, I see she is ready to begin a new day without me in it. Disappearing into the depths of my building, my words forever imbedded in her mind, the truth that anyone around her can become as tainted as I, will whisper darkly just as the guiding hand did to me.

Three sets of feet sounding on the steps following Nimfa's slow walk down, these new footfalls are slow and ominous. Rising up like three dark omens, three figures come up into my prison ready to shift my world.

Robed in shining purple velvet, the figures move to stand in a line before me. Their heads bowed, it is only from their height that I can see they are of Elven descent. Wondering if Nimfa has lied to me to see what I would say before my execution, I stare the figures out willing them to look up at me. And look up at me they do.

Face's I recognise instantly all three hoods falls back as a huge cold gust of wind springs led with icy remanence that snakes into my back. Rock trolls never feeling the cold I see the three beings before me are different, however something tells me the breeze I just felt is not natural. Considering it's is a bright summers day, that breeze has been brought here by a task, one I am still not certain will have me still alive at the end of it. Staring at me dead in the face Nerdiver centre of the three, looks forever changed compared to the mermaid who screamed bloody murder to get me to flee her pond. Taller than the elf next to them, Cyth and Nerdiver have truly formed their own kind, I just wonder if they are fully immortal yet. Or are they holding off on completely there change as who knows what will happen to the world when each Souliune finishes their shift to the new era.

"Are you really willing to send Flighty as my escort Nerdiver? Three times now I have manipulated him. Are you truly stupid enough to risk it again?"

"Flighty is beyond you now" Her voice sings deep into my ears, her words beginning the most powerful spell three creatures could ever perform. Binding me to my punishment of destiny, I feel everything before me alter; my life force quaking at the truth Nimfa told me. I will be banished and the gods shall be the witness to the whole thing.

Letting out a scream I want to hold in so tightly, my life is no longer my own again. My prison sentence being all that was aloud of me to feel the freedom I have always wanted of my own thoughts, I cry out harder than I would want to... my true soul cracking at the darkness still bond to me.

Nimfa

"How does it feel to be a married woman?" Queen Glassadena calls to me from the entrance to my great hall.

Spinning from my own elation of staring up into the high ceiling of this place, I can't help but think now how much my own queendom is linked to hers. Since our ritual trees brought forth by our will to connect together, have cracked up through the earth rising up into buildings and in some cases through building shattering all the harsh mirrors the Elven castle was made out off. Horndon is now once again the place of nature and light. Trees growing even now, the elves are working out a harmony with the new growths on their land, working between keeping some of the original buildings and like Cyth's creation working with the trees to form new homes and places to be. My last image of Horndon when we left to return here was of how stunning all of the falling petals looked which according to Ellamight bloom daily and fall nightly. The power given by the sun and the moon gods.

Not so much breaking everything here, the elves and fairies I have invited to bring some nature into Masters design of our home, they have worked together to bring life to every corner but without taking the rocks which are our core, away. Anywhere you walk inside my now completed complex of building you will find trees of all kinds, silver birch, oak, chestnut and even a dragon trees just at the base of Zeit's school. Helping keep life roaming around, animals have even ventured here to set up home, warming my hearts because all I want is to be connected to everything and Master's Original plan makes this work perfectly.

The grand tree in queen Glassadena's ancient hall did burst up through the roof, something we discovered once we awoke. Finding pretty white flowers dangling down to the ground at the end of the long branches of a weeping willow, the first tree look just as it needed to. Ancient but alive. The first tree to enter this world gives off when I looked at it properly a un- bright hue, somehow being more vibrant than the trees at Nerdiver's grove, yet not as colourful and bright. Giving off a true presence of ancient life inside, when we venture home the elves made communion for the first time in generations, but the difference being this time the tree spoke back.

"I'm not certain yet, it's only been a few hours. I hear you managed to commune with the first tree, though I haven't had a chance to speak with you yet. How did it feel?"

"Speaking of it only being a few hours shouldn't you be with your consort right now rather than speaking with me?" The queen gives me a quizzical look of which I'm sure her daughter would be proud of. "And the first tree is being a bit difficult. She lets me get close but the moment I feel our minds will connect I am blasted out. Physically too I might add. The radius of how far I am flung gets bigger every time although I am taking that as I am making it through to her"

"So you think she is a she?" The assumption of gender I feel being important for the reason I have asked her here is connected to the same thing.

"I know she is. Her mind is my ancestor and only the females have ever spoken or communed with me in the past when I have needed help. You are the same yes?"

"I am. Yet it has become fewer moments with the help of Earth Mother stepping in a lot. My ancestors have left me to her design, well I'm assuming up until the birth of my first litter. This brings me to why I have invited you here"

"Your first litter? I'm sorry to say Nimfa, elves are like rock trolls, females cannot breed together otherwise males of our kind would have died out aeons ago" Bursting out laughing though I feel truth in the world she speaks, I feel a little taken back by this creature being the kind to joke so quick and easy. Always assuming elves would be tight upper lipped from all the stories I've heard of the royal females, by looking at the queen you wouldn't necessarily be able to pick her up out of a group.

A plain Jane as humanoids of legends might say, unlike her daughter the striking image anyone would have of a royal elf, blazing white hair, hard lined face yet so beautiful you want to fall to your knees and beg her to let you live. The queen looks simple. Her hair tied up on a high ponytail, her skin colour is the same as her sons yet her hair is jet black. No grand clothing or face make up, not that elves need any, her face is not as pointed or glam as say Ellamight's. Simple soft features make her look kind; the power she possesses inside is not what anyone would assume by just looking at her. Wearing a simple light linen dress, that flows from her wrists all the way up to her neck and down to the floor with a simple train; the fabric looks comfortable and easy to move in. Her heir wearing a stunning dress that gives you her legs for days, I wonder if this queen is ready to pass on the crown and concentrate mainly on finding the truth of her races past by delving deeper into the mystics of her magic.

"No dear elf" I say joining in on the laughter as I move up to my throne I have grown use to sitting in. Signalling for the queen to truly enter the hall and join me, I wonder how it will feel one day to have guard's stationed near my every move, clocking her guards standing just outside the door. To be fair though after what happened with Master I don't doubt this queen will always have guards with her no matter where she goes. "I asked you here for your help. Help I am in need of for my first litter."

"Oh! You wish to weave." A burst of loud laughter breaking her breast again she glides up to me, her movements so much like her sons I wonder if queens in the elf community are like my kind, gifted far more than the rest of their people, even more than I have already witnessed.

Looking up and around at the trees of heaven which have been grown straight from the earth on both sides of my hall, my throne is no longer the only green in the room. Having to say I much prefer it. My position in the hall makes me stand out enough so having these tree with me bring me comfort and a reminder that my goal to bring our races together has worked. The only race we await to hear from to join our alliance is the mermaids.

Prilance working alone, she is making changes to the fairy colonies her training coming only to those she trusts and sees true potential inside of. Essentially becoming queen of the fairies, she is taking her new position well while continuing the training of her granddaughter before Ellamight and Spitfire set of for the secret mission the queen in front of me set many moons ago.

"I wish for a spell to be weaved which I believe you would be the best creature to help me do so. I cannot do it to myself and even though Ellamight has such raw potential, the delicacy of this situation calls for a more practised spell caster. With you joining us at our wedding I could not think of a better sister queen to perform this upon me" My voice softening as what I ask of her will make me truly vulnerable to anything she would wish to do to me, I take a beat to ready myself.

"What spell do you need me to weave Nimfa" She turns stern, the seriousness of what I ask clear and apparent to her also.

"I ask of you to weave a spell upon my womb. One that will guarantee my first litter to be of only girls. It is what my race and I need, and I want my first to truly be of girls alone."

"There may be consequences of such a spell"

"I am aware of consequences bound to such personal magic in single creatures but I feel I must have this for my races future." I plead my own fearfulness slightly breaking through.

"You may not be able to have a second litter. How many trolls does one usually have as a rock troll?"

"Usually four, five at a push. It is what I need to start my race again, I cannot risk only have one." I answer true.

"I understand." Sliding up to take my hand in hers I see she truly does understand why I need this. How she could let a creature like Kia control her people in her stay I may never know but what I do know is a sister queen she really is. This beginning of our personal friendship is what will continue the future of equality we shall spread around this land. The sigil now forever engraved on our hands will forever be a daily reminder of that.

A half-moon leaning on a sun. Just like the image I saw before we all blacked out from the incredible power flowing through us in the hall of the ancient tree, each creature that helped bring nature's power and life back to Horndon's mirror queendom now has the sigil that binds the moon and the sun to forever look over us. Our goal is to push forward peace and light through Tylimantrica and for me it continues with the birth of my girls I have always meant to have.

Getting to my feet, we move to the centre of the hall, the light of the setting sun is perfect for spell, the warm golden glow filling the space around us cooling any nerves I known I have. Getting pregnant is the easy part but hibernating in Earth Mother's womb for six months to protect the creatures inside me will mean leaving my queendom in the hands of men. Knowing my men are kind hearted I still worry that something could go wrong while I am away. My friends will all be back to their own lives, leaving a male run kingdom which I will bring a group of babies girls back too. Hoping Zeit snaps out of his mourning just enough to help Leach keep order, queen Glassadena clicks her fingers in front of my eyes bringing me back to the first part of all of this. The crafting of females.

"Are you ready?"

"As I'll ever be. I have to admit. After all these years waiting to have the first set of rock troll children in years, I am slightly terrified."

"Every excepting Mother is terrified of the thought of birthing a child. In your case four or five" She expands her eyes making a nervous laugh escape my mouth. "However. Once your girls are here and they look up to you Nimfa, you will not be disappointed or nervous at all. All you will care about is making them happy and making them safe. Trust me you are going to make a fanatic mother. Ellamight has told me of how you have helped her and Spitfire, and Nerdiver with my Cyth. You were born to have these children so let's make sure this litter is the best you could possibly have."

Placing her long fingers to my stomach, queen Glassadena eyes sparkle a bright peach colour as her spell aims for my womb. The last part of the puzzle for me and my rock trolls to come out of extinction, I relax myself to the knowledge I have done everything I can to bring the next generation of rock trolls to this world.

An unknown future
Nimfa

This is it. I feel the growth of them inside of me, a mother's natural instincts clicking on as Earth mother pulls at me begging me to fall into her warm embrace for the duration of my pregnancy. Ready to rest and I mean really rest from the world for a while, I move around my queendom in search of the one I am to leave in charge.

Ellamight giving me a smile as I pass, I am glad she has decided to stay here with us working on growing the natural life that this place has needed. Spitfire off training with her grandmother, I know once I return back to my throne my two friends will be off on the quest Ellamight so longs to finish.

"I will see you in six months" I call out to her

"I'm excited to meet them! Hurry it alone already" Her light hearted laugh echoes in the courtyard as I move down into the earth searching for him.

Of course the day I am leaving, my consort is nowhere to be found. Usually I would have asked him to come with me, yet I feel there is another of my kind in need of a good rest in which he can hibernate and mourn.

Stepping through a few of the rooms on the upper floors quickly there is no life down here what so ever. With us rock trolls being the only ones with the ability to come down here without help, the fairies and elves visiting us have mainly stayed above ground. A place I know will one day be crowded with creatures of my own kind I take in the serene silence, enjoying the emptiness of the snake green stonework. Warm and comforting, I drop a few more levels down, willing my consort to come to me.

Hearing the small tapping sound which helped me decided which consort I was going to take in the first place, I follow the noise like it's his way of telling me where to go. Taking me unexpectedly into my children's future bedroom, I feel a funny happy sensation running through my toes. The knowledge that he is as excited as I am to meet our girls is so fantastic I cannot help but put on a massive smile.

Standing up on a platform that will be a sleeping space for one of my girls, I see he is on one of the five platforms which Master crafted going by our usual birth-rate. With the queen Glassadena's spell performed, we as sister mystics are unsure what the consequences will be for such a spell as unlike with Nerdiver I show no physical signs of difference to me. Wanting to make a safe and welcoming space for our girls, Leach looks to be tapping the sigil that covers each of the creatures involved in the ritual at Horndon's hands onto the wall.

Peaking to the other platforms I see he has crafted our sigil of my head above another one, an old style one our people would have used long ago above a third.

"What are you going to do for the final two?" I say making him jump slightly, his concentration taking him off to another world.

"You quiet little troll. Sneaking up on your consort is not well advised"

"And why not?" I give my best flirty smile, before bringing my hands up to ask him to come to me.

"You could have frightened me to death." He jokes jumping down from the platform placing some fine tools down before coming to place his hands in my belly. "You'll have to wait and see what the two other designs I have in mind are."

"Are you sure your fine with me taking Zeit with me into hibernation? You're not offended?"

"No never! I lost a brother too and I am finding it hard to cope. What he must be going through I cannot imagine. We need him ready and full of life when the girls come. He's going to be there professor after all." Leach gleams, his light letting me known he is okay with whatever decisions I make.

"I am thankful for you. I never thought I would have this with any of you." My words making his face crease with confusion. "Nothing true I mean. The feelings I have, it's something I thought only fairy tales were filled with. But since we have been able to truly see inside what we both have is light, I know I have chosen the best rock troll I could to be my consort. And the best of my kind to watch over our land until I return with our future" Leaning down just a smidge, I love that fact that Leach, unique for our kind, is just slightly taller than me. Strange for a male in our race, it is nice, for when his blue skin gleams in the light, it send a shiver through me as he leans in to give me a kiss.

"I am here for whatever you need my queen. I only wish we could hurry the pregnancy along and have you back with our girls straight away."

Pushing at his shoulder lightly, I quickly hug into him, his orchid on his face a bright yellow today for joy, as he is clearly as happy as I am.

"I will miss you" I say into his chest.

"And I you."

Holding me back by the arms, he drops to his knees where he begins to tell our girls how excited he is to meet them and to hurry along already. "I don't want them to come to quickly!" I squeak. "I am in need of some rest. I haven't stopped since Tylimantrica set me off on my task over hundreds of years ago."

"This is the last one is it not? Then you can rest in your rule happy you have done what was excepted of you" Leach shoos me a little clearly wanting to return back to his artwork.

"My leach. It is foolish to think that this is over. That sigil you carve out is the sigil that bounds us to a fight that is in the horizon. It's just a question of when it comes. Not if"

Leaving him to his work, I move up out of the under city and head right to where I know my best friend is.

Right on time, Zeit exits Master's prison tower, his empty tray showing the last meal he will ever serve to the demon up there. How he became so filled with darkness I did not see, is a mystery. I only hope I am doing the right thing by allowing him the chance to return and redeem himself one day.

"Zeit"

His silent face looking up at me, any joy of the friend I use to know has completely gone. Not knowing that I'm taking him with me, he just gives me a bow before heading in the opposite direction to me.

"Where are you going?"

"To study. I know you think the spell that Cyth, Nerdiver and Ellamight did on Master will keep him from this land until the gods find him worthy to return but I want to triple check." Without stopping to actually converse with me, his need to not be with others comes of him in waves. A complete change to the creature he was before the invasion began.

"I need you to come with me instead" I put on my most commanding of voices, making him stop.

"Come where?" He sighs, the weight of everything he feels on him, like I had just picked up one of our buildings and placed it on his shoulders to hold.

"To heal" Holding my hands out to him, he turns so slowly, his trust in the world going when his love was taken from it. The longer he stays like this the deeper he will get to the depression eating him up. He needs the warmth and cuddle of the goddess just as much if not more than me. If my friend

is to find the creature he was when his love was alive he
needs to accept Thadus is gone. He would want him to live
on; heck his love will live on through him. He would not want
him wasting his life on mourning the loss of their life
together, no he would want him celebrating the time they
did have.

"Take my hand." I plead, shaking my fingers so he gets how
much I need him to come with me. "Please Zeit" Dropping
the tray I know someone will find soon, Ellamight has already
promised me she will take over feeding Master, that tray
being a signal we have definitely left. My best friend gripping
my fingers, the touch of another troll makes him become
slightly panicked. Not giving him time to break away, I yank
him into my opening arms, his body relaxing in the
knowledge he is safe with me.

"We are ready Tylimantrica" I call out, our goddess easily
phasing us down pass the rooms below our feet so fast we
don't even see them.

Time to sleep my children

My goddess's voice whispering through our souls as she
squeezes us warmly, she holds us tightly in her earthly body.
Knowing nothing can get to us, my safety is complete until I
come to full trimester. Zeit letting out the longest of breaths I
know he has been holding in since Thadus's death. I breathe
with him. The growing queens in my womb feeling us relax;
they ready themselves for the growing they can now do in
peace.

Soil cocooning tightly up against us, Earth Mother relaxes in herself, her plan for our race nearing its end.

Master

Laughter. Child's laughter. And I mean more than one child's laughter bounces against my ears. Recognising a rock trolls laughter anywhere with the sound of two stone rubbing together as the vocals cords react, these sound are so high and pure they have to be from child. If that is right it means Nimfa did it. She has actually brought new life to our race.

Arriving at my cage earlier than normal I have been brought down from my prison by Ellamight, her power matching that of her queens when she bounds me in chains. White gold, the chains are heavy, easy to keep me subdued and my hands knotted together near my chest. Certain these will not come off until I am escorted fully from this land; I see the tall elf duck her head as we exit the pearly white building.

Sunlight hitting my face, I am quickly taken to the courtyard I built solely with my two bound hands, the wildlife that now roams it shocking me. I knew they had been planting trees and plants everywhere but to see the likes of deer's, rabbits, raccoons and birds dotting themselves all around making a life, I can't see how this is separate from the world outside the walls I crafted. Why bother having this castle of your letting the natural life inside wonder in and out.

"Beautiful isn't it" Ellamight's happiness at the image before me makes me gag.

"Beauty is in the eye of the beholder is it not? This is not beauty. It is chaos" I huff as she pushes me further into the courtyard, her happiness easily shattered by me.

"If you cannot see the beauty here, you are seriously going to struggle getting back into this land in ten thousand years Master. Remember the gods will be watching you at all times. Redemption can be earned but it is just as easily taken away."

Laughter once again filling my ears, I look over my shoulder ignoring Ellamight's play of teaching me right and wrong. That may be there plan with this banishment, but at the rate darkness is circled around me so tightly, I shall never be seen again.

"Come back little one!" Zeit's voice echoes over the space between us as I lock eyes on one of the first toddler rock trolls to have been born in thousands of years.

The most gorgeous image I have ever seen in my whole entire life, I see not just the one running in my direction now but counting, there is at least ten of them. Ten girls in fact. Young and filled with such raw life. Laughing together, Zeit catches the breakaway troll as she tries her best to climb into the fountain I so beautifully designed, the time I had here alone feeling so long ago.

Naturally grey like I once was, the little troll has all of her mother's features including her one orange eye and one pink eye. Light veins which you can only see when the sunlight reflects against the water to her skin, this little trolls looks to have gold pulsing through her. Her perfectly smoothed stone skin shows the beauty female rock trolls always have over males. Their status born higher than our own, I notice something not just about this little one but about all of them. Every single one has a crown growing out of their head. Small bunches of curling moss bunches up from there crowns as Zeit and Xen look after the girls. Their Mother, not two steps away is in a light-hearted talk with my guide out of this land, the little fairy in a warriors outfit, looking ready to fight whenever needed.

"How long have I been locked away?" I ask, now only realising the length of time when trying to consider how old the girls are.

"A year and a half. The world is on cause for equality and your race is set for a definite regrowth of life. Nimfa, to the shock of us all is about to re-hibernate with a second litter while Spitfire and I can finally leave on our quest"

"Second litter? Surely you mean third? Rock trolls cannot birth ten trolls in one litter. They would die instantly and so would the young." Ignoring her comment about her and Spitfire, I could care less of the adventures of a fairy and elf.

"Goddess Tylimantrica has helped Nimfa through any struggle she may have faced down in the earth. But this is of no concern of yours. Flighty will come over in a minute and this is the last you shall see if any of us for a long time. Remember Master, the gods are watching. Do not think of them as fools. One toe out of line and your return may never come" Her patronising tone makes my blood boil as I see Nimfa sadly glance my way before telling her girls to return into the earth. Being here for my exit is clearly to show me her power is one I need to follow, though I can't help myself in trying my best in giving a patronising bow.

Calling all the younglings to phase to the levels below, Zeit clearly was here only to show me the future of our race is here. One of these creatures may choose me after my banishment. The last youngling to fall into the earth is the original one I saw. Her cute little face lighting up as she takes me in, giving me a tiny smile, a force flying straight off of it as if it is her teeth twinkle with light. Power like her mother, her face is the last thing to drop into the ground as I feel like I have been shot into the heart of my dark soul. Tying it's best to replant light in there, my body convulses as I trip like a fool, Ellamight giving me a confused look as I feel something imbed inside me.

Growling as I shake it off, I punch my oozing chest with my bound hands, doing whatever I need to smoother the spell this child has tried to place upon me. How foolish are these creatures to think such a pure ball of light could stop me in my tracks of killing this land one day. My fairy guide giving his sister's lover a quizzical look in my direction, I give him a gooey smile, his muscled body looking a little slimmer than the first time I met him, his physique becoming that of a flyer.

"Let get going Master. It's time you start you sentence"
Taking the chains end from Ellamight anyone would wonder how he is strong enough to take the weight of the chains, his small body nearly being the same size at the chain itself. Yanking hard, his arms barley react as his pulls me forward, my whole body jilting from the strength this tiny creature has.

M

"We are nearly there Master. Keep going already" Flighty's incessant voice bangs at the back of my head driving me insane. My body being so weighted down by the chains around my hands I want to slump to the floor and not move, I force myself on. The sooner I make it to the border the sooner I'll have my strength back, though my soul twinges again, the little troll truly doing something to me.

Looking at the fairy I see no change what so ever in him from the angry and scared little fairy that stood on the edge of the well a few years back. Powerful now I give you however strong hearted I think not. Not certain if the darkness has been taken out of him since I last saw him, he does look lighter, as if a weight has been lifted from him. I cannot see any other reason Nerdiver would allow him to escort me alone to the edge of our land, like I said to her three times he has let me manipulate him, do they truly want there to be a fourth.

"So did they kill demon?" I slip in the mention of Psyc to see what reaction I can get from him. His face a mask of fear at the mention of demon dying I take it as an astounding no.

"Unlike you Master, we are not barbarians. Psyc is doing a lot better actually. Though he will never be what he was before you cursed me and I cursed him. His mind is once again his own."

"And where is this Psyc now as you call him?" I edge my voice to sound like I have a plan for him, when really I don't care for anything back in the forest behind us. The way ahead is long for me yet I feel my bounds buzzing, signalling that I am getting close to the barrier that will hold me out of Tylimantrica for as long as it wants.

"Psyc is out finding who he is. Not as a fairy or a demon but as something more. Thanks to me he has new gifts that allow the fairy colonies to leave him alone..." Flighty's words break off as a thought seems to come to him.

"Does he leave you alone now? I know all about the crush he had on you little bug. Did he ever get to tell you how he felt" I laugh directly into his face as I spin to look him. My oozing skin no longer a soft as it was, it still runs all over me as my face becomes inches from the fairy who hasn't noticed me spin at first.

"Keep walking" He spits at me through a clench jaw. Yanking on his end of the chains I'm bound to, my body starts to fit in place like a seizure until I succumb turning my thoughts to walk the way I'm meant to again. How I hate these creatures for having such a power over me. Cursing them silently, the buzzing doubles as I take a few more steps. The forest around us ending, it makes way for the only place that connects our land to another.

Mountains far taller than anything else in this land, they spike up sharply into the sky, looking as if they wait for a giant to step down on this place only to receive an unpleasant welcome. Spreading off in both directions, this is the barrier to our land, the mountain range making it all the way to the ocean on either side of it. How far this barrier goes I am not positive though a block of rock so harsh and dangerous that no creature, not even a fairy could fly up and over it makes this piece in our land impenetrable. A break in the centre, there is a thin valley only big enough for one creature at a time to pass through, meaning no invading army can get through here. At this particular moment I feel the valley has been made solely for me. The cold sound that whisper out of the pass, aims its harsh unknown at the little bit of light that toddler troll planted in me.

On either side of the entrance of the valley are two high towers guarding the outpost. Around the bases of them are broken mirrors, showing the last signs of the old mirror queendom. Looking far more powerful than they did, the towers have jagged looking tree branches growing up and out of the towers stonework, many more guards than there used to be patrol the border line of this land. Gazing closer I see they are armed and ready with armour made by my kind. The first defence against any invading army, no creatures could get through here quick enough to do any real damage but these towers wait here just in case. If nothing tells us of how powerful anyone could be, the journeys we have taken to get to this point never would have happened.

My last chance for a conversation with anyone for a long while, I try again with Flighty, needing a little more time before I get to the border. The ooze coating my skin feeling itchy, I want nothing more than for it to be gone. The curse the three elvens types put on me, have made me itch from inside. The toddler troll only making it worse, I feel like I cannot step out of this land without this itching gone. This can't be my life, this itching oozing skin of mine needs to depart like I am about to depart this land.

Feeling the light force shot at me, the little troll I once was before the guiding hand found me feels to want to come out. The spot of light edging it way out further into my soul, some kind of clarity is finding its way to me. Maybe if I leave the darkness here, I have a chance at a better life out there, one free only expect to the view of the gods.

"So I take it you haven't seen Psyc for a year and a half then. What of your sister and her girlfriend? Have they morphed any more since there Souliune began? Ellamight hasn't seemed any different since she's been bringing me my food?" I pause as I position my hands to my chest, slightly difficult with these chains. "And what of Cyth and Nerdiver? Are they complete in their transformation into new creatures?" Putting my best Nimfa voice on, I do my best to sound interested. I just need to stall long enough so I can push my hand into my chest and get through the ooze of gunk I now am. My last gift to this world will be one I bound Flighty too long ago.

"No I haven't seen Psyc in a long time now. My sister has been off training with Prilance my grandmother so before you think you can over power us one day. Think on this Master. Since you've been locked up, Nerdiver and Cyth have completed their Souliune. The Mellifine's are immortal now, and soon Ellamight and Spitfire shall be the same once there quest is complete. I tell you this so you know our land is becoming one of only true light..." Pushing my hand deeper into my oozing flesh I feel my fingers connect to my original grey stonework, the place where I placed mine and Flighty's oath waiting for me to tap it.

"Equality will be the ruler of this land; the elves are stronger than you ever wished them to be. The fairies are on track to unlocking powers you could only wish off. Rock trolls are entering the world again and by the looks of the little princess's they will be more powerful than any of us combined. A treaty meeting with the mermaids is set and by the time you may return on good terms. Which I highly doubt as you are as rotten as it comes. Or by the time you try to break back into this land, you will be defeated. Give yourself a chance in the next ten thousand years as you see Master you cannot beat us. You lost. Just remember that."

"Remember what sorry?" I ask as I circle the orange flame circle brunt into my stone, tapping it three time as I feel the chains on my wrists about to blow apart, my concentration so fixated on getting this ooze out of me I ignore every creature around me bar Flighty. The border line coming up fast, my chains feel as if they are going to incinerate me with how much they are buzzing now, though flighty hasn't seemed to have noticed once.

Two steps away from entering the valley, my chains are buzzing like mad, making it harder to bind Flighty to his oath. The guards in duty looking at me with puzzled eyes, they seem to be trying their best to listen in on our conversation, one giving me a quizzical look at my hunch exterior.

"This is your opportunity given by your queen to redeem your soul. Don't waste it. Darkness ate you up... but maybe you can spit it back out and find the small rock troll that was born with goodness in his heart" Sounding genuinely hopeful I may find light out in the unknown in front of us, I hate him even more that he thinks, telling me I need to change. I know I do but I've had enough if others telling me how and what I should be and do. They've never tried to help me, no. The creatures of this land have only ever blacklisted me, turning me further to the dark.

"How would you know what was born in my heart?" I cry out, pulling my hand from my chest as I turn before the last step into my banishment.

"Knollica showed me why goddess Tylimantrica chose to save you personally above all the rest of your kind. She saw a light in you that could burn brighter than the sun god himself" He looks to plead at me. "If only you didn't let yourself be warped by that stuff covering you"

"Why would you care so much about me after what I have done to you?" I feel I need to know before my final step takes me away.

"Did you know your kind are born with intelligence of an adult?"

"Of course I know"

"That youngling rock troll you saw aiming herself to go swimming in your fountain?"

Not letting him change my mind and soul by his words, I click my fingers on both hands summoning my orange flame, so small flighty doesn't notice, his presence looking calmer than I have ever seen him before.

"She said she chooses you. You are the troll she will wait ten thousand years for to change. Master. She is but a child but she believes in you and wants to know you can change, you can be worthy of her. The goddess is giving you one last chance to join our fight against the darkness. Don't ruin it already" Signalling at the flames above my palms, his nice leather vest he's wearing beginning to burn where his oath circle lies, he clearly isn't as foolish as I thought. He knows what I have planned; maybe he has excepted it all along.

"Our oath was bound when darkness guided my hand. To finish this connection between us Flighty. To let me truly find if there is goodness in me on my ten thousand year journey, I need to be free of anything the guiding hand gave me. I'm sorry Flighty but this is a curse you will need to free this world from. Not me."

"I know" Flighty gives me a genuine smile of friendship, his strong muscles arms opening up to embrace what I am about to unleash upon him.

Stepping back my foot breaks the border line, my chains breaking free instantly, sending a shockwave of sound and light out in all directions making the elves all fall to their knees. Throwing all the dark ooze flowing over my skin at Flighty, my orange flames and our oath lock him in place as the tiny amount of light the young rock troll princess smiled at me grow full in my heart.

He's setting me free. The little fairy I cursed so long ago now is setting me free. Willing taking the darkness I brought into this world. Who could be such a soul, one who is free of darkness again until we are alone once more. Feeling utter sadness for the first time since I was a new-born, I feel bad as I turn from the world. The sight of what I am creating again is something I wish not to see.

Leaving the darkness behind with this land, I feel myself set free as the Elven guards first aimed their swords at me until Flighty's cry of pain from his oath takes hold. Turning to a growl as the ooze changes him once again, Flighty the small fairy who was an outcast from the rest of his race, the fairy without dust has woefully accepted my curse, I now born again.

Not being around this time to see the repercussions of my last decision, I feel what I have done is right; Flighty took the consequence of breaking our bound oath. Nimfa isn't mine, not that I want her anymore but that was an oath we bound together, an oath both of us couldn't end unless it was this way.

Calling out to one another I hear the guards all jumps into action, my presence forgotten as Flighty becomes a new being. My body back to its classic grey stone; I touch my face feeling an orchid alive and well planted into my cheek. Stepping away from the cries behind me, the horror the beast that was Flighty is about to rain down on the land I have left is something the creature who hated me will have to deal with.

Tylimantrica warmth tickling at my feet, I feel the presence of my goddess return. Even though I have cursed Flighty once again, for the first time since I was a youngling I am free of darkness and ready for a new beginning. Feeling ready to embrace the light she has so long to fill me with, I smile, my skin no longer feeling jagged and rough, my cheeks are smooth and shiny as it my belly and hands.

Sounds of pain and blood behind me, I feel hope for the first time in my adult life that the creatures Flighty has so much faith in will be able to save him. The infection that has plagued me for so long vanished; I wonder what creature I am going to be. My future unknown, I walk against a small gust of wind. My first opponent in an uncertain land.

Tylimantrica will return in...

Ellamight
&
Spitfire

Elven Dictionary

Thimen – Time

Frezzon - Freeze

Protect – Tracon

Shelter – Lethin

Guard – Gurrat

Preserve – Forine

Forever – Ethial

Souliune – Soulmate

Chifferen – Change

Enjoy Nimfa & Master?

Leave a review on Goodreads or Amazon

hdapratt123.wixsite.com/hdapratt

A Sneak peek into one of HDA's other series

Book one in The Elemental Cycle

HDA PRATT

Prologue
Terra

Not a cloud in sight above her dreadlocked head, Terra knew. Knew that the first full day of summer had finally arrived and the sun was granting them, the newly unemployed friends the perfect weather. Complementing the elation running through her soul, Terra's warm laughter rings out at the sight of her dog being bested by the brute that is Eline's beast.

Lika's bronze fur catching the light of the sun so perfectly; it reflects a shine any freshly polished armour would be jealous of. With her brute force and German Shephard descent, Lika is not a dog to be messed with. Master of the uncontrollability Lika, Terra cannot help secretly liking the fact that her soothingly calm best friend Eline holds the power of taming such a beast.

Crushing soft sand between her toes, Terra lets the riverside's beauty sink in. Looking to her friends, she notices the weight-fullness that they all shared, has vanished. After one simple act, one of defiance, of not living a life placed upon them. All it took was to throw away what was expected and embrace their deserved freedom.

Jumping to her feet, water rushes at her and Eline, soaking her giant friend's legs. Kicking the water at Eline, a look of mischief covers the Dutch woman's face, her revenge ensuing. Giving off a screech that could only match that of a mountain lion's roar, Eline drags Terra back down into the liquid. Watching their owners copy their play fighting, the two dogs jump into the water, attacking the giggling girls.

Splashes and barks echoing down the river's water that for today was somehow blue. A warm breeze blowing under the arching bridge high above, it throws itself at the drenched group. Laughing down at them, Terra sees Donald watching from above; happy he chose to not sit at the water's edge. Distracted by him, Terra feels her golden dreads soak up a massive amount of water from Eline splashing a wave over her.

Helping each other up, they move out of the water quickly, having had enough of being in the murky Suffolk water. The only one unhappy to leave it, Eline's puppy buzzes with constant energy, deciding in a second that she is finished with Terra's Maggie, Lika barrels herself at Donald. Licking his face, the dog pins him on his back, over-powering him easily.

Stretching to the height of six foot two, Terra was sure Donald had not stopped growing even after making it to the age of twenty-two. Combined with his build, Donald could easily hold back the power of Lika, if he truly tried. His pale skin and ever-changing green eyes show the English/Scottish mix that his parents created. With a round shaped face, his neatly trimmed beard tinged by a ginger glow, hides his baby fat beneath. Shaved to one length, Terra thinks how much older her handsome friend looks with his brown hair clipped to its new style.

Laying down a few feet away from the attacking puppy, Terra's Maggie watches the younger pup fire a constant stream of energy at Donald. Rubbing Maggie's wrinkly head, a pair of watery eyes shines out from the droopy skin that has dropped with Maggie's ever growing age. With her puppy-like spikes of energy dwindling, Terra can't help but wonder how many years her boxer has left.

"Nee Lika" Eline shouts in her native tongue, clicking her fingers. Hearing Eline use her first language of Dutch, it sparks an ever-recurring reminder that her best friend originates from Holland. Apart from the tang in her accent and that she towers even above Donald; Terra always forgets that fact about her. Two years they've known each other and the only question about Holland Terra had had been short and sweet. Did Eline think in Dutch or English.

"Nee Lika" Looking to her owner, Lika's ears flop down, her eyes turning a pure black as she contemplates her next move. Holding back a smile, Terra watches the power struggle between master and canine. Clicking her fingers as one last warning, Lika gives a last ditched effort at licking Donald.

"Heir Lika" Eline calmly speaks her words, pure strength and no anger coming off of her. Scolded, Lika slowly shuffles over to Eline's side, before thumping herself into a seated position. Glancing at Maggie, her tongue hangs out as she showers her in a loving gaze. Thanking the heavens Maggie was never like that as a puppy, she pats her girl's soft head.

"Thank you. I thought she was going to lick me to death." Donald chuckles.

"I still can't believe we did it guys." Squeezing water out of her dreads onto the sand, Terra changes the subject. "I cannot stop thinking about it." Splashing some water in front of her bare chocolate coloured feet, a few droplets sprinkle onto Maggie's head, making her scamper away in irritation.

"It felt exhilarating didn't it" Donald beams.

"Exhilarating" Eline repeats. "It was one of the best decisions I could have ever made!" She shouts gaining a bark from Lika.

"Seeing the look on Red's face, I wish I had filmed it. Just so I could see the way her mouth fell open in utter surprise." Terra laughs, so happy she will not have to see the patronising girl ever again.

"CCTV would have picked it up if the cameras were facing in the right direction." Donald states, taking his name badge off his now unneeded uniform. "If only it hadn't been in the moment, we could have set up hidden cameras. Being able to see that for the rest of my life would have been priceless."

Copying him, Terra rips her brown square shaped name badge off and leans forward to the sandy part of the riverside. Creating a hole in the sand, she places her broken badge inside. "Come on guys let's keep walking. I still have so much energy to burn."

Joining Terra, her friends drop their badges in the hole before she smothers the sand back over. Grabbing their shoes, they whistle to get the dogs on track and start walking again.

"We should continue this feeling and go on an adventure" Donald puts out there.

"What kind of adventure?" Eline asks. "Though you know I'm definitely down for an adventure anytime" She adds quickly.

"I don't know something with a kind of goal to reach." Donald thinks aloud. "Maybe-" Clicking his fingers, Terra sees the light go on inside. Certain she knows what he's going to say, he proves her thoughts right. "Let's walk the Great Wall of China."

"You and that bloody wall." Terra chuckles "China's quite a way to go. Let's start smaller by walking to Shotley first." Unsure if a huge adventure is what she wants; Terra picks up the pace of her walk.

"We don't have to go to China. I just want to -" Spinning on the spot he shouts. "Go somewhere!" Arms raised he acts like he's in a movie by dropping to his knees for dramatic effect.

"Oh god" Terra huffs

Shocking Donald out of his acting scene, Terra huffs gaining an odd look of disgust from Donald, before he realizes she isn't looking at him. Seeing the approaching figure coming their way, Terra knew this is karmas way of payback.

"Shall we run?" Donald suggests

"No, I want to see his reaction when we tell him what happened." Eline's eyes bulge at the thought of shocking Sirel.

"Imagine if he had been there as it had unfolded." Laughing aloud, Terra pictures the man's already red face, burning as bright as Red's overly dyed hair.

From the first time she served the approaching figure, he seemed to have some sort of radar of when she was out walking Maggie. Always bringing with him the monster that is his bosses' dog, it would always go for her boxer. Out for a leisurely stroll on his own, Terra couldn't help instinctively looking to see if the odd customer had brought the horse-sized dog like usual.

Working for a very well respected Suffolk council member, Sirel's boss had family money running back to before the wheel was invented. Ignoring her whenever he came into the shop, Sirel only had a soft spot for Donald. Never having anything in his own life when he came into the shop, Sirel only came in with a list from his boss. Sadness emanating around him, wherever he goes, the loneliness is soon understood whenever he decides to speak to them. Although being a groundskeeper for his boss's estate, working alone must be enough for him.

Unfortunately, disliking him comes easily for Terra. Based on his views of life and how he speaks of many people, her dislike is understood but the way he treats Eline and her, it pushes her hate even higher. Coming from Ireland his annoyingly toned voice hasn't kept any of the Irish pleasantries. In fact, he has completely lost his accent, though what is left is a squeak that scraps its way out of his throat.

Wearing his signature dark green fishing coat, it hangs like death around his knees. Covered head to toe, she's confounded that the heat of the sun doesn't make him pass out.

"Ah Donald" He squibs

Looking at the group in turn, he passes over Terra for a greeting, but not before managing to give a dirty look at Maggie. Bitterness towards the man rising inside her, she turns her face into a dirty look of her own.

"Dutch girl, fantastic weather we're having. Shame you're not sailing along the river." He motions at the calm water. "Is your boat every going to be finished?" Without taking a breath he continues, cutting her off before Eline can answer.

"I don't doubt when it is finished, you won't make it far" Bursting out in a fit of laughter, his pleasure at his insult is clear.

"Hello Sirel" All three friends chime together, biting back their hate.

"Are you not hot in your coat?" Terra asks.

"Hot?" A puzzling look crosses his face. "No, the breeze sends a chill right through me, I cannot stand the wind." Answering Terra question to Donald, Terra watches with happiness that a flush of red heats his face giving away his lie.

"Oh, that's a shame. I was about to say you could come for a ride on my boat now it's finished." Pointing out onto the river, Eline shows Sirel where the Reis floats upon the water.

"But the wind will definitely be blowing when my Reis sets off."

Sparkling clean, the top shines white in the sun while its bright red underbelly bops in the cloudy brown water. Unlike Sirel who only glances, Terra makes out the design of a mystical creature stretching the length of the boat, designed by one of Eline's many talent friends. The boats name coming from Eline's own language, it means journey, Terra's mind releasing maybe Donald's idea isn't a bad one after all. Maybe somehow they were always meant to have the events happen today; maybe Eline somehow foretold an adventure to come by naming the boat Reis.

"It looks so clean Dutch girl"

"And why wouldn't it be?" Donald asks

"Well, you're from another country so you can never tell" Sirel says contradicting his own origin.

"You are just a dick aren't you?" Donald snaps his pretence of liking this man is truly gone now he no longer has a job to keep.

Taking Terra by surprise, the anger in her friend's voice matches the devil. Understanding Sirel was no longer a customer, she still couldn't believe he really just shouted at the old fool.

"Seriously what is wrong with you?" Donald raises his voice "Firstly you can't even register Terra's existence. Then you never call Eline by her name, as you clearly can't be arsed to learn it. All you seem to be able to do is make rude snarky comments about her boat and country. How old are you six? Even a six year old wouldn't be so rude to people!"

"I don't get it Sirel, you yourself are from another country" Eline adds

"Holland is a forward-thinking country. Way more than the one I'm standing in with you around"

"Donald you should-" Terra begins but Donald turns on her.

"What! I shouldn't finally tell this insolent man what we all think of him. I've had enough"

Taking a step back Sirel looks shocked, still not understanding what he's done wrong. Motioning for Donald to continue Terra hopes her angered friend is nearly over.

"Being respectful of someone, means you don't have to say every horrible thought that comes into your head. It's someone who knows not to say something at all. I so hope I never have to see you again Sirel... have a great day" He finishes, signing off like he is at work.

Storming pass the man, Donald heads up the water's edge whistling for the girls dogs to follow. Giving Maggie the nod her boxer is waiting for, the dogs run off after the angered man. An awkward silence following Donald's rant makes Terra look to the Reis wondering if she could swim out to it. If it wasn't for the horrible water stuck between them, her and her friends could already be sailing the seas.

"What did Donald mean by never seeing me again?" Still oblivious to anything her friend said she wants to shake the fool.

"You won't see us on the deli anymore," Eline says "None of us in fact."

"Ah! Why will I not?"

"We no longer work at the shop!" Done with the conversation Terra snaps. Pushing her tall friend in Donald's direction, she gives the old man a final look.

"I'm sure you'll hear all about it next time you go in." Eline says over her shoulder "Goodbye Sirel"

Available **now on Amazon Kindle and Paperback!**

Worthy
by
HDA Pratt

The Sleepless
Night Creature

HDA PRATT

A Night Creature Trilogy

Cayden McNigh is Immortal.

For over three hundred years he has hunted, killed and even tormented his prey. But what happens when the hunter becomes the hunted?

What does it mean to be a powerful and fearsome creature to feel fear?

For one Immortal a sleepless time is about to begin.

Printed in Great Britain
by Amazon

64447171R00163